FOREVER
Footprints

FOREVER
Footprints

Based on a True Animal Rescue

KATHLEEN F. CELLURA

Library of Congress Control Number:		2011917581
ISBN:	Hardcover	978-1-4653-5527-0
	Softcover	978-1-4653-5526-3
	Ebook	978-1-4653-5528-7

This book was printed in the United States of America.

Cover illustration by: Joel Ray Pellerin

To order additional copies of this book, contact:
Xlibris Corporation
1-888-795-4274
www.Xlibris.com
Orders@Xlibris.com
102778

DEDICATION

───✦───

To

Catherine

Frances

Sister Aurelia

Oprah

───✦───

IN MEMORY OF
MY FELINE FUR PERSONS

C. C. Cat

Muffy Cat

Tina

Tangie

Sha-Sha

ACKNOWLEDGMENTS

With sincere gratitude, I wish to acknowledge those who, over a lengthy period of time, assisted me, encouraged me, who sought out information on my behalf, and most importantly, believed in me and my novel.

Thank you, Donna . . . Stephanie . . . Bonita . . .

MESSAGE FROM THE AUTHOR

Dear Reader,

This is a partly fictional account of a true story.

The story is centered on the actual rescue of an abandoned dog. The rescue did include a local affluent family, a teacher, her students, and some of the parents. Much of the story is a blend of fiction and nonfiction. Names, places, and the sequences of events have been altered to ensure anonymity and privacy. During the writing, I used some composites of various existing personalities and romance interests and changed some specific sites.

I hope the reader will carry away some lasting memories, profound images, and a renewed outlook on how one caring, responsible act can snowball into all kinds of positive possibilities. It is with sincere hope that readers of all ages, once they have completed the story, will move toward establishing in their communities clubs and advocate movements that will demonstrate an outcry and a demand for the humane treatment of animals. Spaying and neutering programs nationwide are essential in order to avoid the statistics as illustrated in the story.

Kathleen (Kathi) F. Cellura

INTRODUCTION

This is a tale based on a true story that occurred several years ago. I found myself offering the oral rendition of this special animal rescue experience to students and friends throughout the years. Over this lengthy period, I had been urged by friends, colleagues, and students to put the story into printed form. As I wind down from life's demands, years of serving and giving to others, it seems that the time is right to write—to fulfill my dream, to fulfill a commitment I made to a dear lady long ago.

By all the usual measurements, I can say that I have experienced an energy-packed, often tumultuous, life filled with extraordinary challenges, loves, and passions. It's been quite a ride, but each chapter has been a preparation for me to fulfill my destiny.

The realization that I do, indeed, have something special to share has been an integral part of my thoughts for some time. I strongly believe in this story of devotion and commitment and all its dimensions of heartache, joy, and unconditional love. I invite the reader to ponder upon the life lessons revealed and perhaps expand on them. I have deliberately left areas open for individual interpretation, to fill in the blanks.

The story demonstrates the actions of ordinary people making extraordinary sacrifices. They display courage and lead by example. They display love in the deepest sense. Their spirits exude loving kindness. And yes, one person can make a difference.

It is a privilege to tell this story as seen through the eyes and felt deeply within the heart of a teacher named Klee. Make this journey with Klee. Become one with her, her students, and an extraordinary woman in the community, and the special Labrador retriever named Allie who brought all the characters together . . . who made the story possible.

CHAPTER 1

1984

Her home, nestled among the Florida oak and pine trees, immediately caused a sense of peace within Klee as she entered the crushed stone driveway. After a long day dealing with the responsibilities and the usual stresses of middle school teaching, she embraced the seclusion of the two-acre sanctuary. At the end of the long driveway, the stucco split-ranch house framed by the surrounding woods was attractive to the eye and a balm to her wounded heart. The house had been built on virgin land on 1978, two years after Klee's emotional escape from New York state to Florida.

Once the land was purchased and the time arrived to prep the building site for her new home, Klee rode into the two-acre parcel on the bulldozer along with the operator. To ensure that only the designated area would be cleared was her main goal, since she wanted to save as much of the natural habitat for animals and birds.

The building project had a twofold purpose in Klee's mind. Not only did she want to create a nature preserve for herself, but she also kept in mind the resale value it would command in the future. She realized the plethora of opportunities offered within the real estate world; new homes, resales, lot sites, and new construction had always piqued her interest even as a youngster as she observed her father's dealings.

Each time Klee returned to her refuge, her heart skipped with anticipation. She felt that she entered her own private paradise. She was filled with gratitude when she surveyed what she had created. The natural beauty that surrounded her was spectacular. All this helped ease the pain of errors in judgment and the disappointments she left behind in her other life.

After dinner, she made it a ritual to plan an evening of relaxation in the airy great room. The fireplace with its brick façade that extended to the ceiling was the focal point of the room. The ten-foot-wide window span that overlooked the woods and the circular drive often framed the outline of evening visitors. The bobcats and foxes liked to stretch out on the circular cement drive in order to absorb the heat. This was especially true during the winter season.

The large room was welcoming and generated feelings of coziness. Situated in a special designated space was the organ. The handsome instrument was dear to Klee. The hours of pleasure it gave her were immeasurable. Her other prized possession was the free-standing grandfather clock. Her parents presented this gift to her when she moved into her new home. Its six-foot height and massive oak cabinetry made it an imposing sentinel overlooking the room. The Westminster chimes singing from the clock echoed within Klee's soul creating feelings of contentment.

That evening, while relaxing in her recliner in the great room with a financial journal in hand, Klee drifted off in thought. Flashbacks of that particular, unforgettable December of 1974 when she lived in western New York state flooded her mind. It all seemed so vivid to her, although it was ten years ago. She was surprised that her memories were so keen that particular evening until she reflected that it was that time of the year once again. The month of December, with thoughts of cold snowy weather and the holidays, seemed to trigger her annual reverie. She remembered the lovely home she had shared with her housemates until each moved away to follow personal pursuits and dreams. The sights and sounds of the past flooded her consciousness.

To subdue her restlessness, Klee went over to Tangie's basket and picked up her feline pal. Tangie was accustomed to this ritual in the evening. Usually they both took a catnap in the oversized recliner. The chair retained Klee's perfume fragrance, and the cat seemed to enjoy the scent of her missy.

The name Tangie was short for Tangerine. The cat had been abandoned in a new development project named Tangerine Forest. Seventeen acres of Florida live oak and slash pine trees encompassed the development. The contractor was unusual in that he retained many of the trees rather than stripping the land naked. Upscale manufactured homes would be offered in this planned community for retired folks who wanted to spend five or six months in paradise each year escaping the Northern winters. The "snowbird season," as the locals referred to it, usually extended from October through April.

The building boom was once again in full swing in most of Florida after the terrible economic setbacks of the early eighties. Shortly after moving to Florida in 1976, Klee decided not to return to the teaching field for a couple of years. She wanted to pursue new experiences. However, she calculated that eventually she would engage in two jobs—teaching and real estate part-time. With this goal in mind, she studied and interned for one year with an established real estate broker then passed the state exam for the broker's license. It all unfolded nicely. It was a good time to be a realtor in Florida she often mused, especially since that's how she met Tangie.

She had been showing property sites to a potential buyer when she came upon a cat in Tangerine Forest. The cat appeared to be living off food from the work crews and found shelter among the rubble and construction material. Once Klee had finished with her client, she returned to the development with one intention—to rescue the cat. The abandoned animal was captured with the enticement of a freshly opened can of tuna. Klee was an old hand at this. It upset her terribly to observe such treatment of animals. She could never walk away.

Once in Klee's home, Tangie was washed and brushed to remove the fleas then fed and nurtured. She was a tabby cat with a black back and a hooded black top, which patterned her head. White fur enhanced her face, neck, and underbody. The most striking features were her black nose and greenish eyes. Those eyes were mesmerizing. The most comical part of her anatomy was a buff shaded patch that extended from her nose to her mouth and lip area. She looked as if she had been in a bowl filled with butterscotch syrup.

Suddenly, Klee was startled from her memories by the phone's piercing ring. She surveyed the face of the grandfather clock. To her amazement, it read 10:00 p.m.

"My word," she said aloud to Tangie, "who would be calling at this hour?"

CHAPTER 2

Picking up the receiver, she heard a voice say, "Hello, is this Klee?" Hesitantly she replied, "Yes, this is she."

"Well," came a brisk reply, "this is a voice from your past. I have had quite a time locating you."

Klee's interest was piqued. She tried to connect the voice, but before she could respond, the woman on the other end of the connection cheerfully exclaimed, "It's Bethany Winslow from Pittsford, New York. Do you remember me?"

Klee's heart flipped, and like a speeding bullet, many images and sounds of joy and pain rapidly penetrated her memory.

"Why, Bethany," she exclaimed, "how wonderful to hear from you. Of course I remember you. What a nice surprise."

Klee imagined the lovely lady who at one period of time had been so much a part of her life when she taught at Fairhaven Central in New York state. Bethany was a strong woman of character. Klee had respect for her, and although they had lost contact over the years, she continued to retain warm feelings for the woman. However, Klee often felt guilty when she thought of how she left Pittsford. She had never said good-bye to the Winslows nor to precious Allie. She was ashamed of her actions and for walking away from the legal commitment she had to them. Yet at that time, Klee was so emotionally fractured and disillusioned that all she wanted to do was retreat. Klee wasn't proud that she had given in to such behavior, but she had.

"Klee, you can't believe what I had to do to get your address and phone number," Bethany replied. "I called Fairhaven Central School District, and Judy, the secretary, was reluctant to issue your stats other than to indicate that you had moved to Florida. Anyway, after a long explanation about our past relationship and telling the secretary something about Allie and your students, I was finally successful. She did remember the story of Allie. We sure lost contact with each other, Klee! You left without a good-bye. I felt so hurt."

"I do apologize, Bethany, truly I do. It was a difficult time in my life, and I just wanted to slip away."

"Of course, I understand. I had a feeling something had occurred. I have no intention of prying. I'm just glad I found you."

"Thanks, Bethany, for your understanding. I am glad you persisted," Klee replied. "Judy has kept in touch with me over the years. Actually, I hear from her every Christmas. I must say that I'm in semishock because this very evening I was reminiscing about the entire episode with Allie. I seem to do this each year when the holidays are around the corner. It's eerie that you should reach me on this particular evening."

"How amazing," Bethany sighed. "Klee, when are you going to write Allie's rescue story?"

Klee chuckled, "Someday, someday . . ."

Bethany and Klee caught up on so many things. Allie, their precious Labrador, was doing just fine, but the aging signs were obvious. Bethany expanded with the disclosure that Allie had her up-and-down days, and yet she had given them many years of pleasure. All the Winslows couldn't imagine being without her.

Daughter Laurie had finished her studies at Wellesley then became a licensed clinical social worker and married. Son Tom completed his studies at Harvard and graduated from Harvard Law School. He was following in his dad's footsteps. His dad, Shepard, was busy as ever with corporate law and special projects at Xerox.

"Bethany, I'm so very happy to know that all is well with the Winslows," Klee said. "It has been a pleasure chatting with you. I wish each and every one of you the best of holidays."

"And to you, Klee, and please do keep in touch."

Once Klee put down the receiver, she recorded Bethany's contact information in her telephone directory. She was pleased to reconnect with the Winslows even though recalling her entire relationship with them and Allie would serve to ignite personal, heart-wrenching memories.

Retiring to bed that evening, Klee's thoughts danced with a variety of possibilities as to how to approach the penning of Allie's special story. She couldn't get over the fact that Bethany called that particular evening. It almost seemed like a special message—a good omen.

Sometimes to actually pen a meaningful event served as an emotional catharsis, which ultimately meant revisited pain. Maybe that's why Klee hesitated. The procrastination kept her from the multilayered emotions that would surface as she wrote. She would be required to factually relive the past, to look deep into herself, and ultimately find who she was.

CHAPTER 3

The next morning ushered in once again, another sunny December morning in southwest Florida. Klee had adapted beautifully to Florida. Not only did Lemon Bay and the Gulf of Mexico provide her with water indulgences, but she appreciated the moderate temperatures of the Florida winter months. No snow tires, no shoveling, no boots, no heavy clothes to tolerate ever again, and no more gloomy, repetitive dark days. The easy lifestyle of Florida suited her just fine.

The driving route to and from the middle school each day was like driving along a gigantic painted scene displaying acres of flowers, magnificent trees, flowering shrubs, and man-made lakes. How she loved the freedom of living in the midst of such beauty.

Klee's Florida teaching position required her to make several adjustments, however. Specifically, the suite configuration for the middle school grade-level pods was different compared to her previous career in a self-contained classroom. Because of the connective classroom design with a huge office and workroom in the middle, it demanded more person-to-person interaction on a daily basis with students from other classrooms and teachers within the pod.

Klee parked her blue Chevy station wagon in the same parking space each day. It was closest to the office, which provided her with a shorter walking distance. She grabbed her briefcase and headed for the office to check the mailbox. This was her routine every morning before entering the domain of the pod office.

The school had been constructed recently. Everything installed was top-notch from lighting fixtures to acoustical ceilings to carpeting. The green chalkboards were easy on the eyes. Large windows with miniblinds brought the outside into the modern room design.

Once the buzzer tone signaled for the beginning of homeroom period, Klee walked to her lectern to greet her eighth-grade students with announcements about holiday week scheduling and period changes . . . then she lost concentration for a moment. A peaceful feeling came over her . . . a flash crossed her mind, and at that moment, she knew that she had reached the time in her life to begin writing Allie's story. Maybe it was the unexpected phone call from Bethany that prompted her to do so. Whatever it was, Klee felt the stirring within to move forward with the story.

That evening in her study, she began typing the indelible experience which occurred in a suburb of Rochester, New York, during the onset of the winter season of 1974. She began the story by outlining on paper key words that described all the sounds, sights, instincts, emotions, devotion, and ardor of those who were involved. The faces, with their expressions of concern, tentativeness, and joy were vivid pictures in her mind's eye. It was an experience that was very much part of her. The tears still flowed without hesitation when certain stimuli prompted Allie's face to appear.

CHAPTER 4

1974

Darkness began closing in on the winter sky. The piercing cold penetrated every muscle of Klee's body. This was typical for a western New York state winter. Months of unfriendly skies, inches and inches of snow, and lots of cabin fever were the norm.

"It appears that another snowstorm is on its way," Klee called out to Lisa as they came from the regular Monday afternoon faculty meeting and headed toward the school parking lot. "We sure are getting it early this year! The wind is up too. It might be a fierce night."

"Right you are, Klee. I hate it when snowy winter weather comes so early, but let's take advantage of it if we get more snow. Maybe we could get out for some cross-country skiing this weekend. I think there is enough of a snow base now, and if we get more of the white stuff, it should be perfect," Lisa replied.

"Now that sounds good to me. I do believe they are calling for more snowfall, but how much, I don't know. Which is better for you, Saturday or Sunday?"

"Probably Sunday would be best. I want to do some shopping on Saturday and some catch-up. Also, Rob will be leaving Saturday morning at ten o'clock. Kodak has him traveling again," Lisa called back.

"Okay . . . we'll think Sunday."

Klee enjoyed being around Lisa. They always had some good laughs together. Klee was noted for her antics and making people laugh, while Lisa played the straight character. They made quite a team when they got together at faculty get-togethers or house parties. Lisa's husband, Rob, teased them and labeled them "The Comedy Sisters."

Both women were sport enthusiasts. From appearances, one would never guess Lisa's athletic ability and competitiveness. She gave the impression of being more model than athlete. She was small in stature, precise with makeup, and had the interesting trait of swishing her long auburn hair.

Klee loved all athletic activities too. From childhood onward, swimming, sailing, water skiing, softball, golf, tennis, hiking, and even football captured her heart. The football games at the corner lot with her cousins and neighborhood pals were fast, strenuous, and energetic. All the kids were rapid in their movements, and they never seemed to be idle. Calories were burned, and their lean bodies were proof. Actually, all the sports Klee had pursued throughout her life, as well as the interactions with other teammates, provided experiences that enhanced her life.

She was a wiry gal who never sat still and hated to take naps as a young child. Often, when she was confined to her second-story bedroom for a nap, Klee would climb out the window and down the cherry tree. She also adored the water and lived in the water most of her waking hours at the family's lakeside cottage during the summer. Klee mastered every kind of boat along the lakefront even as a youngster. As an adult, these experiences prepared her for her sailing days at the Canandaigua Yacht Club and for motorboat ownership.

As a young thirty-something with a trim body, she was of average height, with short brown hair. Klee dripped energy. She was a woman with a mind that never stopped seeking the answers to the why of things or new ideas. She was a stickler when questions of principle or integrity surfaced. Some individuals truly despised her for her strong values and would deliberately set her up so she would appear in a negative light, but that would not change her position. She had the courage to stand alone, but that was part of being true to oneself as far as she was concerned. Her principles were about to be tested that wintry afternoon.

CHAPTER 5

K lee slid into the seat of her trusty Malibu Chevrolet, with its champagne gold body, white vinyl top, and white interior. This was her dream car. She was at an age in which a sharp car translated into happiness. One of the great bonuses of this dream car was that it always started no matter how much the temperature had dropped. The ACDelco battery did the job and gave Klee a secure feeling. The Delco stereo radio was the best also, and it included a neat tape deck. The Chevy's heater produced warmth fast. She really appreciated her Chevy and got a kick out of driving it. Klee wasn't any Diana Shore—the gal who sang "See the USA in Your Chevrolet," but she sure was a Chevy fan!

As Klee journeyed home from school, she felt some relief from the stabbing chill. The soothing music from the car stereo filled the warming environment. "Bless the Beasts and the Children" by the Carpenters was playing. Each time Klee's heart was touched by the music and lyrics, and every time she heard the Carpenters' rendition, she lamented the lack of compassion in the world. That song, those lyrics, "Bless the beasts and the children for in this world they have no voice, they have no choice," became her theme song, not only in her teaching, but also in her private life. In the classroom, she used her guitar to bring these words firsthand to the students—for their enjoyment and for reflection—during the Circle Talks, in which the students participated weekly and sometimes biweekly.

The Circle Talks were designed to give each student the opportunity to share sunshine experiences or hazy events. She felt that students needed to feel free to express whatever they needed to say. They needed to share their joy or something that might be gnawing at them. She, of course, served as moderator in order to guide, should the topic or conversation begin to head for troubled waters or get too personal.

Klee was proud of how readily her sixth-grade students had adapted to the Circle Talks. Their enthusiasm to arrange the chairs in a circle for the session was a strong indicator of interest. Once the session was completed, chairs and desks were returned to their original positions. The students appreciated putting things back together and keeping their classroom neat. The majority of the wall space displayed their attractive map work, graphs, science charts, and drug prevention posters. They took pride in their daily assignments and classroom displays.

Looking at her watch, Klee anticipated the weather report on radio station WHEC so she switched off the tape and tuned in the radio station:

"Six inches of heavy, wet snow are expected this evening. This is an early, severe visitation of winter for us, folks. It's going to be a healthy storm due to the Lake Ontario effect. Make sure you have those snowblowers and shovels ready come morning . . . think about stocking up on a few extra groceries just in case we really get socked in or lose power because of the weight of the snow. The trees can hold so much before branches start spiraling downward onto power lines. The high winds that are predicted will cause havoc too. It will feel like twenty degrees out there. So as usual, I caution you to remember to provide proper care and attention to those of the animal kingdom," said the popular DJ, Eddy Rogers.

"Hole-ly macaroni!" Klee muttered. "That kind of dumping already!"

She decided to stop at the Star Market for supplies before returning home in case the storm turned into a whopper. She always leaned toward the cautious side. The impending storm also meant rising even earlier in the morning to shovel the one side of the driveway to free her car. Although it was a two-car garage, her major goal would be to clear a single path for the Chevy. Contracting a snowplow clearing service was out of the question because the driveway was dressed with gravel for the country-look effect, and that meant the plow would invariably scrape up the gravel and gouge the drive bed. One such experience had been enough for Klee.

With caution, Klee negotiated a left turn into the Star Market parking lot. She began searching for a space. Cars lined the parking lanes. It seemed that everyone had the same idea to stockpile for the predicted early-in-the-season snowstorm. Proceeding down the lightly dusted snow lane, Klee spied a parking space. Spinning the wheel, she made a left turn into the free spot and abruptly came to a halt. Leaning forward to turn off the ignition key, she found herself peering through the windshield of her car at a scraggly, lonely evergreen tree. Beneath the tree, a dog huddled.

"What in heavens is this?" Klee exclaimed. As she peered through the windshield, beautiful, soulful brown eyes engaged hers. Its thin body shivered in the piercing cold, and the light wind ruffled its pale-yellow coat.

She took a deep breath, gingerly opened the car door, and, as quietly as possible, shut the door while all the time keeping her eyes fastened on the dog. It looked like a yellow Labrador retriever or maybe a Golden retriever she thought. In a soft, caring voice, she began to speak to the dog as she approached.

"Well, who are you? How did you get here?" she whispered.

Suddenly the dog rose and bolted across the parking lot toward the wooded area that surrounded the Star Market.

"Oh no," she gasped in a low audible voice. "You are injured!" The dog obviously had something wrong with its right hind leg as it limped away as fast as its weakened legs could move.

Her heart raced. Her eyes, upon realization of what she had just witnessed, filled with tears; her emotions hit the red alert button. Klee wanted to scream out . . . no . . . no . . . not another distressed animal! She could hardly handle anything that had to do with animal neglect or cruelty. She had seen it as a youngster when she and her dad had cruised some of the back country roads, seeking fields to pick young dandelion greens for mom's salads.

Klee never had forgotten what she had seen on some of those pastoral roads. Exposure to neglect and cruelty at such a young age had done a job on her. She was such a sensitive kid, and yet openly she faced what she observed. She faced what was true. She did not bury the impression. She did not rationalize it away either—maybe outwardly it would seem so—but never in her soul. Also, at the tender age of seven, she felt things that she did not know how to articulate in the adult world. What she did realize in her observations was the fact that she and her family had a comfortable lifestyle. Her dad was an extremely hard worker, a successful businessman. How she lived was not always the same for others. The inequities often made her cry. When asked why the tears, the seven-year-old couldn't verbalize what she was feeling nor the images that held her attention.

With determination in stride, Klee dashed to the market entrance. She inquired after the store manager and was directed to his office cubicle at the front corner of the store.

"Hello, Mr. Sloan," she said as she took notice of his name tag. "My name is Klee Cato, and I am a teacher at Fairhaven Central. I am wondering if you happen to know about a dog . . . maybe a Labrador retriever in the parking lot area that appears to be injured and probably abandoned."

"I certainly do," exclaimed Mr. Sloan. "That dog is a yellow Labrador from what I have been told, and it has been out there for a long, long time. Some lady has been trying to rescue it. She comes in here to buy food for the dog, often she gets a nice cut of meat too. I understand that she is a surgical nurse at the Strong Memorial Hospital in Rochester. Go over to the message board. There is a card with her name and phone number if you want to contact her."

Mr. Sloan impressed Klee as being a nice man—a little hurried, but that seemed to go along with his job position. He was lean in stature and wore rimmed glasses. His sandy color brush cut appeared to be a remnant of days passed, probably the military. He exuded precision and quickness in his appearance and speech.

Klee moved quickly toward the board while calling out, "Thanks, Mr. Sloan." She copied the name, Bethany Winslow, and the phone number from the neatly printed card, and left the store with a pulsating sensation in the pit of her stomach.

Her heart was weeping, her mind's thoughts chasing each other, and she knew this would be another challenge in her life that needed to be resolved. Klee never walked away from what needed to be done. She fully realized that there were so many unknowns—the abandoned dog, the woman named Bethany, and the winter elements. Somehow, and at some point in time, all these essential unknowns had to collectively work together . . . somehow.

CHAPTER 6

As she drove away from the parking lot, she began to verbalize aloud, "Girl, you need to take some deep breaths . . . you must remain focused . . . this is happening in your life at this particular time for a specific reason . . . please, please don't let your emotions bungle what you need to do!"

Klee's tumbling thoughts competed with concentrating on the road. She was planning on what she would tell her class in the morning, if the storm didn't close the schools because of possible power failure. She wanted to discuss her discovery with her students. She was curious to know if anyone was already aware of the plight of the Labrador at the Star Market area. Klee felt deep within her that this was going to be an exceptional learning experience and quite a journey for both students and teacher.

As she negotiated her driveway, she became aware of the fact that she never did pick up extra groceries. She was so preoccupied with thoughts of the pending weather and what would happen to the dog during the long, fierce night that purchasing emergency staples flew out of her mind. Her worried spirit throbbed. Her heart felt like a trip-hammer pounding within her chest. Obviously, groceries were the last thing on her mind!

Once Klee entered her home, she couldn't get to the telephone fast enough. She didn't even take time to greet the beautiful calico cat that waited to be recognized. Muffy Cat hung around anyway while Klee plunged into her task. Impatiently dialing and hoping that someone would answer, the connection was made.

Klee blurted out in one sweeping breath, "My name is Klee Cato. I am a teacher at Fairhaven Central. I am looking for Mrs. Bethany Winslow. I got her name and phone number from the Star Market information board, and I am inquiring about the abandoned dog."

"You are speaking to Bethany Winslow," a gentle voice responded.

"May I do anything to help? I understand that you have attempted to rescue the dog," Klee stated.

Klee could hear Bethany gasp.

After a brief hesitation, Bethany unfolded her tale. "Oh yes, yes! I, along with my family, have been trying to rescue that dog for a couple of months. I go to feed her twice a day. When I can't do it, my daughter Laura and son Tom carry on with the mission. I've even had our vet, Dr. Kate Tanner, out there twice to tranquilize the dog so we could bring her in. It's been so frustrating . . . so heartbreaking! The dog gets away even after ingesting the drug. Instinct must kick in. It sure is powerful because the dog wins, and we lose each time. By the way, my husband, Shepard, is an attorney who is working on the Allid Project at Xerox. Shepard has named the dog Allie because that's the closest to the project's name. It has stuck . . . we all refer to her as our Allie. She knows her new name. When I call to her to feed her, Allie comes dashing out of the woods. The wooded Perinton Foothills of our area certainly have provided fantastic shelter for her."

Once Bethany finished with her detailed description, Klee said, "I noticed that Allie has a limp. I wonder how she sustained such an injury."

"We think she was a passenger in a car that was in an accident at the corner of the Fairport and Moseley roads. We remember seeing it reported in the newspaper and on television. The injury probably occurred during the crash. She was able to bolt from the crash site, and being so traumatized, the dog just naturally sought refuge. Mother Nature probably directed her to go to the wooded area for safety," Bethany replied.

Klee sighed. "What an amazing story! It is unbelievable! Obviously the dog has survived only because of your diligence and loving care and, of course, her innate smarts."

"Yes, we have tried everything. We hope she'll make it through this winter."

With a determined voice, Klee stated, "Bethany, I want to help you and your family and most specifically Allie. At this moment, I cannot accurately describe what I am feeling, but I realize that you have already been there so you do understand. I will say this to you . . . I make this commitment when I say we will rescue Allie. We will bring her in from the wild to enjoy your loving care—your family. You see, I have a special guardian angel, and it will happen. My angel and I work together on many special projects and often too."

There was dead silence.

"Bethany, Bethany, are you there?" Klee called out.

A tearful reply came, "Yes, I am here. If this rescue will only happen for Allie, we will all have closure to a heartbreaking episode."

"Although my heart aches along with yours, I am demanding of myself that my thoughts and all the positive energy I can muster will somehow, someway help us rescue Allie," Klee firmly stated.

After hanging up, Klee's thoughts went to the possible wind-chill factor that was predicted for the night. The tears began to stream. She could only imagine what a night Allie would endure. She could only imagine all the abandoned animals and suffering children that she did not know by name or face, but who were facing circumstances of neglect that very moment. Her spirit was deeply immersed in that realization and the unexpected situation she found herself facing. She felt so helpless.

A thought then flashed through her mind. She had learned to follow such moments of inspiration. She realized that if she carried out the thought, it would relieve her of some of the vulnerability she was experiencing. She would deal with it following supper.

She truly had little appetite for her supper. Muffy Cat, on the other hand, had no problem eating hers. Muffy Cat, the beautiful calico, was so special to Klee. The little ten-pound fur person had several endearing names that Klee had assigned to her—Muffy Cat, Muffy, Muffin, and Petite Chat.

Often when Klee looked at Muffin, she'd recall the quote of Jean Burden, an American writer: "A dog, I have always said, is prose; a cat is a poem."

Once Muffy Cat's needs were met, Klee carried out the thought that had previously visited her before suppertime. She bundled herself up with ski jacket and cap and went out to the garage. After rummaging around, she found some pieces of scrap plywood from a previous project. Klee always had projects. She hoarded all leftovers once the job was completed. Each plywood section discovered was about fifteen by eight inches. Foraging a little more, she selected some pressure-treated wooden stakes that were often used for bracing when planting a new shrub or tree around the property. Next, she grabbed the hammer and heavy mallet. Everything went into the trunk of the car. She was going back to the Star Market.

Once there, she would locate the original scraggly evergreen tree where she first encountered the dog. The picture she saw in her mind was to take the plywood pieces and build a three-hundred-forty degree circle shelter under the tree. The makeshift hut would keep out the wind and most of the snow she calculated. Maybe—just maybe—the dog would go back to the tree and use it during the night.

CHAPTER 7

The snowfall was as heavy as predicted. The plow drivers diligently worked throughout the night. The roads were cleared for morning traffic. Luckily, there were no power outages. It was business as usual, and school buses were able to roll.

Klee could hardly keep her wandering thoughts under control as she drove toward the Star Market parking lot on her way to school. Bodily visceral sensations alerted her to the fact that she was feeling anxious. Had the Lab used the plywood shelter she had erected the night before? She thought of Allie and the cruel night she must have endured with the driving wet snow, the whipping wind. Approaching the lonely evergreen tree, Klee saw immediately that the dog did not occupy the handmade shelter. The snow was fresh and there was no indentation whatsoever that would suggest that Allie used the area during the night hours. Facing this fact, she became more determined to resolve the situation. She had the reputation of charging forward as an event unfolded; this event demanded a full charge.

With a heavy heart, she dismantled Allie's intended hut. Opening the trunk of the Chevy, she tossed the building material into it. The rapidity of the toss made her realize that she was experiencing not only disappointment but anger. Once everything was thrown in the trunk, she took hold of the trunk door and slammed it hard.

Klee entered her classroom and glanced at her lesson plans. Today she would veer from those plans and let the students share in a first-hand life experience. *What could be better?* she thought. Something real, something tangible would provide meaningful lessons.

Once the opening exercises were completed, Klee, dressed in an attractive paint suit, addressed her class:

"This morning, I want to take time away from the planned lessons and discuss with you something that is very special. In fact, it is very important, and I do believe we can work on this situation together. Are you ready?"

Greg raised his hand and asked, "Ms. Cato, does this mean we'll get out of doing our lessons this morning?" Many of the students began laughing.

"Well, partially, Greg," Ms. Cato replied. "It's possible that one of the subjects might be shortened this morning. The time we spend on the topic I have in mind will offer the opportunity for many valuable lessons—both academic and life lessons that you can embrace, I hope."

Klee recounted to the students her experience at the Star Market the previous afternoon while she was on her way home from school. She outlined in detail her observations, her conversation with Mr. Sloan, the store manager, and the woman, Mrs. Winslow, who had been trying to rescue the dog for many weeks. The students listened intently.

They sensed from the tone of their teacher's voice and her facial expressions that she was extremely concerned; she was dead serious. Usually she spoke with her hands. This day, it was no different, but her movements were more exaggerated. Whatever came out of her mouth was dramatically emphasized with her hands, her arms, her entire body. Her body language revealed her intensity. She walked back and forth in the space directly in front of the students. The nervous energy that consumed her was obvious with each stride.

When she finished, Debbie said, "I have seen that dog." Some of the other students chimed in also, indicating that they had seen the dog when they went shopping with their moms.

Klee was taken aback. She was surprised that the dog's plight seemed common knowledge. Once she regained her composure and with a tender tone, she asked, "Am I to understand that you are telling me that people have been aware of this abandoned dog for some time? Do you know if anyone has attempted any kind of involvement?" Klee was known for her candor. She was always a straight shooter. The students fully understood this. One could hear a pin drop! No affirmative reply came forth.

"So . . . if we think no one has taken issue with the abandonment other than Mrs. Winslow, then we need to address the problem. I think if we begin discussing actions—possible solutions like we do in our weekly Circle Talks—we'll come up with good ideas to resolve the incredible suffering of this injured dog. We have good minds, kind hearts, we will find a solution!" exclaimed Ms. Cato

Klee decided that this would be an appropriate time for a special Circle Talks session. At least once a week, the students arranged their chairs in a circle and prepared to "talk." It was both social and therapeutic in which each student had the opportunity to share, if he or she wished, something fun or exciting in his or her life or something bothersome or distasteful. The students were taught listening skills, the techniques employed to resolve the problem, and how to share different options to resolve the problem. Reported outcomes and evaluations were discussed at the following session.

Although this time Ms. Cato didn't have the students arrange themselves in a circle, she was certain that the techniques previously learned would come forth.

Ms. Cato approached the chalkboard and readied herself to record the students' suggestions.

"Maybe someone could call the Humane Society."

"Could we collect some blankets to keep the dog warm?"

"For right now, the dog needs shelter . . . like a doghouse."

"Maybe we could build a shelter."

"I bet my dad would help us build one."

The responses flowed, and Ms. Cato was so proud of their input and general discussion. The learned skills in the weekly talk sessions were coming into play with ease during this particular exercise. Her heart smiled.

Ms. Cato said, "We have a lengthy list of ideas on the chalkboard. Let's check off the ones we think we want to pursue. Let's be realistic and determine what can be done in the least amount of time. Remember the dog is surviving in severe conditions! Please, take out your papers and pencils, then carefully select from the chalkboard those items you think are most important and the ones we can accomplish quickly. You may select only five from the list. Think and feel it from inside yourself as you make your choices."

Once the students had narrowed the choices after a lengthy discussion and brainstorming session, certain goals were determined.

Eric Williams spoke up, "I am sure my dad will help build a shelter."

"My dad will too!" piped in Andy Regina.

"That will be splendid if they can do this," responded Ms. Cato. "I'd like to call Mr. Williams and Mr. Regina this evening to discuss our plan. Will you please tell your dads that I will be calling?" Both boys smiled with pride.

Joanie Cohen blurted, "I know my mom has a lot of old towels around, and I can get some. The dog would be kept warm with towel wraps."

"We have an old rug in the garage," offered Robin Alberta.

"This all sounds helpful. In addition, I will also call Mrs. Cohen and Mrs. Alberta this evening. I am counting on you to tell your moms I'll be calling."

The suggestions continued to flow. It was a productive, positive hour spent that morning. Klee was so pleased with her students.

Concurrently threading along in the recesses of her mind, she was certain that a lengthy research unit would evolve once Allie was rescued, but at this point in time, she didn't want to introduce the idea of a unit plan. Klee thought about the brief reading she had done from her home encyclopedia about the characteristics of Labrador retrievers and what the students would eventually reveal in their reports. Labs have a soft downy undercoat that keeps them dry and warm from the cold water of a lake or river as they fetch a falling bird. The coarse outer coat helps them repel water. These characteristics most likely gave Allie the ability to survive up to this point. Labradors' best feature is their temperament; they are loving, people-oriented, and easily bored. Hopefully, this loving temperament would surface once Allie was rescued. Along with that hope was the nagging question, "How did Allie dispel the boredom associated with her breed during her isolation in the woods?"

Snapping herself back to the present moment, she continued to explain to the class that she would go to the Star Market manager right after school to get authorization to build a shelter alongside of the store. She was sure that Mr. Sloan would give the okay, but it was important to be courteous and ask permission. Once she secured the go-ahead from him, she would call the parents.

"This very day, after school, the Allie Rescue Project will begin," declared Ms. Cato.

CHAPTER 8

Klee hurriedly finished her duties that afternoon and dashed off to the school parking lot. She had one thing in mind: to get to the store manager. She rushed through the faculty parking lot, catching her fall as her boots glided on a patch of black ice. Once situated in her car, she turned the ignition key with full confidence. The trusty Chevy engine promptly kicked over in the extreme cold. The car tires creaked over the snow-covered parking lot until she entered the cleared main road that would take her to her destination.

Once inside the Star Market, Klee had to wait to see Mr. Sloan. He was on the telephone. She paced back and forth and formulated in her mind what she would say to him. She finally decided that she would simply be forthright in her request and to the point.

Mr. Sloan emerged from the office cubicle. Klee extended her hand. "I am Ms. Cato, a teacher, from Fairhaven Central. We recently spoke about the abandoned Labrador retriever."

Mr. Sloan nodded. "Did you get in touch with the lady that has been trying to rescue that dog?"

"Actually I did. I, along with my class, and some of the parents are going to launch a rescue mission. The first phase of the plan needs your authorization."

A questioning, look came across Mr. Sloan's face. "What do you want from me?" asked Mr. Sloan.

Klee went into the plans laid out by the students and the need to build a temporary shelter along the side of the building. She explained that the project was twofold: one to rescue the dog and the other for the students to acquire new learning skills and knowledge during this venture. She assured Mr. Sloan that all evidence of the shelter would be removed once the dog was taken into guardianship.

"Well, I don't see why not. Go ahead and try to save the dog. I agree with you that this will be quite a learning experience for your kids—probably for everyone involved. I wish you all good luck. Just keep in mind, that is one smart dog out there!" exclaimed Mr. Sloan.

He raised his arm and with his right hand gave Klee the *V* for victory sign as he walked away. Klee felt lucky that he was such a personable, accommodating guy.

Back in the car, Klee shouted, "Great . . . this is great!" Next, she looked forward to her phone calls with the parents that evening.

Klee's conversations with Mr. Williams and Mr. Regina went very well. Yes, both fathers had some building material. Mr. Regina agreed that he would contact Mr. Williams once Klee hung up. Both fathers said there was a great deal of conversation going on at the dinner table about the dog rescue.

Next, Klee reached Mrs. Cohen and Mrs. Alberta. They were very sympathetic and eager to assist in any way. They offered to call some of the other parents and ask for their support and involvement. It seems that the parents were tuned into the plight of the dog named Allie; her students were doing a good job of spreading the word about this special Lab—about the need to be proactive.

CHAPTER 9

The magic hour of the Allie Rescue Project would take place late Wednesday afternoon after the dads left their workplaces. Everyone agreed to assemble at 5:30 p.m. at the right side of the Star Market building. Klee thought that Allie could last in her hiding place for two more days. She just had to. On the one hand, if the plan didn't work, then it would be back to the drawing board. They might have to face a detour in their plans. However, on the other hand, because of the weather, she recognized that time was of the essence to save Allie.

An appointment with Mr. Dean Cappelli, the vice principal, was next on Klee's agenda. He had a reputation as a calm listener and one who was willing to be supportive of faculty members and students alike whenever there was a need. He didn't give lip service in his dealings. His talk matched the walk. This coincided with her belief system. She admired individuals possessing such a positive, strong character trait.

Klee felt comfortable approaching Dean. Besides his professionalism and pleasant personality, he had those movie-star looks. Most of the faculty women commented on his dreamboat appearance, and even the guys had to admit to his handsomeness. However, Bill, the physical education teacher, took a slow burn whenever he was in Dean's presence. He believed that Dean loved the way the women flocked around him and preened his feathers. He always made some wisecrack but was careful to do it with humor. Dean irked him to no end. Regardless of Bill's ire, Dean's wavy jet black hair and those cobalt blue penetrating eyes usually did a job on almost everyone, and Dean surfaced as the winner. Often at faculty parties Klee found herself giving a serpentine glance or two his way. She wondered what it would be like to be with him on a personal level, but she pushed the thought out of her mind before it progressed too far.

First thing the next morning, Klee was seated in Dean's office. She presented the entire project outline to him in order to receive his support and assistance. She included her projections on the intended outcome and spelled out the multidimensional learning goals she was aspiring to reach with her students.

Dean began to laugh. "Ms. Cato, what will you get into next? Seriously, Klee, I understand where you are going with this and what an assignment you will make of it. What can I do for you?" he asked.

Klee gave a sigh. "Just be on deck for me, Dean. I have no idea how it will all unfold. I may need to come to you on the spur of the moment, my need for your assistance might be out of the blue and urgent."

Dean nodded, "I'll be here for this project and for you, count on me. By the way, I probably don't need to mention this to you, Klee, but I hope that somewhere in your lessons, you'll take the opportunity to deal with the issue of pet overpopulation and the importance of spaying and neutering. Educationally, we are all so lacking in this area, the whole nation is. We need to do more to educate our students concerning this national disgrace. The students are a natural resource. With the proper knowledge, they could make a difference in their communities. My brother is a vet, and he has many upsetting tales to relate to our family members. So you might say that the topic is near and dear to me."

"Dean, I totally agree, and as a teacher, it has always been foremost in my mind. Mention on the topic is expanded whenever appropriate. I have also found that a mini-unit encompassing the powerful statistics of overpopulation is usually very successful with the students. With the millions of cats and dogs facing euthanasia each year, it is hard to imagine that we refer to ourselves as a responsible society."

Dean proffered his hand, and they firmly shook hands. Klee felt assured that she had a strong ally. It was reassuring to know that he had powerful feelings about the runaway, explosive pet population. What a pleasure it was to be working with a responsive guy! She realized more and more that Dean was some package!

CHAPTER 10

All day Wednesday, Ms. Cato used every skill to keep her students focused and calm. She could feel the electricity in the atmosphere—feel the anticipation of the afternoon and what it would mean for everyone. A mix of emotions surged within her as she internalized more and more each hour, realizing what a commitment she had made. She would not waiver, however, because she truly believed this rescue would have a happy ending—if not today, well, then another day. Besides, she had her guardian angel! Klee constantly called out to her angel for guidance. She had never tagged her angel with a specific gender. Rather, it was a spirit composed of all that was good, and it encompassed both genders, if one needed to be specific.

At 5:30 p.m., some cars and a few pickup trucks began entering the Star Market area. Then more cars came along. Parents and students disembarked—what a crowd. Klee muttered to herself, "Allie, you are the real star, and just look at the audience that has assembled for *you* . . . to help *you*."

Mr. Williams and Mr. Regina began unloading lumber. The students carried the tools and nails, and one twosome stumbled along trying to carry the heavy sawhorses. Ms. Cato encouraged everyone. Mrs. Cohen had laundered all the towels, and Mrs. Alberta and her daughter Robin hauled the three-by-five rug.

A cloak of dimness, what was left of the day's light, broadened across the wintry sky. It wouldn't be long before the thermometer would cascade downward. The elements played such a role in the entire saga of Allie's rescue! Mother Nature was ultimately in control. She held the trump card.

It was amazing to see how fast the shelter was erected. Klee had asked that the shelter be built high enough to allow a person to occupy the space with the dog. This was accomplished.

Some mothers and children assisted as gophers, others huddled together to keep warm and spoke in low murmurs. Klee shared with them what would happen next. From her pocket, she withdrew the food she had packed for Allie and explained that she hoped to coax Allie into the shelter with the food. Regarding the blanket she was holding, Klee explained that she had scented it with her perfume fragrance so that the dog would remember her. When Allie encountered the scent thereafter, she would be preconditioned to expect a positive experience.

Mr. Regina called out, "Okay, Ms. Cato, the job is done. All is ready if you are."

Ms. Cato gave a smile of relief and said, "Thank you, thank you everyone."

There wasn't much light, but there was enough visibility to carry on with the mission.

Klee continued, "I am asking that we refrain from any movement or sound once the dog appears. I am asking that each person be very, very still."

Klee took a deep breath. She hoped with her whole heart that this would work. As she called out for Allie, some of the mothers caressed their children. The builders stood at attention.

"Allie . . . Allie," Klee shouted as she cupped her hands around her mouth. "Come out, girl . . . Allie, come . . . come, girl."

With great joy, everyone watched a limping but fast-paced yellow dog barrel down from the hillside plowing through the accumulated snow. Injury and pain did not slow the basic drive to satisfy hunger. Previously, Klee had requested that Bethany refrain from feeding Allie that afternoon.

Allie didn't seem wary of the assembly. It was obvious that she was more hungry than cautious. Klee extended her hand so Allie could smell the held food. Then Klee moved toward the shelter all the while coaxing Allie to follow. Eventually, both teacher and dog entered the man-made hut. Klee crouched down on the rug. *Bless Mrs. Alberta for the rug,* she thought, and Allie began to sniff and come closer. When the moment seemed right, Klee removed the entire wrapper from the chopped beef, and Allie had most of it down in one gulp. Once Allie finished the food and seemed to settle, Klee covered her with the scented blanket and the towels that had been provided by Mrs. Cohen.

Softly she spoke, "Allie, this is your home for now until we can extricate you from your wooded fortress. Please stay here during the night."

She held the dog close to her beating heart. Allie didn't struggle. It seemed that the dog and the woman connected. Unconditional love flowed between the two like a torrent. Klee looked upward. She knew her angel was there with both of them. She felt the mingling of her spirit with that of Allie's.

Klee emerged from the shelter. She had a somber expression and said, "All we can do is hope that Allie will remain in the shelter throughout the night. We have done our very best at this point in time. I'll return later this evening to see if we were successful. Students, parents, I can't thank you enough. Well done, well done," Klee said as she raised her hands and gave a silent applause.

As the assembly quietly drifted to their cars, Klee waved adieu with a grateful heart. She wondered if Allie instinctively sensed what was being done for her.

As she walked to her own car, the tears flowed. She thought once again of all the abandoned spirits of both the animal world and the human world. It was a refrain that played over and over again in her thoughts.

She drove the sparsely lighted roads to her home, realizing how emotionally drained she was feeling. She loaded the Carpenters song into the tape deck. She clung to the emotional impact and meaning of the words. Intuitively, she knew that her guardian angel would guide her to the next step, no matter what it might be.

She lived alone at that point in her life except for her loyal companion, Muffy Cat. The calico was Klee's shadow. She was smart, demonstrated ESP so often, and, while vividly spirited, she was cuddly and loving too. Muffy had the ability to fill Klee's heart. Klee needed that emotional boost once she arrived home, especially tonight.

As soon as she opened the door, Muffy greeted her and sensed her mood. When Klee entered the kitchen from the garage, she scooped Muffy into her arms, hugged her, and listened to the deep purr. Her soul experienced loving relief.

While Klee caressed Muffin, she whispered into the cat's ear, "The first part of the mission has been accomplished."

Klee prepared her supper half-heartedly. She was hungry, but the thought of actually eating didn't set very well with her. Yet she knew she must nourish herself and keep her strength. Emotions should not rule.

After clearing the dishes and straightening the kitchen, Klee descended to the next level of her home—the family room. The informal room with fireplace, TV, and organ was the focal point of social gatherings, especially during the winter months. The roaring fire in the raised hearth seemed to beckon everyone to its glow and warmth. The cozy room certainly was inviting to her this particular evening. She decided to have some quiet time before she checked on Allie at her new residence. It was time to reflect and to meditate. Klee stretched out on the couch and opened the inspirational book she was using for meditation. Her eyes fell upon a passage about angels written by Sophy Burnham:

> Angels . . . come as visions, voices, dreams, coincidences and intuition, the whisper of knowledge in the ear. They come as animals or other people, or as a wash of peace in an ailing heart. Sometimes a stranger may come up and give you just the information or assistance you need. Sometimes you yourself are used as an angel, for a moment, either knowingly or not, speaking words you did not know you knew.

She reread the passage several times; she believed. Yes, all involved—students, parents, members of the community—filled many of Sophy Burnham's descriptions. Klee's reflective nature gradually gave rise to personal evaluation.

CHAPTER 11

Sometimes Klee felt lonely. It would take her many years and abundant experiences before she understood the difference between loneliness and solitude. Later in life, she came to understand two glorious gifts that solitude provided: the gift of knowing oneself and the gift of freedom and all that freedom encompasses. Once the authentic meaning of solitude is attained, and its worth measured, the freedom and peace that come with it are extremely rewarding. Solitude affords time and quietness to go into oneself and to ultimately find the real person. All the roles one has played throughout life in order to meet certain expectations no longer mean anything. One learns the blessing of finding the . . . *I am.* The awareness of the real self is powerful. The heart truly sings. Solitude is beautiful; it needs to be embraced, not shunned. It need not be feared.

After having a decent supper and a quiet time to meditate, a hot shower was next on the agenda. This would be the final ritual of relaxation before Klee was ready to call Bethany Winslow and report to her what had occurred after school that day.

As she dialed Bethany's number with Muffy in her lap, Klee anticipated that her account would give Bethany some hope and encouragement and something positive to share with her family that evening, even though the ultimate goal of rescue had not been reached thus far.

"Hello, Bethany, I am so glad you answered the telephone," Klee said. "This is Klee Cato, the teacher from Fairhaven Central."

"Oh yes, Klee. It is good to hear from you again. I have been hoping you would call," Bethany replied. "Do you have any news for me?"

"Well, it just so happens that there is. A great deal has transpired since we spoke. There is a movement . . . positive involvement to help rescue Allie. Not only is there student involvement, but a number of the parents have been mobilized into service. What took place today in the late afternoon at the Star Market with the students and their parents was most heartwarming. As a teacher, I'll never forget the mental picture of the entire episode, the students and the parents working together. Good is out there. Often it just needs to be rallied and given a boost."

Klee recounted in full detail the actions of the late afternoon. She explained that she was planning to return to the market that evening around eight thirty to see if Allie remained in the shelter. It was a fifty-fifty chance she realized. Allie most likely would like the warmth of the rug, towels, and blanket and the protection of the shelter, but there is always a "but." Her instinct might dictate to her to go back to the wooded area where she could hide from passersby, car engines, and any other threatening sounds. The wooded place, after all, had been her refuge for weeks, a place that was safe.

"It is wonderful, *wonderful* to hear your description," exclaimed Bethany. "I cannot thank you enough, Klee, for what you are attempting."

"I am living this saga of Allie right along with you, Bethany. There has to be relief—some liberation—and very soon. This is a learning experience for me, and it is my strong desire to make it one for my students too. I do believe everyone involved will glean from the exercise at hand. Just think, Bethany, you are responsible for bringing to light the plight of this abandoned dog."

"You are very kind," Bethany said in a faltering voice. "I, along with my family, have truly tried."

"Your efforts are genuinely appreciated," Klee responded. "There is an adage, and I'm going to paraphrase, that says that it takes only one person to make something positive occur out of a miserable situation, and you are living proof of this axiom. We will remain in contact and do what we need to do for success."

"I am available at any time, or I will make time . . . thank you, Klee. I hope you find Allie in her new home tonight. Should I drive out also?"

"Right now I think it would be best if you don't appear during this establishment of a new person and a new routine. Go ahead, however, with your feeding schedule, but please don't make any other changes if you will agree," implored Klee.

"Certainly, I agree. Just call me when you need me."

CHAPTER 12

K lee bent over to give Muffy a pat on her soft furry head. Muffy looked up at her with deep penetrating eyes. Klee believed that her calico cat understood what she was preparing to do as she slipped into her parka and pulled on her stadium boots.

"Well, Muffy, I am off to check on another four-legged friend. Maybe someday you'll get to meet Allie. I'll return soon, Petite Chat."

Klee's mind raced as she drove to the Star Market parking lot. She wondered why she was guided originally to the Star Market and not the large Wegmans supermarket. She could have just as well gone off to Wegmans on that particular afternoon after the faculty meeting. True, there weren't many store choices because the area was still countrified, although there was definite evidence of growth. It was only a matter of time and the area would balloon into another burgeoning suburb of Rochester. For now though, she was savoring the remaining country atmosphere. She was a country girl at heart. She took pleasure in the simple life and the open spaces with the beauty of nature all around her.

Why Star Market? Klee believed that it was Star because she was supposed to be there at that particular time . . . that particular moment to find the dog. It was ordained to happen that way. The universe has its magnificent design planned out for each individual. Unfortunately, too often, the plan is not accepted or relished too much when presented to the intended receiver. It depends on what the universe is offering! The key is to accept the offer whether one likes it or not.

While parking her car once again in the Star lot, Klee decided that if Allie had remained in the crude shelter, then she would nestle with her in the hut for a reasonable duration. Speaking soothingly to Allie would give the dog a sense of familiar security, she thought. Also, Allie would have the scent of Klee's perfume once again. She had some of Muffy Cat's dried food in her jean's pocket. The chicken flavor should gain the dog's interest. She wasn't concerned about water intake for Allie—there was plenty of snow.

Klee parked her car a distance from the building. She walked slowly toward the shelter, not wanting to display any rapid movement. She was softly humming the upbeat song "I'm Sitting on Top of the World."

Reaching the entrance, Klee bent down and peered into the temporary home. She waited for her eyes to adjust to the darkness. Would Allie's body outline appear?

There wasn't any movement. There was no body outline. Allie was gone! Klee's stomach went to ice. As she meandered to her parked car, Klee kept telling herself that it was only a fifty-fifty chance that Allie would remain in the home. Maybe Allie would return later during the night as the temperature plummeted. There were so many maybes, so many possibilities. Then she concluded that she might have to accept that the plan simply failed. She also acknowledged that Allie was one savvy dog! Obviously, the next phase of the rescue was required.

While driving home, Klee felt the emptiness engulf her. It was a natural reaction, but painful nonetheless. Muffin greeted her by sprawling and rolling on the floor right in the entryway. There wasn't much else to do but pick up Muffy and give her hugs and reassurance. This was one keen cat, and she knew exactly what to do to steal Klee's heart. Klee caressed Muffy and buried her face into her soft body. She felt the moisture from her eyes on the cat's fur. Klee accepted the disappointment, although it hurt.

Facing her class in the morning would be difficult. She had offered encouragement that the shelter would be the first step in gaining the animal's trust. Once the trust was firmly established, she had explained to the students that there was a strong possibility of an easy rescue of Allie. However, with her empty-nest discovery, she had to encourage them to accept that phase 2 would need to be called into play.

CHAPTER 13

After strengthening her resolve to rescue Allie, Klee thought about calling Bethany to tell her that Allie was nowhere to be seen. Of course, Klee wished that she could convey some good news, but she had to be forthright and tell Bethany that the shelter efforts didn't work. The only thought she allowed in her mind was the positive mantra: Allie, you will be saved! Allie, you will be saved!

Klee made a successful connection to the Winslow home. A voice answered, but it wasn't Bethany's. It was a young girl on the other end of the line.

"Hello there, this is Klee Cato calling to speak to Bethany."

"Oh, I know who you are. Our mother has told us all about you. I am Laura, her daughter," she replied. "You are the teacher who is trying to help us rescue Allie. We want to save her so very much."

"It's nice to speak to you, Laura, and I do know how much you want her. Be assured that you will have Allie soon. I'm not exactly clear in my own mind how this is going to unfold, but the rescue will occur."

"My mom tells us that you have such perseverance and faith."

"I have both in abundance. We'll talk again, Laura, I am certain. Now, I'd like to speak with your mom, please."

While Laura summoned her mom, Klee tapped her pencil on the desk. What would be the best approach with Bethany? In her heart she believed that a frank but kind discussion would be best. Frankness was Klee's general method of operation anyway.

When Bethany picked up the phone, Klee explained that she had recently returned from night patrol. With sympathy in her voice, she described her findings at the newly constructed shelter. After all the coordinated efforts, the shelter served for naught, she went on to explain. The disappointment in Klee's voice resounded.

"I thoroughly understand how you feel. It is such a letdown realizing that Allie is still out there. Regardless, I am so grateful, so impressed,"

Bethany exclaimed. "I can only imagine all that was involved. My entire family is appreciative, and we understand the huge undertaking on your part. We are uplifted by you, Klee. I do believe that this will be a year you and your students will never forget!"

"Thank you, Bethany, I appreciate your comments. Yes, you are most likely correct that this will be a banner year. Although there has been a setback, another attempt needs to be taken." She decided to go for it! "I will need your assistance and that of your vet, Dr. Kate Tanner, if you are willing to join with me."

"Of course . . . of course, I'll do whatever I can," vowed Bethany.

Klee outlined her plan. She stated that she, Bethany, and Dr. Tanner should meet at the Star lot early one morning at Allie's usual breakfast time. Once again, some hamburger needs to be laced with a tranquilizing drug before giving it to the dog.

Bethany responded, "Oh, we have tried this more than once, and it didn't work! It was so frustrating and upsetting. I am reluctant to have Allie tranquilized again."

"I do understand, Bethany, but—and it is a big 'but'—I strongly believe it will work this time. I feel such positive energy, and I earnestly believe my guardian angel will be with me. I say let's go for it. Please!"

Klee keenly felt Bethany's hesitance, her doubts, her concerns. In her heart, she hoped that Bethany would try again with the drug approach. If she did refuse, then Klee was prepared to go ahead with the rescue in some manner, although she did not indicate this thought to her.

After a considerable pause, Bethany said, "Okay, we'll do it. I'll get a call into Dr. Tanner first thing in the morning. She's in her office very early. Hopefully, she'll give me a time, and then I'll call you before you leave for school. You understand that we will need to work around her clinic hours, and that means she'll set the time and day."

"Absolutely," Klee quickly responded. "I also need to make arrangements with my vice principal, and I must be sure my students are provided for in the event that I should be late returning to school."

"Good, Klee. Dr. Tanner will make it quite early in the morning if she follows her former pattern. I'll make the arrangements and get back to you."

With a sigh of relief, Klee walked away from the phone. She knew things were beginning to perk again. Patience . . . patience was the key word. Also, visualizing the upcoming rescue event was vital for success. Visualizing success, believing it will happen, and the input of positive energy are the best ingredients for success, indeed.

CHAPTER 14

It was time to call her trusted buddy, Lisa. It seemed that with all that was happening in Klee's life, it was ages since they had had a hearty conversation, but in reality, it was not so.

Klee got comfy in her recliner and picked up the phone. She was anxious to tell Lisa the latest concerning the Allie saga.

"Hi, Lisa, it's Klee. I thought I'd give you a ring with an update about precious Allie. I know we don't have much time to talk at school, so this call seemed the best bet."

"I am so glad you called. You have been on my mind," Lisa warmly replied. "So what's happening?"

Klee filled in the time line of events, detailing the successes, the failures, and the lessons thus far. Once she finished, she turned the conversation to the next hopeful plan to which Bethany agreed.

"I have some good news. Although Allie didn't use the shelter the parents built for her, I am going forward anyway. Fortunately, I do have a commitment from Mrs. Winslow, that's Bethany, the woman I told you about. She is one fantastic lady. Anyway, I'm going with her and her vet to capture Allie. Notice I am using the word *capture*. If it takes an actual capture, then so be it. That's my mind-set."

"I know you, and you'll do whatever it takes," responded Lisa. "I don't know what you have in mind, but please be careful with this undertaking. Remember you are dealing with an injured dog. Allie might become frightened once she feels the sensation of the tranquilizer, and dogs have sharp, tearing teeth!"

"You are so right. I must consider the teeth. I don't know what or how this is going to be resolved. I do know that I feel anxious at times . . . I'm plain old scared. I feel like a kid when scary feelings surface. Hole-ly macaroni! Why do such matters seem to fall at my door? Why don't I just walk away? It would be so much easier, but I know I won't and can't now.

There are so many relying on success. I hope that angel of mine trots right alongside of me!"

Lisa laughed. "That humor of yours always kicks in. Seriously, I believe in you, Klee. I believe the rescue, or capture as you put it, will take place. However, friend, if you should not succeed, remember the two phrases you always use."

"I know," Klee sighed. "If it is meant to be, it will be, or if it doesn't flow, then let it go. Presently, I demand of myself that both phrases remain on the back burner for now. I don't want to even think about them, but I will not completely abandon them either. Thanks for your support. Say hello to Rob for me. Good night, my friend, and I'll see you on Sunday for our cross-country ski trip, if not before."

CHAPTER 15

1984

Klee often recalled her cross-country ski adventures, but she had traded skis for riding the gentle waves of the Gulf of Mexico.

Klee's escape to Florida in 1976 eventually became the best decision for her. She had maintained a permanent residence for eight years. The lifestyle was so much easier and healthier.

The December of 1984, like all her other Florida Decembers, continued to offer delightful experiences in paradise. The temperatures were delicious and the skies filled with marching, billowing clouds with their various shapes were fun to observe. The month of December was especially astounding around holiday time since folks and businesses offered spectacular light displays. Car caravans by the hundreds drive throughout designated areas to view the extravagant light displays and tableaus. The decorations are brilliantly orchestrated and depict every known holiday nuance from snowmen and elves to angels and stars.

Klee didn't miss the cold and snow of the north. She had settled into life in southwest Florida. In place of cross-county skiing, she went sailing on the bay. Her folks had a lovely home on Lemon Bay, and Klee had inherited her love of water from them. She adored visiting their waterfront home; the view was breathtaking.

Canandaigua Lake, one of the Finger Lakes, was Klee's childhood experience. She knew every inch of that lake. So it wasn't unusual now for her family to be settled on the water's edge once again in Florida. Klee used whatever free time she had to sail. Frequently she could be observed tacking to and fro across Lemon Bay. She was in her element and totally contented. To sail along and follow a couple manatees and observe their graceful movements was totally magnificent. Sometimes a few dolphins swam alongside and kept pace with the boat. Their eyes were so large; their sleek, smooth bodies glided effortlessly through the water. She was thrilled to have these creatures move through the water with her.

Holiday break was coming up, and Klee's eighth-grade students had their reports and mini-research papers to hand in before the break. That meant that Klee was accountable for 150 packets from her eighth graders, which needed to be thoroughly read and corrected. The grades needed to be recorded and the packets ready to hand back in January when the second semester began.

Her thoughts, however, were on the fun she would have with her mom especially during the Yule season. Going to her parents' home for the preparation of holiday goodies was a tradition. Baking cookies was an art performed by her mom, Fanny. Revered recipes from Grandmother Catherine's recipe box would be laid out. Fanny too was a fantastic baker in her own right, but Grandma was the master and teacher. Although the kitchen would be void of the petite white-as-snow-haired lady wearing her starched apron, the spirit of Grandma would be with them.

While fussing around in the kitchen with her mom, Klee loved to reminisce and often used the phrase, "Mom, do you remember when . . . ?"

Fanny would purchase all the special ingredients for the cookies, the Brazil nut loaf, and her famous Florida fruitcake in advance. She never took shortcuts in her baking; that's why her goodies were so delectable. Fanny had a huge kitchen, which overlooked the bay. It was special baking cookies and peering through the large slider window at passing boats of all descriptions and sizes out on the water. It sure beat the cold, snowy, and most often ominous cloudy days of winter in New York state.

"Klee," Mom asked, "when do you want to plan time to make the homemade sausage?"

"Once I'm home from school on holiday break, my time is open to you, Mom. Give me a call when it is best for you, and I'll come over."

"I'll need to order the meat in advance and also order the casings for the sausage," Fanny responded. "I'll prepare the hand meat grinder for our use in advance. A good hot-water wash and a light coat of olive oil will do it for us. We'll need to make a great deal because Uncle Albert and Aunt Mary will be coming in from Rochester this year, and the rest of the family from Naples will be arriving too."

Klee's thoughts drifted back to many past holidays she had spent with her Aunt Mary and Uncle Albert in Rochester. They had six children, which always meant a high-spirited gathering when they came together on Christmas day. Ever present in her senses were the delicious aromas of baked goods, ravioli, marinara sauce, Italian sausages, and filet mignon on the grill. Her senses remembered the aroma of the meats. The picture of huge shrimp with cocktail sauce, a block of provolone cheese, Italian olives, and seasoned artichokes flashed in her mind. She was beginning to salivate while reminiscing. She remembered with great fondness the joking and laughter she enjoyed with her cousins as they joyfully participated in the family celebration.

Working at chopping the walnuts, Klee said, "Mom, I have something to tell you. I'm excited about it."

"What is it, Klee?" Fanny asked.

"Do you remember the episode I wrote to you about a dog named Allie? It goes back to the time when I was teaching at Fairhaven Central. The year was 1974. It was a snowy, nasty winter for me in New York state while you and Dad were enjoying the sun and surf of Florida."

"Why, yes, I do. I seem to remember that the experience impacted many lives. It gave me concern and some anxious moments as I thought about your involvement. I was so worried knowing that you were involved in a rescue with an injured animal. Without a doubt you were consumed with the task at hand."

"Yes, I was, and it truly did have a far-reaching impact. Now I'd like to communicate this chronicle to a wider audience," declared Klee. "I have begun typing the story."

Klee told her mom about the recent phone call that came unexpectedly from Bethany Winslow. It had been eight years since they had spoken. Klee explained how embarrassed she felt about the lost contact with the Winslows. She reviewed with her mom some of the deep personal situations that occurred at the time. These events made Klee withdraw mostly from her past, so she let many individuals drift from her life. She explained that the call prompted her to begin to write the story of Allie. It was okay to delve into the story and her past because now she had a handle on that difficult bittersweet period. She was prepared to revisit the time in her life that occurred in New York state during the 1974-75 school year.

With the rhythmic chopping of the walnuts Klee let her mind drift back to 1974 . . .

CHAPTER 16

Klee felt over-stimulated and not ready to prepare for bed after experiencing the failure of not finding Allie in her newly built shelter and her plea with Bethany to engage the services of her vet once again, so she decided to do some schoolwork.

She settled down in her study and began outlining the steps for a play she wanted her students to present to the entire school. On Thursdays, she assigned a flextime period for anything special she wanted to introduce to the class. So she needed to have something prepared for the next day. She was playing around with various ideas—a possible theme or two. A *Space Odyssey* theme might appeal to her sixth-grade students. She felt that with proper guidance, the students could write the script and build the scenery. She would seek the help of the music teacher, Jane Marco, to compose the appropriate music.

The concentration mode was not cooperating, however. Since she heard the six o'clock weather report while having supper, she was distracted and felt unsettled. Stretched out on the desk, Muffy Cat kept a close surveillance. Another four to six inches of snow was predicted for that night. The only consolation was that the temperature would not decline drastically. The weather wasn't cooperating at all with the rescue project at hand. Each day that passed, Klee felt a pronounced urgency—and the true significance of the phrase that "time was of the essence." The phone jangled.

Grabbing the receiver before the phone managed to sound its second ring, Klee said, "Hello, this is Klee."

"Klee, it is Bethany. I know I said that I'd call you in the morning, but I decided to call Dr. Tanner at her home, which I did a few minutes ago. She previously had given me her personal number in case some emergency came up with Allie. It seemed to me that I couldn't prolong this matter much longer, so I called her. I believe that she wants this state of affairs resolved as much as I do. So, Klee, I have some good news! Dr. Tanner will meet with us on Friday morning at 7:00 a.m. She'll drive the vet ambulance and have everything she needs aboard. She will park at the far end of the Star parking lot so Allie is as far away as possible from the wooded area."

"Sounds terrific to me," Klee stated. "I'll be ready! I am concerned about the weather conditions. There doesn't seem to be any letup!"

"I'm very worried too. I can't imagine how much longer Allie will be able to hold out. Her leg and hip must be paining her tremendously with the weather conditions. One other thing concerns me. I have some unsettled feelings about tranquilizing Allie again. I know I mentioned my reluctance before, and for some reason, I can't shake it off."

"I totally understand what you are saying and feeling, but I am certain that this will be the last time. I repeatedly tell myself that we will bring her in this time around."

Klee was excited yet anxious too upon internalizing the news that Friday was red banner day. She had to make a call. Dialing the familiar number, Klee hoped Lisa wouldn't mind the late call.

"Hello," Rob answered.

"Hi, Rob, it's Klee. How is everything with you? So you'll be traveling again."

"Just great, and yes, I'm leaving Saturday morning. Klee, I understand you are involved in another adventure," Rob responded.

"Well, yes, but it is more than an adventure it seems to me."

"Good luck, my friend. I'll get Lisa."

"Hi, girlfriend, what's happening?"

"I know it is late Lisa, but this is a brief call. I want you to know that on Friday morning at 7:00 a.m., phase 2 of Operation Allie Rescue will take place. I received the information of time and date from Mrs. Winslow, and as soon as I hung up, I wanted to call you right away to let you know the good news. Wow! It's all happening so fast!"

"Oh, Klee, I wish you all the luck, and please be very careful, my dear friend."

CHAPTER 17

Thursday morning after the opening exercises, Klee announced to the class that they would be discussing something special during the regular flextime period. The introduction of the *Space Odyssey* production she had planned for flextime would have to be put on hold. Allie was the first priority. She also wondered if maybe, just maybe, a play might evolve around Allie.

Jamie raised her hand and said, "Ms. Cato, does this have anything to do with Allie?"

Ms. Cato smiled and responded, "Why, Jamie, you are perceptive indeed. Actually it does. I'm going to ask you all to work in earnest this morning so we can look forward to our flextime. I think you will like what I have to say. May I count on you all for solid work right up to flextime?"

Many yeses filled the room; some students smiled, others simply nodded.

Eric called out, "Are you going to tell us that Allie has been rescued?"

Ms. Cato looked sympathetically at Eric's innocent face and hopeful eyes. She said, "I wish I could. If only it were that easy. We'll discuss everything later. I want to be sure that you all are involved every step of the way."

Eric Williams had worked so diligently with his dad during the construction of Allie's shelter. Klee recalled Eric's seriousness and devotion to the project. In her heart, she knew that not only was the rescue of the dog imperative, but what the students gleaned from the experience would be priceless.

The students kept their word and academically produced what was expected of them. Seldom did they let Ms. Cato down. The larger block of time scheduled for reading went along smoothly. Next, math period would be fun. For a change of pace, Ms. Cato often set up teams to challenge one another. This meant going to the chalkboard and performing whatever mathematical operation Ms. Cato called out to them. A different score keeper and timer were selected each time the math challenge was employed. The students relished this exercise. Ms. Cato used judgment, depending on the student, when issuing the level of the math operation. Her main goal was to make math enjoyable and to allow everyone to have as much success as possible.

Once math class was completed, the students would be off to their thirty-minute music class. Prior to morning classes, Klee had entered the office and asked the secretary for some time with the vice principal during music break.

About five minutes before the students were ready to go to music class, the intercom static could be heard. The static sound occurred first, and it was the signal that an announcement would follow. All eyes automatically glanced up at the speaker located above the classroom door.

"Ms. Cato, Mr. Cappelli will see you in his office at eleven twenty," announced the secretary.

"Thank you, I'll be there," replied Klee.

Her students looked at her with questioning eyes. The vice principal wanted to see their teacher . . . hmmm? Klee looked at her students and began to chuckle, "See, even the teacher is called to the office by the vice principal!"

The students laughed. This day's unfolding was different for the students. Usually, Klee kept an atmosphere of consistency because it offered a sense of security. The students knew what to expect, and thus, they performed with greater ease. If changes had to occur, the class was totally briefed and understood the why and how of things that brought about a deviation from the daily routine. The exchange with the students explaining departure from the regular routine and the courtesy of interaction concerning alterations resulted in the least amount of resistance from the students. Ms. Cato was a stickler on taking the time to explain the "why" of things. Ninety-nine percent of the time, the explanation technique worked among her charges. They understood and felt comfortable with the change; they became part of it.

Dean smiled broadly when Klee entered his office. His tweed sport jacket with woven threads of light blue and navy slacks with razor-edge creases complimented his jet black hair and cobalt blue eyes. He was not only considered a good-looking administrator but also a well-dressed one too. He was an impressive, tall, muscular man. To add to his physical attributes, he had a keen mind and always tried to be accommodating.

"Hi, Klee, what can I do for you today?" Dean asked. "Could this have something to do with the dog rescue?"

"Hello, Dean, and yes, it does. A great deal has taken place. My students and several parents are involved."

Klee recounted the cooperation of the parents, the students, Mr. Sloan, the store manager, and the building of the shelter on Wednesday.

"So I understand that you have lessons not only in your classroom, but also beyond the confinement of established walls," Dean stated. He expressed how impressed he was that so many parents became involved. "This is great for the kids to see their parents in action."

"Basically, that's all good, but there is a 'but'!" Klee sighed. "After all the energy expended, Allie never remained in the shelter. To my knowledge, she never returned to it—not even once."

"I sense that you are very disappointed, but knowing your personality, you won't stop until you are satisfied nothing more can be done," Dean confidently stated.

Klee explained the phase 2 of the operation, which included the presence of Mrs. Winslow, the vet, and herself, of course. She indicated that Allie had to be rescued this time because Mrs. Winslow was extremely concerned about the overuse of tranquilizing the dog.

"Dean, you asked me how you could help," Klee said. "I am sure I'll be back on campus and in my classroom on time, but in case something goes awry, will you please be available to cover my class? This is short notice I realize, but Mrs. Winslow only called last evening and said the vet could assist on Friday—tomorrow."

Laughing with a twinkle in his eye, Dean affirmed, "Yes, it is short notice, but such adventures can't always be planned, can they?"

Dean perused his planner. Then, looking up with a reassuring smile, he announced, "Consider it done, Klee."

After thanking him, Klee almost glided down the long hall to her classroom. One more concern resolved! One step closer to the liberation of Allie!

CHAPTER 18

As the clock's hands approached one thirty, Klee sensed that her students were ready for flextime. She asked them to clear their desks and settle in for the special period. There was some chatter, but the volume seemed to be at a much lower decibel than usual. Many eyes were upon her. The students appeared to be assessing her demeanor and mood.

While the students were in music class, Klee had prepared an outline of what she wanted to report to them. She wanted to be sure she mentioned all that needed to be said about the Allie caper thus far.

Picking up the outline, she walked to the front of the classroom and stood there as she usually did, waiting for the class's attention. A hush settled among the students.

She began, "I have a great deal to report to you, class. You know that our shelter efforts, in a sense, failed. I use the phrase 'in a sense failed' because, when something isn't successful, it often means that there is more learning that needs to take place. I'd like us to keep that thought in mind. Rather than use the word *failure*, let's use the word *relearning* . . . or a need to reevaluate."

Bob raised his hand and asked, "Do you mean we just go on to the next plan, Ms. Cato?"

"Exactly, Bob. Life is filled with detours, curves, and stop signs, but those are temporary obstacles. We need to work to the best of our ability around the roadblocks that present themselves. When our best is exercised, success is usually the reward—the gold star. Let me say this, however. Sometimes we give our very best and the result isn't what we had hoped for. When that happens, we need to let go.

"Ms. Cato," Jennifer, a bright and articulate student, asked, "are we going to do the relearning bit now?"

Ms. Cato broke into a hearty laugh and said, "We're going to do the relearning bit. Are you with me?"

The nods, smiles, and light in their eyes were reassuring to Ms. Cato. These beautiful, innocent spirits who occupied room 119 made her career special. She explained that matters were moving along rapidly and the plan for the rescue would take place on Friday, tomorrow morning at 7:00 a.m. Their part was very important. They needed to be exemplary students and get on task just in case she was delayed during the rescue. She made it clear that she expected them to do their best for Mr. Cappelli if he should need to take her place for a while. She encouraged them to think in terms of a successful rescue but cautioned that what was meant to be will be.

CHAPTER 19

The Thursday routine at school went off like clockwork. Klee made sure the students stayed on task and avoided any more discussion about Allie's preplanned rescue for the next morning. She wanted everyone to remain calm and focused. Truthfully, however, during the day as her thoughts drifted to the challenge of the next morning, the churning in her stomach underscored her nervousness. Outwardly, she did a good job in covering up; inwardly, she was so anxious that her stomach whipped like an eggbeater.

That evening, there were unexpected but welcomed phone calls from some of the parents. The good wishes for success on Friday morning were the tonic she needed. The comments of support, the parents' interest, and the students' high level of connection with the drama made it all worthwhile. Klee stubbornly believed that the ending would be beautiful for all concerned, unless the weather denied Allie's rescue.

Peace settled over the house as Klee prepared for bed. However, once again, the phone ringing stabbed the silence.

"Hello."

"Hi, Klee," greeted Lisa, "I didn't get a chance to see you at school today, but I called to say that I will be thinking of you in the morning. I'm sending all good thoughts your way, girlfriend."

"Thanks, thanks so much, Lisa. I've put so much energy into this. I will be happy when there is closure one way or another."

"I believe you will be relieved and satisfied with the outcome. If I see that little dance of yours and that impish smile as you approach me in the cafeteria, I'll know Allie has been freed from her wretched existence."

"Yes, I must believe that the rescue will happen. I don't know how much of a dance you'll see because I'll probably be emotionally drained and exhausted, but I'll give a little hop at least!" Klee laughed.

"Keep up the humor, girl. I can only imagine your internal pitch. Try to get some decent sleep tonight."

"Will do, and again, thanks for calling, Lisa."

After the phone conversations, Klee busied herself with some household tasks and gave Muffy Cat some special attention. She had happy thoughts that the saga would be over soon. Tomorrow morning, Klee believed that Allie would be liberated. It seemed incomprehensible, but it was only on Monday when this story began. On the other hand, Klee was a mover. Before climbing into bed, she began her meditation time. She enjoyed engaging in this daily custom; sometimes she was fortunate enough to squeeze into her busy schedule an added reflection period. This was pleasurable and relaxing. It was a precious time to connect with her spirit.

Finally settling into bed, Klee realized that Muffy had already burrowed under the bedcovers. She smiled down at the cat and thought how fate had been good this particular night because temperatures were predicted to stabilize in a normal range. Thirty-nine degrees was certainly better than below freezing.

She was eager for bed that night, and sleep visited her within seconds. She awakened with a start. The clock read 5:00 a.m. Had she been dreaming? Her pj's were damp; she apparently had been perspiring. She felt disturbed, off-center. Her subconscious had played havoc with her; fears and all the what-ifs had surfaced during her slumber. She gathered Muffy into her arms and held her for a short time to calm herself. Then, slowly rising from her bed, she knew that the zero hour was not far off.

The pulsating water from the showerhead felt delicious. She loved the sensation of water in any form at any time. Sometimes she thought that she should have been born under the Pisces astrological sign rather than the Libra. On the other hand, she was a true Libra—weigh and balance, fairness and justice fit her to a tee. Next on the morning agenda was the exercise routine—stretches, sit-ups, and knee bends. This was an invigorating way to begin the day. It helped to ease the unpleasantness of the fitful sleep of the previous night.

To her surprise, her appetite was healthy. She had a hearty breakfast and so did Muffy. She loved to hear Muffy cracking her dried food nuggets. While they were having breakfast, the TV was on with the morning news. Klee was anxious to hear the weather report. This particular morning the report was music to her ears and a delight to her heart.

"Muffy Cat," Klee cheered, "it's going to be a beautiful day, sunny skies with the mercury ascending. What a beautiful day for Allie!"

All the ski apparel had been laid out the night before. Sturdy ski boots, knit cap with face mask to protect her face just in case Allie had a negative reaction, thick ski pants, and full parka were at the ready. As she surveyed the gear, something unexpected happened. She felt light-headed. She began to perspire and felt weak. Her mind raced; her heart pounded with apprehension. Later she was told that she most likely had experienced a panic attack. Klee wasn't sure what was happening to her, but next she found herself on her knees along the side of her bed.

Calling out in a tearful voice, she said, "I have tried my best right along, and I will see this through . . . there is such an investment by so many, and there is a living creature with a beautiful spirit that is waiting to be liberated. I can't keep out of my mind all the animals and children of the world that are desperately waiting to be freed, to be rescued, to be loved. I need you, my dear guardian angel, to be with me. I fully realize that I am a mere instrument playing my part as a member in the huge symphony of life. I do believe it will work out for the best. Oh, but please, dear angel, be with me."

Klee heard some strange sounds then realized those sounds were explosive sobs from the depth of her soul. Finally, she had released the internal tension that had built up over the days. The sobs were consuming. It was a blessing that she had such a powerful release. Tears and sobs clear the soul—refresh the mind. She was a unique individual, and no matter how much she tried to hide her sensitivity from others with her humor, antics, pragmatic approach, and firmness of resolve, she remained an extremely thin-skinned person. She understood, even in childhood, the hurt life served up. She believed that she was probably an old soul and, therefore, looked at situations differently and more intently. Suddenly, she felt a soft sensation on her cheek; Muffy Cat was licking away the salty droplets from her tear stained face.

Klee rose to her feet and straightened up. She patted Muffy's head and said, "Thanks, Petite Chat. I needed to let that all out, and I needed you too!"

Now feeling an inner serenity, she began to dress and selected with care each piece of apparel she had previously readied. While dressing, she imagined a successful mission. Once she was decked out in her rescue attire, she strode to the garage and flipped the ignition key to fire up the trusty Chevy.

CHAPTER 20

At precisely 6:55 a.m., Klee rolled into the Star parking lot and parked at the far end. A minute or two later, Bethany Winslow and Dr. Kate Tanner arrived separately. Dr. Tanner was a tall, slender woman with long wavy brown hair. She was in her whites and emerged from the hospital van holding a collar and leash in her left hand. Klee was introduced to Dr. Tanner, and for the first time, she actually saw Bethany in person.

Klee extended her hand to Dr. Tanner and said, "I am very happy to meet you, Doctor. This is a banner day I do believe."

Dr. Tanner smiled and responded, "Nice to meet you, Klee, and yes, I hope this will be a banner day. I've heard a great deal about you from Bethany."

Klee approached Bethany warmly. "So we finally meet face to face." She embraced the woman with strawberry blonde hair that was meticulously coiffed into a French twist. The navy car coat she wore made her nurse whites more pronounced. Even with the winter coat, it was apparent that she had a petite frame. Bethany was dressed and ready to go on duty at Strong Memorial Hospital once the women completed the task at hand.

Bethany responded to Klee's warmth, "Yes, at last we meet!"

Once the introductions were made, everyone was ready to get down to business.

Dr. Kate planned on placing the collar around Allie's neck once she ingested the laced dog food. She would control the leash that was attached to the collar so she could stabilize Allie's movements. Bethany had a container that held the freshly chopped beef, which was mixed with Heart's dog food stew. According to Bethany, this was Allie's favorite meal combination.

Klee looked at the collar and leash. She felt a red flag go up, and she knew what that signaled to her. Usually her intuition was right on target when her insides sent a strong message to her brain. She was quick to assess the scene. She'd have to speak up. She realized that this would put her in jeopardy, but like all the other times in her life, she would not allow herself to stand by and go along when her gut feeling told her otherwise. Her integrity level often got her into trouble. It was far easier to go along and be part of the crowd or to sit on the fence. This was the name of the game in life, but more often than not, she could not fit into the game mold. In fact, she did not want to play the game—period.

"Dr. Tanner," Klee spoke up, "I can't believe that leash will sustain and control the power of the Labrador once she feels the sensation of the drug. Do you have another type of leash you might consider attaching to the collar?"

"This will be fine," responded the doctor. "I use this in my practice all the time."

Klee realized that Dr. Tanner's tone sounded a little defensive, but she persisted. "Have you ever used this leash with Allie?" asked Klee.

"Well, no, I have not. Allie has always taken off before we could employ the collar properly," responded Dr. Tanner. "Usually we were only able to manage to get the collar on her, but not fully secured." Klee was taken aback by the use of "we." She wondered who was in charge, the vet or "we."

Klee began shifting her feet. Body movement was necessary for her when she was beginning to feel upset. She also could feel the heat ascending her neck.

"Well," said Klee, "I am not comfortable with this at all."

Bethany realized that there were two distinct points of view emerging. Both women were firm in their positions. She also realized that everyone needed to go forward, and naturally, she would lean toward what the vet said.

"Let's try it," Bethany declared. That being said, she clapped her hands twice and called out, "Allie . . . Allie . . . come out, girl. Come, come, Allie."

Right on cue, the yellow limping dog appeared at the edge of the woods. She stood there for a moment whipping her tail as fast as a rotor on a chopper.

Bethany called out again, "Come closer, Allie . . . come, girl."

Allie seemed to have gathered reassurance and mustered courage to leave her safe place to enter the vastness of the parking lot. We were all positioned farther away from the woods than Allie was accustomed, but she trustingly hobbled along to where we were standing. She approached Bethany with unquestioning eyes. Allie was eager for the food she knew Bethany would offer to her. It was a long time between meals, and the cold temperatures required food for energy and heat in order to survive.

When Bethany opened the container of dog food, it emitted a tempting aroma. She placed it directly on a plastic plate that she had brought along for this particular procedure. She used the plate in order to delay Allie's ingestion. This would keep the dog closer to everyone—even if it was only for a few added seconds.

This technique would give the vet her chance to gently place the collar and firmly secure it around Allie's strong neck. Dr. Tanner emptied the prepared syringe into the stew on the server. Once this was accomplished, Bethany gently stooped and placed the feast on the ground. Allie was accustomed to hand feeding and was familiar with Bethany's daily scent. The plate business was a new twist for Allie, but she was hungry and went for it. Dr. Tanner was ready. Her face was fixed and her eyes glued on the dog. She had one shot to collar Allie and control the leash without injury to anyone.

Allie's eyes widened as she anticipated the offering. Her legs appeared to perform a little dance movement as she began to ingest the food as fast as she could. She started to salivate. Her legs appeared to wobble. Dr. Tanner moved forward and, with skill, slipped the collar around the neck of the Labrador. She tightly gripped the leash. Allie went into panic mode; she was feeling a strange sensation. Her instinct demanded that she flee.

Twisting her head, she opened her mouth, and her powerful jaws and razor sharp teeth came down on the leash. Dr. Tanner was struggling to hold on. Again, Allie repeated the same action. Her second attempt was successful. The leash snapped between Allie's vice-gripping jaws . . . Allie was free!

Bethany cried out in a shrill voice, "She's getting away again . . . My God, not again!"

Klee's reaction was fierce. She wanted to pound the hell out of something—out of anything! She was at such a pitch, but her self-control reined her in, so she simply muttered, "Damn it."

Dr. Tanner seemed to resemble a statue because her body was rigid. Her face looked like a carved stone, which reflected disbelief.

CHAPTER 21

During this entire scene on the day of the Allie Rescue, there was a gallery of spectators. Watching from the interiors of their cars as they awaited the early morning commuter bus to downtown Rochester, commuters had a show. One can only imagine what they were thinking as the drama unfolded. It was curious that no one left the warmth of a car to help after observing Allie break free from the restraint.

Hearing Bethany's distressed call and watching Allie fleeing from her temporary rescuers, Klee took off after the dog. Her throat was constricted from the anger she was feeling. She was slipping as her ski boots hit some icy patches and ruts. As she struggled to hold her balance, she flashed back to those days when she was a youngster at the corner lot playing football with her cousins and pals. How glad she was that she had learned tackling skills early in her life! This had to be her best tackle ever. Hopefully, her guardian angel was striding in cadence with her.

Klee called, "Allie, Allie, it's all right!" Finally catching up, she lunged forward while targeting where her hands and arms must be placed on the dog's frame in order to capture her. She would grab Allie around the entire girth of her body, certainly not her coat. She felt the dog's body in her arms and pressed tightly. Allie quickly turned her head, and Klee saw the stark white, sharp teeth. Lisa surely gave her a correct heads-up on the teeth possibility. Instinctively, Klee buried her face deep into Allie's back fur to protect herself. With each twist Allie made, Klee continued to maintain her protected face position and to hang on, waiting for the tranquilizer to take effect.

"Allie . . . Allie . . . it's all over, girl," whispered Klee convulsing into tears. Klee continued holding on, even as she began to feel Allie's body go limp. The tranquilizer took effect. Allie lay motionless. Still Klee would not let go.

Bethany reached the two spent bodies stretched out on the frigid parking lot lane, shouting, "Klee! Klee, are you all right?"

"Yes, everything is fine. It's all over!" Klee exclaimed breathlessly. "I think I could use some of that tranquilizer stuff myself!"

Klee finally released her hold on the dog and gingerly lifted herself. She felt a twinge in her right knee. That knee was always a concern, and the recent tackle made it come alive with pain.

She had experienced an injury several years previously when she taught in the inner city schools of Rochester. She had been assigned, by her own request, to an all-black elementary school that also had a section for special education students. The total school population was over one thousand. Her entry date to the new assignment was in September 1964. The summer prior to the September school opening, the civil rights riots occurred in Rochester, New York. As a result, the school year of 1964-1965 was tumultuous. Every day was a challenge, but the insights and learning during this assignment made Klee a better person.

Jolted back to the present moment by the sharp pain, Klee noticed the huge blanket with the University of Rochester logo Bethany had in her hands in which to wrap the dog. That logo is a good omen, thought Klee. She had completed her graduate work there and was proud to be an alumna of the U of R. The logo display gave her a warm connection, a reprieve from the recent dramatic episode. The blanket was a symbol of something positive in her life, something reassuring. The Latin word *Meliora* in the logo really spoke to her; "Meliora" when translated meant betterment of self and betterment for the society.

Carefully, both women covered Allie's relaxed body. Dr. Kate drove up with the ambulance van. All three women gently lifted Allie into the prepared stretcher bed in the rear of the van. The cradle seemed to perfectly caress her weak, defenseless body. Klee watched the van lumber along the lane until it reached the main road, and the emergency flashing lights on the ambulance signaled urgency.

Some negative feelings surfaced. It was only human. She would have respected Dr. Tanner if she had given some kind of positive acknowledgement about the leash fiasco. Maybe something like, "I'll need to investigate a new type of leash." Any little courtesy would have sufficed. However, Klee made herself shrug it off. She surveyed the parking area and glanced at the faces peering from the parked cars. Moving slowly toward her own car, she wondered, "What are they thinking? Did they experience any emotional response?"

Examining her watch, Klee realized that she had enough time to return home and change her clothes and make herself presentable for class. She was comforted with the thought that if she were five or ten minutes late, Dean would be present to cover her class. As she drove along, she could feel sweet relief infuse her body. Her heart was beginning to function normally. Emotionally, she enjoyed the pleasure of success and knowing that Allie was liberated—Allie was safe now! Closer to home, she was becoming more excited as she anticipated the wonderful news that she would be delivering to her students in a short time.

Walking from the garage into the kitchen, Klee began shouting, "Muffy Cat, Muffy, where are you?" At that, the cat came hurrying along into the kitchen. Klee scooped up Muffy and began to dance—to hug and kiss the cat. Both Klee and the cat in their own way knew something very special occurred that morning—something far-reaching.

CHAPTER 22

Klee entered the side door of the school building from the adjacent school parking lot. The corridor only echoed the clicking sounds from the heels of her shoes as she stepped along to her classroom. Classes had begun. Students were on task. She had herself under control, yet she felt it was okay to let her students see the human side of the event. She realized that her eyes might fill and maybe her voice would falter, but she also realized that this was all part of the learning, the real-life lessons associated with the Allie saga. Life isn't easy. Sometimes we can fix things, and other times we cannot. This time we did. The fixing, the students needed to understand, took time, patience, and determination with hope and faith sprinkled in along the way. Klee, on the other hand, wanted to make certain that she didn't fully break down with relief and joy; that could upset some students who might misinterpret her behavior.

Taking a deep breath, she slowly opened her classroom door. As she displayed a broad smile with raised clasped hands waving above her head, the students began to cheer. Klee herself began to clap her hands and said, "In a minute class, I'll tell you the entire story. First give me a chance to speak to Mr. Cappelli."

Mr. Cappelli studied Klee's face as she approached him. "Obviously congratulations are in order," Dean said in a low voice.

"Oh yes," Klee responded with a huge grin. "Thanks so much for helping me this morning, Dean."

"My pleasure. Let's do coffee soon and you can give me a detailed account."

Klee smiled, "I'd like that, Dean."

Mr. Cappelli wished the students a good morning that would be filled with happiness and lots of learning. With a wave, he exited into the hallway.

The students had all kinds of questions once Klee retold the events of the morning episode. She was so pleased with their exuberance and connection to this real-life drama. She did tear up as she told certain segments of the episode.

Robin asked, "What do you think will happen to Allie at the vet's hospital, Ms. Cato?"

This first question made Klee realize that the students needed to be assured that Allie was in good hands, and that probably the doctor expected her to be all right in the long run.

Klee responded, "I suspect there will be many tests and probably X-rays on the right hind quarter area. That particular area will need special attention."

"Ms. Cato," Eddy asked, "will Allie need to stay in the hospital a long time?"

"It depends on the examination results and what they reveal. It is a matter of waiting it out. What we all have to keep in mind is the fact that Allie is safe, warm, comfortable, and receiving medical assistance."

The next question, Klee had been anticipating and had hoped it would surface. If one child had this thought, there undoubtedly were others.

"If Allie is real bad, will they have to put her down, Ms. Cato?" asked Jessica.

"We must realize that it could be a possibility. If the doctor came to that determination, then it would be the best and the most humane act for the animal. I do believe, however, that Allie might have some ordeals ahead of her, but then she'll be just fine," responded Ms. Cato.

Eric piped up, "My dad said that animals can be put down when they are real sick or injured, but they make humans suffer and go on and on."

"Eric, the euthanasia procedure for animals is a humane approach. What to do about suffering persons takes on different points of view, which are debated throughout the world. Maybe when you are mature adults, some of you might become involved in such a debate."

Eric nodded. He seemed satisfied.

Ms. Cato closed the lengthy discussion period. She reassured the students that she would be speaking with Mrs. Winslow in the evening in order to get the initial report on Allie. She told them that she would be sharing the information right after opening exercise on Monday morning.

"Now let's move along. Please take out your notebooks, open your Social Studies books to page 165, and we'll begin developing the new vocabulary words for the chapter."

As the students prepared themselves for the lesson, Klee's mind was humming in thought. It could be that some of the students, in their adulthood, might give their time and talents to researching the end of life controversy. As society changes, gains more knowledge, and evolves in its thinking, then like everything else, the day may come when there is a better way to intervene and relieve human suffering. She realized that this probably would not happen in her lifetime, but maybe in theirs.

As she readied herself for the lesson at hand and for the student-teacher exchange, she experienced the surfacing of questions that often preoccupied her thoughts. This is a generation that was born into a time of assassinations, presidential scandals, abortion rights debates, military losses, and a record high divorce rate. It was a time of turbulence. It was a time of insecurity. Klee wondered how all this upheaval would influence the young people of the present day, this very class. As this generation matured and became the future generation to impact the nation, what kind of a world would they create? What had the sixties and seventies taught?

During lunch period, Klee could hardly wait to see Lisa and her class make their entrance. There was no way that Klee could detail the entire saga during their cafeteria encounter, but at least she could give the good news to her loyal friend.

The vast cafeteria was noisy with students talking, laughing, and just letting off steam. This was a time that teachers could use to become more personally acquainted with theirs students' preferences, wishes, and dislikes. Klee was amazed with one of her students who brought a peanut butter and fluffernutter each day. It never varied.

Finally, on this particular day, Klee said, "Sue, I see that you bring the same kind of sandwich each day. To say the least, it must be your favorite, your preferred sandwich."

"Yes, it is, Ms. Cato. I love it! I even have it on the weekend too," responded Sue.

Debbie, her best friend, who was sitting next to her, laughingly said, "We tell her that she is going to turn into a peanut!"

Smiling at the youngsters, Klee said, "Remember that variety—trying different things—makes life interesting . . . makes it fun."

Sue blankly looked at her teacher, but Debbie nodded.

Finishing that interaction with the two girls, Klee looked toward Lisa's assigned table area. She waited until the classes were settled and well into partaking of their mystery-bag lunches before she snaked her way among the tables to where Lisa was standing.

With an impish smile, and as inconspicuous as possible, she performed a little skip and hop. Klee said, "It's done. Allie has been liberated. She is safe."

"I'm so happy for you, Klee," Lisa said as she gave Klee a big hug. "You know, girlfriend, that my thoughts were with you. I knew it would all be resolved."

"Yes, it worked, but it almost ended in failure."

With a puzzled look on her face, Lisa asked, "Whatever do you mean by that remark?"

Klee patted Lisa's arm and, while walking away, said, "I'll tell you all about it with a rendition of the entire drama on Sunday while we are skiing."

Lisa nodded and, with a huge smile, called out, "I'll call Rob at his office during lunch break. He definitely wants to know the outcome."

The remainder of the day went smoothly. The students seemed contented and energized with a renewed sense of reassurance, security, and satisfaction. Before the dismissal bell, Ms. Cato took ten minutes to briefly discuss with the students what they would be working on beginning on Monday. She mentioned the need to dismantle the shelter at the Star parking lot, write thank-you notes to Mr. Sloan, the store manager, Mr. Cappelli, and the parents who were involved.

Fatigue visited Klee by the end of classes. She had expended a great deal of physical and emotional energy in addition to teaching that special day. She longed to get home to enjoy a delicious hot shower, a meditation period, and a little catnap with Muffy. She fully realized that it was time to take care of her needs. Recharging her battery was imperative! One thought repeatedly played in her mind, even though she felt exhausted. Dean had asked her to go for coffee. She was totally surprised. What did it mean?

CHAPTER 23

The Westminster chime from the clock in the foyer signaled seven thirty that evening. In unison with the chime, the phone's loud ring startled Klee. How she wished that she had a way to modify the loudness and tone of the ring. She disliked loud, shrill sounds. The phone simply had a high-low setting for the ring and nothing in between.

"Klee, I hope this is a good time to call. I realize that you gave a great deal of yourself today and must be exhausted," Bethany sympathized.

"Hi, Bethany, I was planning on calling you once I put myself back together. I was very fatigued, but I remedied that little annoyance. I'm much better, thanks. New juices are running through my veins—for a little while anyway. What is the news?"

"It seems that Allie will be okay, thank heavens," responded Bethany. "She must have had your guardian angel watching over her too. Dr. Tanner has given her all types of injections. The hip area will need surgery, and she needs to go through a general renewal program. Dr. Tanner wants a waiting period before the surgery so she can record Allie's vitals for a few days and give her time to intake good nourishment. One very positive bit of information that Dr. Tanner found in her initial examination is that Allie has been spayed. With this information, it would be fair to assume that she had responsible, caring owners at one time."

"Wonderful . . . wonderful," exclaimed Klee. "I am so happy and thankful!"

"I, along with my family, am so grateful to you, Klee. You can't imagine the relief and joy that you brought to each of us to say nothing of the bliss Allie will know. You have filled my heart. I was so afraid to actually believe that we would rescue Allie this time, but it did happen. I want you to know that I was very upset about the leash business, but in spite of that, you made it happen."

"Thanks, Bethany, for all the heartfelt words, but I was simply an instrument whose turn it was to play a specific melody in order to complete a symphonic conclusion. All the positive imaging and meditation did help me, to say nothing of the special spirit that guided me each step of the way. Repeatedly, I say to myself a verse from Exodus: 'Behold, I am going to send an angel before you to guard you along the way.' I know my angel was present."

"What beautiful faith you possess, Klee. I envy your approach. I sense that you are a spiritual person."

"I think that's a fair assessment, Bethany. After much thought, I have come to some conclusions about organized religion and spirituality. To profess religion or to state a religious affiliation seems to be the easiest and safest path for many individuals. They seem to be saying, look at me, 'I go to church, I am a supporter of the church, I am a leader at the church.' They rely on organized religion and its teachings to get through life. The Sunday service rituals and sermons seem to make them feel better. The church connection gives them a sense of security that they are on the right path. Yet very often in daily life, all the teaching and preaching absorbed at church seems to evaporate. The talk doesn't match the walk, so to speak, and it must, and not just on Sundays.

Spirituality, on the other hand, demands a deeper awareness, a real examination of one's actions. It's a more difficult path to follow, and is often misunderstood by others, but the inner awareness by the practitioner is priceless. Spirituality doesn't necessarily have the tenets and rituals of organized religions to lean on. However, the action, the behavior, is what counts. Spirituality is the union of the individual with the great spirit, the universe, with nature, with God. The harmony of spirituality makes the heart sing. It's not relying on what is preached every Sunday. It is relying on oneself which is in union with a greater power."

"Gee, I didn't mean to go on so, Bethany, but I am passionate about what I have just conveyed to you."

"Yes, Klee, your words and actions can be relied on without a doubt. I have the impression that you are not a Sunday Christian. You go beyond the structure of the walls."

Bethany and Klee had a lengthy conversation about future plans for Allie, the students, their general elation and feelings of inner serenity.

As soon as Klee finished the conversation with Bethany, she made her call to Lisa. She was so anxious to tell her the high points of the day's adventure.

"Hi, Lisa," Klee said in an upbeat voice, "do you have some time to talk? I was planning on telling you all about the rescue on our ski outing, but I'm so elated I find that I can't wait until then."

"Of course, go ahead. I've been sitting by this phone all evening hoping that you would call," laughed Lisa. "Rob kept reminding me that it wouldn't ring any faster by being glued to the phone. Tell me all about the rescue."

Klee gave Lisa a sequential report of the entire event while Lisa listened intently without interrupting. She put emphasis on the leash controversy, and how fortunate it was that the miserable leash didn't void the rescue. She candidly stated how furious she was with Tanner and the expletives she had muttered.

"So that's the end of the saga," Klee closed.

"I have listened carefully," responded Lisa. "I can't believe how close you came to having the mission corrupted over a leash! I am so happy for you . . . for all concerned. I'm proud of you . . . you know that."

"Thanks. Remember, I'm just an instrument! I do have some other information that I want to share with you, however. It's funny how things unfold. When I thanked Dean for taking over my class for me this morning, he indicated that we should go for coffee, so I could tell him all about Allie's rescue."

"See, I told you," Lisa excitedly shouted. "I think you two would be perfect together. I know we are all together at faculty parties and other events, but I have been hoping he'd personally ask you out without the crowd around."

"Wait . . . wait, matchmaker. I don't consider this anything like a date. Hole-ly macaroni, he only asked me for coffee and information about this special project I've been involved in with the various players."

"We'll see," Lisa responded with a lilt in her voice.

After completing her call, Klee began to think about Lisa's comments. She knew that Dean was a guy who had lots of appeal, and most of the female faculty members really liked him. She liked him too but she never quite thought of him other than a nice man, fun at parties, and a good administrator. Once in a while Dean brought some gal with him to special doings like at the end-of-the-year faculty dinner, so she figured he had his own cluster of women friends from which to choose. Yet Lisa had planted a seed in Klee's thoughts. Just maybe the coffee thing was a beginning!

*   *   *

Klee looked forward to Sunday—to the freedom of the out-of-doors. Cross-country skiing would provide the opportunity of exhilarating exercise at Mendon Ponds Park. The physical workout would transmit renewed energy in Klee's body. Her knee recuperated and it felt okay.

The park was a favorite among hikers and cross-country ski enthusiasts. The snow-laden tree branches bowed to the passersby. The birds serenaded with their sweet songs in the early morning while they flitted from tree to bush, and rabbit and fox paw prints were evident in the virgin snow that abutted the ski trails. The clear azure sky was picture-perfect. The beauty of nature was so gripping, Klee's spirit soared.

Both Lisa and Klee were adventuresome souls; often they would leave the worn trails in the park and head off to unclaimed areas. This meant expending more energy, but the thrill of going to secluded areas was a driving force. Both women were hoping to come upon a few docile deer or maybe Reddy Fox. Lisa carried her small Kodak camera in her ski jacket pocket—just in case. Although Lisa's teaching career exceeded Klee's by several years, Lisa's spunkiness, energy, and wit were a pleasure to experience. The two women had a special bond.

CHAPTER 24

On Monday morning, Klee stopped in the faculty lounge before going to her classroom. She felt more relaxed and better equipped to socialize. The days of the demanding challenges were behind her, and she had recaptured more energy to be her high-spirited self. She didn't know if by chance her last adventure had circulated among the teachers, but if it had, she would at least be ready to briefly recap the event with enthusiasm. In her heart, she had hoped that it was not common knowledge. Those who were supportive were always a pleasure. They would come to her privately to express their good wishes. Gentle hearts lifted one's spirit. On the one hand, Klee was not one who tolerated dealing with those who engaged in nonsupportive conversation, jealousies, and school politics—especially the politics. She became infuriated by the brown-nosing. Those that did engage in such behavior were most likely insecure individuals. The draconic behavior often reminded her of a junior high mentally. On the other hand, Klee ascribed to being who she was, period. She remained an independent thinker and a self-determined entity. Her dedication to individualism was obvious.

"Good morning . . . good morning," Klee called out as she entered the faculty lounge.

There were murmurs of "hello," "hi," some nods, and from others no acknowledgement. Often it was a subdued group early in the morning. This was such a morning. Some were discussing a specific problem occurring in the cafeteria. Two teachers were involved in private conversation.

Marie looked up and smiled at Klee. Klee made her way over to her.

"Marie, I haven't had a chance to talk to you in some time. How is everything going for you?"

"Just great. The kids are fine and so is Don. He is coaching basketball on the weekend now."

"He never sits still, that's for sure," Klee laughed.

Klee and Don had been close friends after his divorce. She liked Don and his children. They were great kids, and they were fortunate to have a caring, responsible dad. The children lived with Don. He exercised both parental roles very well. Then Marie came along. She became Don's love and his children were crazy about her too.

Marie told Klee about the children and some of their involvements. Klee listened intently. She also realized that those present in the lounge were not aware of what she and her class had been participating in last week. This was just as well for many reasons, Klee mused.

She would share the story of Allie someday with Marie and Don. They were her good friends along with Lisa and Rob. The five of them seemed to naturally form into a congenial group. Besides the two married couples, cousin Salena, and the two bachelors, Dave and Jacob were also part of the group. They had such fun at the social gatherings or during the faculty parties Klee hosted. Klee had a four-level home, and that meant there was ample space for a large crowd. Not only were faculty members present, but also some foreign exchange students from the University of Rochester. Forty to fifty people attending such parties was the norm.

Often, the small, congenial group remained after the others left to have breakfast at three or four o'clock in the morning. The aroma of bacon and eggs wafted from the kitchen, enticing them. They kicked off their shoes and flopped into relaxed positions. That seemed to be the ticket after an evening of partying. Usually they got into discussions on current events. Muffy Cat was always a true trouper during these parties. She demanded her own chair in which to observe the party and let no soul invade that chair. By the early morning, she could hardly keep her eyes opened, but as a sentinel, she remained on her throne.

The teachers were beginning to pick up their coffee cups and file out of the faculty lounge for their classrooms. Finally, Klee said, "I'm going to run along, Marie. It has been nice catching up. I hope your day goes well for you. I'm anticipating a wonderful day!"

Klee entered her classroom and immediately went to her desk to peruse the lesson plan book. She realized that everything that had been planned for the week was out of whack because of all the changes and interruptions involved in the Allie Rescue Project. The buses would be pulling into the traffic circle in fifteen minutes. She needed to outline new plans for the day and pronto! That wouldn't be a difficult task because there were matters to finish up concerning the Allie Project. The emphasis would center on language arts exercises in the form of thank-you notes to so many who had given of themselves during the Allie caper.

The students came into class chatting as usual. While the students settled into their seats, Klee sensed that they could hardly wait to get through the upcoming opening exercises so they could hear what Mrs. Winslow had to say about Allie. Dr. Tanner's findings and assessment of Allie's condition were of high interest to each student. They had invested themselves in various ways into the rescue project, and now, as all interested investors would be, they wanted the results of their investment while fully understanding that the end results could be either positive or negative. The previous class discussions made that premise very clear. Real-life lessons were unfolding indeed.

Once attendance and the opening exercises had been completed, Ms. Cato approached the student desk area. With a twinkle in her eyes and her hands clasped, she began, "Class, I have wonderful, joyful news for you this day!"

Before she could go on, the class began to applaud. A spontaneous burst of cheers and excitement filled the room. The hubbub was quite loud. Klee drank in their enthusiastic exuberance and their beautiful innocent faces. As she observed their glee, she wished in her heart that life's problems for each of them could be solved as it had been in this situation. She wondered what road each student would travel and hoped that she could prepare them with the inner understanding that life has its own way of unfolding. The important lesson was acquiring the skill of rolling with the punches. All endings, all investments did not always result in winning. Yet each experience, regardless of the result, must be viewed as a learning experience and thus, ultimately, a real win.

Klee mused that each student's mind was like a garden that needed to be tended and cultivated. She was serving as the gardener who had the responsibility to plant seeds and to nurture the young plants. Each student had special attributes, beautiful spirits, and each was worthy of the finest gardening care. What kind of flower would each become as he or she matured and entered adulthood? Realistically, she accepted that there would be weeds also. Yet the weeds served a definite purpose because the beauty of the flowers would eventually overcome the weeds.

When Ms. Cato raised her hand in a familiar gesture that signaled to the students that it was time to settle down, everyone gave her their attention.

"I want to share with you the report from the vet, Dr. Tanner. Allie basically is a healthy dog. The doctor estimates that she is about two and a half to three years old. She is consuming the food offered to her with great relish. This is all good news for us to hear and for Allie. However, there is a 'but.' The X-rays reveal a great deal of calcium buildup in the area of the injured hip. Dr. Tanner will perform surgery and clean out that area. In time, Allie will have a normal dog walk."

The students laughed at the phrase "a normal dog walk."

"Mrs. Winslow said that we will be hearing from her once Allie is fully recuperated," reported Klee.

Debbie raised her hand and said, "Ms. Cato, do you think that we'll ever see Allie?"

"Yes, I do. I think there is a strong possibility. We'll hold that positive thought. Also, I need to mention this. Dr. Tanner, during the exam, discovered that Allie had been spayed. This indicates a responsible pet owner and one that truly cared about the dog." She let that bit of information settle. She then continued, "Now that we have finished with the discussion, we'll need to select team captains for a special writing exercise. The objective will be to write thank-you notes to all the helpful persons during this project. I'd like each team to gather their thoughts of appreciation. I'm not looking for the ordinary 'thank you,' but notes that express examples of heartfelt appreciation. Share your ideas and follow the same procedure as you would do during Circle Talks. In the notes, it would be a good idea to tell what this experience has meant to you and certainly to Allie. Then we'll take time to edit.

Also, I must tell you that I have already stopped in to see Mr. Sloan, the Star Market manager, to tell him the good news about the Allie rescue and to inform him that the shelter will be dismantled and removed. Eric Williams, I'll call your dad tonight and ask him to get in touch with Andy Regina's dad so they can plan a time to dismantle the shelter and haul away all evidence of the temporary housing. It should be soon since that would be a gesture of thoughtfulness and courtesy on our part. Even though it is placed along the side of the building, it is unsightly, and we don't want to wear out our welcome."

As a teacher, she found it best to always explain the reason for the action to be taken or for the behavior to be performed. This way, the recipient of the request requiring a specific action found it more agreeable because the reason for the action was made clear during the request. It was a far more successful and respectful approach than making the demand that one must do it—period.

It was a busy morning. The tasks were of real importance. The thank-you note assignments had meaning and worth. The feeling of pride and self-worth floated and bounced from one student to the next. Klee so enjoyed these types of exercises, these lessons of life.

Later that day, Klee ran into Dean in the hall corridor. She felt somewhat self-conscious since Lisa made personal comments about her and Dean.

"Hello, Dean," Klee called out with a big smile on her face.

Dean replied, "With that happy face, may I assume that the Allie quest is concluded?"

Laughingly Klee said, "Yes, it is. It's just wonderful, but I don't think this story will ever be entirely concluded this year."

"So how about coffee after school on Friday if you are free?" offered Dean. "I want to hear all about it. Maybe we'll even celebrate with a glass of wine rather than coffee."

"Yes, I am free, and it sounds nice, Dean."

"Fine, let's meet in the village at Geraci's Cafe at five o'clock, if that will be good for you."

Klee felt somewhat surprised at this new interest that Dean was demonstrating. What brought this on? Bottom line, she felt flattered, but she cautioned herself to think only in terms of a professional exchange of information. She didn't think she was Dean's type at all. Some of the gals he brought to parties were . . . well, real lookers and sophisticated. True, she had nice looks and a shapely body, but she never flaunted what she had. Besides, she was a homebody. All the sophistication and show were never her milieu. She enjoyed the simple life and nature, period. She could just imagine Lisa's take once she was provided with the new terms of the invitation.

Klee was pleased with herself and with the upbeat tenor of the day. She left school as soon as possible because she continued to feel unusually tired. During her travel home, she recapped the day's events. The students did a great job with the thank-you notes. Klee also personally wrote notes to the homeroom parents that had any involvement in the Allie adventure. Students and teacher had been on task simultaneously.

Once home, her intention was to take a hot, luxurious bath and go into a relaxed mode. Usually, the relaxed mode was short-lived for Klee but enough to refire her spark plugs. She felt a delicious relief and a sense of well-being. She wanted to enjoy these feelings and let her body bathe in the embracing peace. The Allie saga seemed to be under control for now; it was time to focus on other matters.

CHAPTER 25

On Thursday, Klee remained after school to meet with one of the parents on a very confidential matter. It was an eye-opener. Klee empathized with the situation as she listened, and especially with the student involved in this family triangle. Once apprised of what was going on in Steve's life, she committed to assist in any way possible. Steve was a nice lad. He was quiet and downright timid. Klee had wondered about him and always kept a vigilant eye out for him.

After what his stepmother had shared with her, Klee had an entirely different approach concerning Steve. She realized that the stepmother, the dad, and the biological mother would be in her life because she was Steve's teacher. *So be it*, she thought as she left school and headed for her Chevy. It was another situation plopped on her plate. She would do her best for Steve, even more so now that she was privy to personal information and all the emotional and legal ramifications.

As she negotiated the turn into her driveway, she decided to pick up the mail right away because she had no intention of bundling up later to go out in the cold to retrieve the delivered post. Klee was delighted to find three special letters among the bills.

One letter had a White Plains, New York, postmark, so Klee anticipated it was from her former roommate, Beets, who had left the Rochester area to pursue her career beyond the classroom. The other was from Elmira, New York, from her former eighth-grade teacher—her mentor, her beloved friend. Eighth grade seemed so long ago, and it was. The last letter was from her mom. As the holidays approached, Klee always looked forward to her mom's special greeting.

As Klee entered her home, she engaged in the welcoming rituals with Muffy Cat. She was eager to get to her letters but wanted something soothing to drink. She placed the shiny stainless steel kettle on the range to boil water for some herbal tea.

While waiting for the water to boil, Klee freshened up. Muffy followed her into the bathroom and proceeded to scale to the edge of the sink vanity. She liked to play with the water whenever Klee turned on the faucet. The next part of the routine always brought a smile to Klee's face. She would fill Muffy's special glass with cold water and present it to the cat whose noisy tongue lapped the cold water eagerly. It was a comforting picture. As for the hot tub soak Klee wanted to indulge in, she decided it would follow the letter reading and the hot tea.

Settling down in her recliner in the family room with Muffy in her lap, she placed the steaming mug of tea on the end table. With warm anticipation, Klee opened her first letter.

Hi, Klee,

Well, girl, this is my first chance to take some time for myself. I am so behind in my letter writing. You probably thought I had dropped off the face of the earth, but I really have been snowed under. I can say that both literally and figuratively. However, our snow accumulations are not as bad as what has been dumped in the Rochester area. To me it's nice not to worry about frequent loads of the white stuff.

I have some good news. I know you will be happy for me. It is my dream, and I have been working toward this position since I entered the public school arena. I am being considered for a district-wide position—chief consultant of elementary education. I am thrilled to be considered by the powers upstairs. Working my derriere off just might pay off. The announcement of the selection will be in early March. Then the new appointee will shadow the present chief until June. Beginning with the new fall semester, the new chief consultant assumes the reins. If I make it, I'll be on top of the world. My sister, Jenny, will be so proud of me. She remains a principal in Ogden as you probably remember. Our parents will have lots to talk about. My dad is such a braggart, but really, he is proud of his daughters.

Remember the vice principal I told you about? He remains such a jerk in my opinion. I hate it when I have dealings with him. Believe me when I say he is a jerk . . . guess he feels the same way about me. However, I am always professional in his company, although I cringe when I see him approaching me. If I get this new district-wide position, his socks will rot.

I am anxious to know what is happening in your life. What new involvements are you into—you know the ones you can never walk away from, dear Klee. Hope to hear from you soon.

Big hugs, kiddo.

Beets

Klee smiled as she sipped the hot tea. If Beets could only see her vice principal! She wouldn't cringe when he approached her; she'd melt. Klee missed having Beets as one of her roommates, but she enjoyed the fond memories of her.

Next, Klee slid the envelope opener under the sealed flap and anxiously withdrew her mom's letter.

Dear Klee,

I find that I have been reminiscing of late. I drift back to Canandaigua Lake when you were a little girl. Maybe the flashbacks occur so frequently because Dad and I live on the bay, and I watch the fluctuating moods of the water. Maybe *it's because I know that bodies of water and you go together just as animals and you have a special connection.*

I keenly remember the hours you spent outdoors exploring along the creeks and waterfalls when we were at our summer home on Canandaigua Lake. I remember all the poison ivy bouts too, but your love of nature drew you into a world of calm and beauty, poison ivy, and all! Of course, if you weren't off exploring, you kept me on my toes with your long hours of swimming and playing in the water. Do you remember when you and Billy Wingate deliberately capsized his dad's large canoe, and I thought you had really gone under? Klee, you kept me in a state of anxiety so often. Yet this is who you are and all the early experiences were preparing you for the woman you have become today, my daughter.

How I wish you could be with us for Christmas. My heart feels empty knowing that you are so far away. We will call you on Christmas eve night.

Take good care of yourself, Klee.

Your ever-loving mother . . .

Klee felt some sadness after reading her mom's letter. She too wished that she could be with her for Christmas. If her mom only knew where Klee's love of animals had taken her these past days, she'd probably vicariously join right in on the adventure. She would write her a long letter soon and tell her all about her last challenge—all about Allie.

Klee truly missed the special fun she and her mom shared, not just around the holidays, but all the time. She missed the laughter and the humor. The pet name she tagged on her mom was Duck, and Klee was her Duckling. She sure missed the Duck!

Too bad she couldn't board an airplane and zip South for the holidays. Because of medical reasons, she was unable to fly. This restriction curtailed a great deal of her dreams and plans. She knew she must not dwell on the inability to travel because it only elicited sad feelings, so she went to the kitchen to boil more water for another cup of tea before opening the last letter.

My dear Klee,

From your brief note, I understand that you are involved in a special project. Your words indicated your passion to rescue Allie and to make this a memorable learning experience for your students.

I know you so well, and I am exceedingly confident that you will succeed. Please let me know what has occurred. Also, I realize that you are struggling with the human element.

I understand, Klee, how strongly you feel about errors of omission and commission. Please accept that most individuals will adhere to omission. This way, they do not have to become involved. By using the omission mechanism, it becomes a way of protecting oneself. Probably that's why so many ignored the plight of the dog. It takes a great deal of character to stand up and to be counted, and yes, it takes only one person to make a difference. That person's example becomes the banner call for others to follow.

We have discussed this very point on other occasions, but I realize that you have not internalized what we have discussed. The day you do, you will find greater peace and not become so disappointed in your fellow man.

You are in my daily prayers . . . you know that, my dear heart. On Sunday, the sisters' recreation period is from two to four o'clock, so if you would like to telephone me during that time, it would be so nice to speak with you about your latest challenge and, of course, to hear your voice.

With deep understanding and love,

Sister Ann Mary

Klee would definitely call Sister and bring her up to date. How she missed visiting with her at the convent. Since she had been transferred to Elmira, that pleasantry, that need was unfulfilled. It was a healthy drive to Sister's new convent assignment and not the easiest to accomplish in one day's drive, but it was doable.

Sister Ann Mary had been such an influence in her life. Over the years, Klee realized that she could thoroughly confide in Sister who listened, guided, and loved Klee for Klee. Even with all her duties and the restrictions placed on her as a nun, Sister somehow was always there when Klee needed her.

Klee went through several operations early in her life beginning at age twenty-five. Each physically altered her life, and each took its toll. Sister Ann Mary, along with a sister companion, was at her bedside when she could be. Her loving care never faltered. Her encouragement sustained Klee, as Klee realized that her life was about to take a new path after the surgeries. She never dreamed that a former teacher would be such an integral part of her life. With Klee's mom so far away, she was fortunate to have the continued connection with Sister Ann Mary.

CHAPTER 26

Classes went along as usual on Friday. However, Klee had to admit to herself that as the school day came closer to dismissal time, her thoughts began to meander to the meeting with Dean at Geraci's Cafe in the village of Fairport. She decided to do her lesson plans and prepped for the next week following the dismissal of the class. She would have plenty of time to complete her tasks before meeting Dean. Then she wouldn't have to bring her work home over the weekend.

Scanning the huge wall clock in her classroom, Klee suddenly realized that it was already 4:30 p.m. The time seemed to fly by like a speeding bullet. She gathered her materials and placed everything in order on her desk for Monday morning. She freshened up before leaving for the village. Good thing the drive to the village was a mere five minutes away.

Klee arrived at five o'clock. Punctuality was important to her. She had been taught as a youngster that punctuality demonstrated respect for the occasion and the other party involved.

She had always liked the café. There were murals depicting scenes of Italy. One mural depicted Venice, and another large one portrayed the golden fields of Tuscany. Hanging clusters of grapes were appropriately positioned throughout the café. Upon the red-and-white checkered tablecloths were ornate candle holders supporting red candles. The general ambiance of the café was warm and welcoming. All the holiday decorations made it especially festive.

Upon entering the café, Klee scanned the cozy setting, and sure enough, Dean was waiting for her.

Dean stood up as Klee approached the table. He flashed his pleasant, inviting smile. Even his perfect white teeth were nice to look at.

"Hi, Klee. Please sit. Did you have a good day?"

"Yes, I truly did. It's been an exciting period of time for the students, me, and the Winslows."

Before Klee could go on, the waitress appeared at the table. Both Dean and Klee ordered wine. Dean's choice was a sauvignon blanc, and Klee specifically asked for a Taylor Lake Country red wine.

"I am partial to Taylor wines because of the local area production. They are excellent tasting wines. When I was a kid, my dad sold the grapes from his small vineyard, which overlooked Canandaigua Lake to the Hammondsport wine industry. Hammondsport is south of Canandaigua, situated at the south end of Keuka Lake."

"I didn't realize that there was a wine industry just south of us," Dean responded.

"Hammondsport is the home to numerous wine companies," Klee explained. "A visit to the Greyton H. Taylor Wine Museum is pleasurable, and the lake area is most inviting."

"I have very little knowledge about all the Finger Lakes, but I'd like to become more acquainted. One Finger Lake I am most familiar with is Cayuga Lake . . . not far from Ithaca. My family enjoyed it while I was a kid. We'd spend the month of July on the lake each year. My dad rented it from a priest who was a pal of his. Father Patrick and my dad had gone to elementary school together. So it worked out nicely for us to use Father Patrick's cottage each summer. We were lucky kids. My brother Sam never forgot our days on the lake, and now he has a cottage on Cayuga. His kids love it as much as we did.

"I'm thinking that maybe one Saturday we could make a day trip to Hammondsport, so I can experience another lake in the Finger Lakes chain," Dean suggested.

His invitation took Klee by surprise. She never had expected such an invitation from him, but she was enthusiastic in her reply.

"Why, Dean, that would be a fun outing! I haven't been to the area since I was a kid. It would be a nostalgic trip for me and an informative one for you I suspect."

Klee went into her teacher mode and began to explain that originally the village of Hammondsport, which was founded by Lazarus Hammond, was incorporated as a village back in 1856. Later it became the center of the New York wine industry. So it was a natural that the harvest grapes from her dad's vineyard found their way to Hammondsport.

Both agreed that they would enjoy an appetizer. Once the shrimp cocktail was selected from the menu, Dean opened the conversation about Allie. He wanted to know all the details about the rescue. Klee obliged by enthusiastically giving a replay of the events. Dean listened with interest as he sipped his wine and gazed at her with his penetrating cobalt blue eyes. His intense quality of listening was appreciated by most individuals since he cared enough to listen with full concentration. This trait certainly made the other person feel a connection, feel an appreciation as a special individual.

Once Klee concluded, Dean said, "Tell me more about the Winslows."

"Well, they are exceptional people—and an exceptional family. The old saying that it only takes one person to make a difference certainly applies to Bethany Winslow. She led the charge. Of course, she had her family's support, which made her trials somewhat less intense. Bethany is a petite woman but strong in spirit. Her loyalty to Allie is evident. She is a strong woman, and I'm glad she came into my life."

Dean said, "Klee, I am sure that she is happy that you came into her life and that of Allie's. As for me, I am happy to have knowledge of this episode. I believe you when you say it is an experience that probably will never have closure. The spirit of Allie will live on. All I can say, and most sincerely, is well done, Klee."

Those words lifted her spirit; her heart felt the glow.

"I'd like to mention to you, Klee, that since we have been working together on the Allie project, I have come to know you better and find you to be an intriguing, unique personality. I must tell you that I find those traits attractive. Even your name is unique! I've never heard the name Klee before. Tell me about it. Is it a family name from a past generation?"

Klee smiled. "Well, it is a nickname. When I was about seven years old, my cousin Ronnie, who was three years my junior, couldn't pronounce my name. He tagged along after me calling, K-lee, K-lee. From that, the named evolved into Klee, and I was forever Klee to family members and relatives."

Dean smiled. "See, even that story has a uniqueness to it, Klee."

Dean and Klee discussed other school concerns, a couple of marriages of faculty members that were forthcoming, and camping. Klee revealed her love of nature that led her to purchase a campsite in the hills of her beloved Canandaigua Lake.

In the spring and fall, Klee would pick up Muffy Cat and the supplies on Friday afternoons and drive to the peacefulness of her camp. She gave a gentle *toot* as she drove along the extensive road winding through the camp area. She'd hear, "The teacher is here." She so looked forward to seeing all her friends, the ease of the camp lifestyle, and the shutdown of all the professional responsibilities. Her summers were spent at the camp and on the lake, if she wasn't taking courses at the University of Rochester.

Dean told her about himself. His family's domicile was in Ithaca, New York. He had three sisters. Rose was the eldest followed by Maria and Catherine. Rose and Maria resided with their families in Ithaca. Catherine, along with her family, had settled in the Cortland area northeast of Ithaca. He explained that his mother was pleased that Catherine's move wasn't very far from the family homestead. His older brother, Sam, also resided in Ithaca with his family. Sam, the firstborn, was a veterinarian with a good practice. Dean was the baby of the clan. He stressed the closeness the family shared. From his comments and little side stories, it was evident that he was crazy about his parents, sisters, and brother. Traditions and religion were of supreme importance to the members of the Cappelli family.

Dean completed his undergraduate and graduate studies for the master's degree at Cornell University. Now his goal was to earn his doctorate. Dean had been accepted for the doctoral program at the University of Rochester. His face lit up and his eyes danced as he discussed the program and his goals. The enthusiasm he exuded was gratifying to observe. He was working on the postgraduate studies by taking night classes and classes during the summer months. Eventually, he would need to spend a year on campus for intense studies, academic residency requirements, and work on his dissertation. Although he wanted to accomplish his goal, he disliked the thought of leaving Fairhaven Central for that year or maybe even two. He truly enjoyed his work at Fairhaven.

Before they realized it, the ornate wall clock chimed. They both looked up, and to their surprise, it was six thirty. Dean suggested that they order dinner. Klee had made up her mind right from day 1 to go along with the flow, and she stuck to it. She really hadn't expected dinner, but why not.

She said, "I think that's a good idea. I admit that I am hungry!"

Dean smiled. "Consider it done."

As the last drops of the second glasses of wine were drained, and the meal came to a close, there was a pause.

Dean finally said, "Klee, I'm going home to Ithaca for Christmas, but then I'll return shortly after to work on a research paper for one of my classes. I'm wondering if you would like to go to dinner and dancing at the Spring House? Maybe we could go toward the end of the month . . . let's say the twenty-eighth or twenty-ninth?"

Now Klee was really knocked off her seat. Actually, she was shocked. Never in a million years did she expect such an invitation. Dean was asking her for a specific date, and it had nothing to do with school. She realized that she needed to display composure and, at the same time, exhibit warmth and interest.

"Dean, what a nice invitation," Klee replied. "I love the Spring House. It is especially lovely with all the decorations around holiday time. I'm sure it will be a delightful evening."

Klee was careful not to make her acceptance too personal or overly enthused. She was aware that Dean had not asked her out for New Year's Eve, but that was just as well because she was going to a house party that evening. She realized that he most likely had a date for the special eve celebration. After all, it was only recently that they had become aware of one another on a totally different level. The shift in their relationship from teacher and administrator to dating had to go slowly, to avoid any potential hurts down the road. The "Infamous Friday," which the first café meeting would be referred to, had quite an unexpected twist to it!

Returning home after she and Dean had parted on a most cordial note, Klee remained in the bombshell mode over what took place at Geraci's. He asked her out for a real date. Although she was caught off guard, the planned evening date sounded great. She decided to call Lisa and get her input on Dean's invitation. She realized that it was a Friday evening and that Lisa and Rob often began their weekend by going out for cocktails and dinner. Looking at her watch, she believed that they would have returned home.

Klee would try; she needed to unload. She needed a good sounding board. After six rings, Lisa answered the phone.

In a racing tone Klee blurted out, "Hi, I was just about ready to hang up, but I am so glad that you are home. I really, really have something to share with you, girlfriend. Do you have the time?"

"Sure I do, Klee," responded Lisa. "We just got in a few minutes ago, so I'm free. From the high pitch of your voice, I sense something has happened. Has something happened to Allie, or might it have something to do with meeting Dean on this 'Infamous Friday'?"

"It's the latter," exploded Klee. "I'm in shock, I guess."

Klee reported the meeting with Dean at the café in explicit detail. When she finished, she gave a big sigh.

Lisa with glee in her voice responded, "See, Klee, I just knew it. This is wonderful, girl. I think the wheels are beginning to turn, and now the trip has its start."

"Yeah, it should be a fascinating trip, all right," chuckled Klee. I'll let you go now. I suspect that you want to give Rob an ear full!"

CHAPTER 27

Saturday was Christmas decorating day. Klee hauled out Christmas decorations and the artificial Christmas tree, with Muffy Cat's curious and mischievous assistance. The cat went into action once she saw all the boxes being carried from the basement to the family room. Muffy sensed that it was time to have fun and games with Klee and especially with all the shiny things that would be carefully unwrapped from old newspaper sheets.

Muffy thought it was her responsibility to use the pile of paper as a dive center, which she happily accomplished as papers scattered all over the room. Klee laughed at her cat's antics. The decorating was as much a fun ritual for Muffy Cat as it was for Klee.

Klee had to give up having a real tree because of her allergies, but when she finished decorating the man-made tree, it was beautiful. Real or artificial didn't even matter because the end product with its twinkling lights, garland, and special ornaments from friends and students made it a sight to behold.

As she placed the ornaments on the tree, she reflected on the givers. Usually she could find a place on each ornament to inscribe the date and either the name or the initials of the giver. If there wasn't appropriate space for inscribing, she placed the data on a card and then carefully placed the card in the box with the ornament. Klee loved to organize. After all, organization saved time in the long run!

Removing three ornate ornaments from India from a small box, Klee thought about her dear friend, Sonya, who had traveled to India a couple of years previously where she purchased them especially for Klee. The ornaments were inlaid with semiprecious stones that actually twinkled as the tree lights shone on them.

One was in the shape of a star, and the other two had the form of a sphere. Klee was particularly fond of these ornaments and often wondered who had made them and what kind of life the crafter led.

Sonya and Klee had taught together in the Rochester City School District in the early sixties. Although Klee eventually went on to teach in one of the suburban districts, both teachers remained friends. Klee always had Sonya come to her home during the holidays. Sonya enjoyed the tree and all the decorations throughout the house. Each woman respected the other's customs and beliefs. Klee celebrated Christmas; Sonya celebrated Hanukkah.

Because Klee had matters well planned, she had the tree up and dressed for Christmas, the mantle above the fireplace decorated, and the rest of the adornments in place throughout the major rooms of the house in three and a half hours. Then off to the kitchen she would go to make coffee. That cup of coffee was exceedingly satisfying as she sipped it and surveyed the ornamentation display.

Muffy Cat sensed that the fun of tumbling and scattering papers was all over! The actual expression of discontent on cat's face made Klee smile. She delighted in the moods, expressions, and ESP of cats. What a companion she had in Muffy.

CHAPTER 28

S unday morning was lovely. The sun was bright, the sky was robin-egg blue, the snow glistened, and the birds flitted back and forth from the snow-laden wisteria bushes to the birdfeeder. Maintaining a full birdfeeder was so important during the snowy, winter months. Sometimes Klee had to shovel her way out to the feeding station to replenish it. However, all was well this stunning Sunday morning. She planned to call Sister Ann Mary that afternoon in order to bring her up to date on the various arenas in her life. In the meantime, there were many household chores that needed to be accomplished.

At three o'clock, Klee made the call to the convent in Elmira.

"Good afternoon. This is Saint Boniface Convent. How may I help you?" a gentle voice said.

"Good afternoon, Sister. This is Klee Cato speaking from Pittsford, New York. I would like to speak to Sister Ann Mary please."

"Why, yes, Klee, I will call Sister from the community room. She will be with you shortly."

"Thank you, Sister."

Klee waited a few minutes and then Sister's voice came through.

"Hello, my dear Klee," said Sister. "Oh, I was so hoping that you would call today."

"It's wonderful to hear your voice, Sister. I cannot adequately express how much I miss having face-to-face conversations with you and always our delightful visits," Klee exclaimed.

"Yes, it is very different since I have been transferred to Elmira," she sighed. "So tell me about yourself and, of course, Allie."

Klee detailed the events surrounding Allie's rescue and the involvement of Bethany Winslow, her class, and Dr. Tanner.

"Sister, Bethany Winslow has something in mind for the students once Allie is healthy and accustomed to commands. I have the impression that she wants to bring Allie to the classroom so that the youngsters can have their first actual meeting with the dog they have learned to love. This will be the best show-and-tell ever, it seems to me," declared Klee.

"What a superb idea. How delightful for the class," Sister said. "Klee, you have provided so many learning experiences via this rescue. I am proud of you, dear."

"Thanks, Sister. Your faith in me, your support, and love over the years means a great deal to me. Remember, you were the most important role model for me during my formative years. You still are!"

"I am happy to be part of your life's journey. Anything I might have done for you pleases me," Sister said. "When I taught you, I often said that you were impossible. You certainly had me praying in the chapel many evenings. I understand now that you are unique in so many ways. That uniqueness was merely attempting to surface when you were a youngster, but you didn't know how to portray it. I admit, along with many others, that I didn't understand initially either, but I have learned. That's why I often close my letters with the phrase, 'With deep understanding.'"

Klee, in a hardly audible voice, said, "I know you do. Thank you, my dear Sister."

Once Klee got herself under control, she talked about her holiday plans. She even mentioned Dean to Sister and told her a little about him. Klee made it clear that they were professional colleagues. She did not indicate to Sister that the future date with Dean was anything spectacular but rather just getting to know one another.

"Do you have special feelings for this man?" Sister asked.

Klee was caught off guard. She had not expected this question. She hadn't really permitted herself to explore her feelings, so she wasn't prepared to answer the question, but she did.

"Well, Sister, he is a great guy, smart, gorgeous to look at, and has definite goals and aspirations. He has all the ingredients for a possible suitor. Am I attracted to him? Honestly, I guess I am."

"It sounds as though he possesses many attributes that are suitable to you. Do you feel that the two of you are compatible?" Sister asked.

"Yes, it is fair to say that we seem compatible in so many areas. Compatibility is such a plus," Klee admitted. "The romance part is great, but the friendship element is what sustains the relationship, I truly believe."

Klee surprised herself when she made the last statement. Realistically, it was best that she had verbalized it—to hear herself say it. Compatibility and friendship were a must. She was glad Sister had put the question to her.

Both she and Sister would miss their annual Christmas visit, which truly saddened them. Klee's mom always had Sister and her travel companion during holiday season from the first year Sister taught Klee until Klee was out on her own.

Sister was thrilled at sharing a little of the holiday at the Cato home. She praised Mrs. Cato's delectable baked goods and savored each bit. Sister knew that Mrs. Cato would send her back to the convent with a box of goodies. This was a real treat for her. Also, she marveled at the festive beauty of all the decorations that engulfed the Cato home. Sister was deeply humbled by the many gifts the Cato family showered upon her at Christmas time. She was thrilled with her new shiny black oxford walking shoes, white linen handkerchiefs, and a good supply of lavender soap. A sheet or two of postage stamps was a treasure because this afforded her the opportunity to do all the letter writing she wanted to do. Keeping in touch via letter writing with family and friends was a small pleasure for her indeed.

Once Klee was out on her own, she carried on the holiday visit tradition at her own home. The thought of not having Sister's visitation during the 1974 season left Klee with a feeling of emptiness. Yet she understood that Sister's life was one of sacrifice. Since Sister was fulfilling her mission in Elmira at the Saint Boniface Convent, the distance, the lack of nearness, compounded the void and disappointment Klee was experiencing. It had been such a tradition for so many years. Resolute, Klee disciplined herself to go with the flow, but the acceptance part wasn't always easy for her.

"Sister," Klee said, "I know I have mentioned this before, and I wish you would truly consider calling me any time and reversing the charges. Please do. It is okay by me. Really, it is, Sister!"

"I know you have . . . thank you, dear heart," replied Sister. "Take good care of yourself, Klee. We'll talk again soon."

CHAPTER 29

The Monday morning drive to school on this particular day was unusual for December. There was another early snow accumulation. Plows banked the snow along the roadways, pushing it much higher at the entrance of each driveway. Once the plows finished with their pass, residents heaped the snow carefully along the driveway entrances so they could reach the road. Children loved climbing these snow mounds then sliding down toward the street. While it was fun for them, it was a concern for the automobile operator. However, the kids were oblivious to the pending danger.

Arriving at school, Klee walked into the office, greeted the secretary, and went directly to her mailbox. Among the papers, there was something out of the ordinary. Klee looked at the writing on the envelope but did not recognize the script. Carrying her mail bundle to her classroom, she decided to open the envelope immediately.

> Hi, Klee,
> Your students have been telling me all about the rescue of the Labrador retriever. I had no idea this was going on in their lives and yours. I'd like to teach a couple of new songs, which would lend themselves to their class project about Allie. I am told that you are planning to begin a unit study in the New Year.
> I'd like to teach them how to write lyrics and show them how we can integrate the lyrics with a familiar melody or a simple tune that I might create. Also, they tell me that you play the guitar for them on

special occasions. I have been informed that you love the Carpenters rendition of "Bless the Beasts and the Children." I'd like to explore that too.

I realize that our schedules do not coincide, but maybe we could meet some afternoon this week after dismissal.

Please let me know, Klee.

Thanks,

Jane Marco

Klee was surprised, and at the same time pleased, to receive this special note from the music teacher. Jane did such a great job with the students. Klee knew the offer would be fun to explore. She looked at her calendar and selected two dates.

On the bottom of Jane's note, Klee responded immediately because she wanted to return to the office as quickly as possible with her reply:

Jane, what a wonderful idea for the students. Thank you so much. I'm free on Wednesday or Thursday. I hope one of these days will be convenient for you.

Klee

Klee was eager to welcome her class that morning, especially since she learned that they had been talking to Jane Marco. She was excited to tell them that their music teacher wanted to explore some new songs that might enhance their learning from the Allie experience.

After the opening exercises, Klee started the day with announcements and one in particular.

"Good news today. Mrs. Marco has related to me that you have been telling her about Allie. I'm so glad you did this because Mrs. Marco has asked me to meet with her so we could discuss doing something special for Allie through music. Would you like that?"

There were nods and smiles as conversation broke out among the students.

"When will we do it?" asked Jessica.

"It will be soon I suspect," replied Klee. "Once Mrs. Marco and I make some plans at our meeting, I think it will be a go. She and I will be meeting this Wednesday or Thursday after school. However, we will need to decide at that time if you'll start the project before the holiday break or when we all return."

Everyone seemed satisfied, and the routine of the day began.

In seven more days, the holiday break would commence. There were many academic items to tidy up before the break, yet it was always difficult to keep focused at this time of year. The yuletide spirit filled the air, and young people would be forever young acting! That was a given!

With all that had been transpiring these last weeks, Klee realized that time had eluded her. She had better get into gear and work on plans for the class end-of-the-semester party, better known as the holiday party. It would be simple but fun for everyone. The students enjoyed punch, an assortment of cookies, popcorn, and of course, candy. Thank heavens for room mothers! Klee would be calling them to make arrangements for all the treats. So many of her parents were delightfully cooperative, interested in their children and their teacher, and they were there when needed. She felt lucky to be living at a time when there was still respect and caring for the teacher. However, she fully realized that it had changed a great deal since she first began her career in the late fifties. In the teaching arena, the fifties were referred to as the golden era. Little did she know the lowly status a teacher would hold as the decades marched on, and as the family unit became fractured, the proprieties and civilities of daily living would become old-fashioned.

CHAPTER 30

On Wednesday after dismissal, Jane and Klee met to decide the music plans for the Allie project.

"Jane, I am thrilled with your idea to have the students write lyrics!"

"I'm so glad, Klee," replied Jane. "I have used this approach before, and it has been successful. I believe it can be again."

"Are you planning to start before the holiday break, or do you prefer to wait until we return in January?"

"I'd like to begin now to ease them into what is required for the lyric structure and method to follow. When we return to begin the new semester, it will be a painless review of what we previously learned, followed by an actual launching of the project."

"Wonderful, just wonderful," exclaimed Klee. "I'll inform the students of the plan. You see them again on Friday so they haven't much longer to wait."

At home that evening, Klee received a call from Bethany Winslow. She was surprised because she understood that Bethany was planning on contacting her once school resumed in January. Klee felt a visceral twinge.

"Hello, Bethany. What a nice surprise to hear from you. Is everything all right?"

"Yes, everything is just wonderful," Bethany gleefully replied. "I just had to call and tell you how much we are enjoying Allie. Shepard put up the tree last evening, and it was so heartwarming watching Shep and Allie during the assembly. Allie was beside herself with excitement. Shep began teaching Allie how to fetch certain ornaments. It was hilarious to watch the new yule team! Cleo, our cat, just looked on with a noninterested demeanor . . . as if this fetching routine was beyond her dignity. Our mouse, Charlie, remained under the wing chair by the fireplace with his beady eyes focused while playing the role of sentinel."

"Gee, Bethany, I didn't know you had other pets," exclaimed Klee. "What a combination! You mean the cat and mouse actually cohabitate?"

"Can you believe it, but they do. They've taken in Allie too," chuckled Bethany.

"Cleo was rescued from the Rochester Humane Society. Cautious little Charlie was liberated from my daughter Laurie's science class. She could not bear having it fed to the snake the biology teacher had on display. It was quite traumatic for her. She, along with other classmates, was so upset that they went to the principal. As the result of the student pleas, the teacher was asked by the principal to allow the students to take home the mice. I think Laurie was correct in her reaction. Not all students can observe what nature mandates, especially when there is a captive audience made to watch."

"I totally agree," responded Klee. "I am also vehemently opposed to that type of exposure in a classroom. I have observed firsthand the reactions of some students. Not all individuals are ready, nor do they want to make such a scene part of their memory."

"Returning to your pets, Bethany, I must say that each member of the Winslow family is an exceptional individual indeed. How very fortunate all three animals are to have their home with the Winslows. You have given them their own Eden. The love and caring you all demonstrate must have been incorporated, maybe by osmosis, into their little spirits. Of course, too, that's one of the special traits of a Labrador. Labs are very social and loyal. They bond strongly to their family and other pets—even cats and mice, I guess."

Klee and Bethany chatted a little longer. Bethany seemed more committed to her plan to bring Allie to school in February. They exchanged holiday wishes. Both women were beginning to experience a special bond.

CHAPTER 31

More snow was predicted, but who would mind more snow during the holidays! That's what all children dreamed about. After all, Santa had to get his reindeer into town. The adult world enjoyed it too. Maybe not the driving and its hazards, but the snow was the special ingredient to make the holiday spirit glow for everyone.

Klee enjoyed being home during this period. She was very much a homebody. She loved her home and worked hard to keep it clean and attractive.

It was a lovely home. Klee bought the house in 1967. She, along with two other teachers, made it their home. It was far less expensive to share expenses than each renting separate apartments. Not only sharing of expenses was attractive, but also living in a four-level home in a new suburb of Rochester made it doubly inviting. Expenses were shared, true, but the division of labor also made it pleasurable for everyone.

However, one can be certain that change will eventually come knocking. And change did come along. The first adjustment was a professional advancement move for Barbara (Beets, as she was called because of her red hair) when, after thorough investigation, she realized that she had the possibility of greater career opportunities in the White Plains, New York, school district. We were thrilled for her and her desire to seek the professional climb.

Two years later, Sue fell in love and moved to the cold north country of Lake Placid, New York. She was a natural winter sports enthusiast, so it was perfect for Sue. Klee was happy for her, without a doubt, but she also realized that she was left with an empty house with all expenses and the entire maintenance load. No more sharing of expenses or division of labor! Many adaptations had to be made.

Klee had the fortitude to go forward and was determined to maintain her home, even if it was only with her pal Muffy Cat. The former arrangements were in the past. It was done—finished! It was time to move on while realizing that each woman had left behind many fond memories.

The upcoming ten-day recess would afford her time to spend on things she enjoyed rather than on all the routine chores. She was already anticipating certain days for cross-country skiing. Thoughts of having time to play the lovely instrument she had in the family room pleased her to no end. The organ was her "get away from it all" instrument. When she played the organ, there were no hands on the clock. Time didn't matter. What truly mattered was the music. The beautiful organ sounds from the cherished instrument provided her inner peace and heartfelt joy. During this free period, simply going at a slower pace and easing up on all the multitasking and all the needs of all the personalities she encountered each day would allow Klee to enrich her spirit and amass new energy.

CHAPTER 32

The next day at school, the holiday bustle continued as the students anticipated the upcoming party.

"Ms. Cato, what time do you want our mothers to bring in the treats for our holiday party on Friday?" asked Andy.

"Well, yes, I think we need to determine the time. On Friday, I plan on shortening the lessons for each subject so we will have enough time for some fun and the food fare toward the end of the school day. You'll return from Mrs. Marco's music class at one forty-five, so I'd like to have all the goodies delivered about two o'clock, but definitely no later than two fifteen. Please tell your moms the plan."

Robin asked, "Ms. Cato, will you bring in your guitar and play for us?"

"Why, yes, Robin, I plan on doing just that," answered Klee.

The students liked it when Klee played her guitar, and she enjoyed it too. She was by no means an expert player, but she mastered enough to get along. "Rudolph, the Red-Nosed Reindeer," "Silver Bells," and "White Christmas" were among the favorites. She deliberately selected songs of a nonreligious nature because she was very sensitive about her obligations to *all* students in her classes in a public school setting.

In Social Studies class, she presented a unit depicting the various holiday customs that were experienced around the world. Most were of a Christian orientation, that was a fact, but Klee also made sure that Hanukkah was included in the students' studies. This particular year, she asked Joanie Cohen if she'd like to bring in the dreidel toy to play the dreidel game, and the menorah to enhance students' understanding of Hanukkah. Joanie promised to bring to class five or six tops so five groups could play simultaneously.

Each year, the story of the eight-day Hanukkah celebration interested Klee's classes. More frequently than not, most students were not aware of the celebration and its meaning, but they liked the idea of eight days of gift giving!

Mrs. Cohen called Klee about the offer she had made to her daughter, Joanie. She was delighted to know that Klee had invited Joanie to participate in the sharing of Hanukkah. Besides sending in the dreidel game and the menorah, Mrs. Cohen offered to make some special Hanukkah treats for Joanie's classmates. Both women agreed to include the Jewish baked specialties at the party the last day of school.

"Ms. Cato, I plan to send in some latkes. They are delicious potato pancakes. I sprinkle powered sugar over them. The kids really like the *sufganiyot*, it's a jam-filled doughnut. I'll bake everything fresh the day of the party," explained Mrs. Cohen.

"That would be terrific. What a treat for us all. I look forward to your arrival."

Klee's strong goal throughout her career was to expose her students to nationalities, races, customs, religions, traditions, and mores in order to bring about understanding and acceptance of others.

Each year she delivered special teaching units with the idea of inclusiveness as her goal. The principles learned were reinforced throughout the year. She wanted to do her part to assist the students to become comfortable with differences and to expose ignorance that manifested itself through bigotry, prejudice, and smallness of mind. In her opinion, prejudicial acts and practices of ignorance were the cancers that ate away at societies and were responsible for the malevolence in the world.

The understanding, sincerity, and respect Klee imparted in her lessons permeated the entire classroom atmosphere. She incorporated lessons not only from textbooks but also from actual experiences she had learned as a child and young adult. She learned early what prejudice did to the soul. This depth of understanding would surface as tolerance and respect within the society of her classroom. In turn, the students reciprocated. Both leader and followers strongly exhibited appreciation toward one another. Mutual respect and courtesy were expected.

A strong focal point for her as a teacher was the concept of collateral learning. She remembered in her studies a significant viewpoint stated by the great philosopher and educator, John Dewey. He wrote in *Experience and Education*:

Perhaps the greatest of pedagogical fallacies is the notion that a person learns only what he is studying at the time. Collateral learning in the way of formation of enduring attitudes . . . may be and often is more important than the spelling lesson or lesson in geography or history . . . For these attitudes are fundamentally what count in the future.

Keeping this quote in mind, she found herself ascribing to the philosophy of collateral learning as an integral part of her teaching methods.

Klee fully realized that learning acceptance and respect for another's lot in life manifested itself whenever a particular incident occurred in the classroom. The unit teachings and daily example did come through. It paid off. She was so proud of the students. Respect and caring shone like a lighthouse beacon when a dark or cloudy situation arose, such as the incident with Adam.

Adam was an epileptic child. He was a tall lad, nice looking, but his spirit was broken because he was always on guard and fearful of a seizure. He had little confidence. The medication made him exceedingly tired. Often, he refused to take his meds.

He would be embarrassed and heartbroken with each episode of a seizure. Yet when Klee gave the command to push away the desks to give her room to administer to Adam as he lay on the floor with his teacher on her knees, the students, without a sound or comment, did all they could to help their teacher and Adam. Compassion and kindness were reflected on their faces. They had respect for their fellow classmate and his plight. They accepted that Adam was different. They wore badges of tolerance. Klee's heart bathed in their performance.

CHAPTER 33

Among the students, a gleeful party spirit and extra high noise levels permeated Fairhaven Central that Friday. The excitement of parties and the two-week recess, which would begin at three thirty, had a powerful effect on the adrenal glands. This day was a showcase of conduct on parade. It highlighted how much control and the expected conduct a teacher had built and nurtured among her students over the preceding months.

The day progressed nicely for Ms. Cato's class. The students were excited about writing lyrics for "Allie's Song." Mrs. Marco had outlined her plan with them during music class.

The decibel level in the cafeteria was higher than usual, but that was to be expected. Talk about having the entire assemblage of students on high C! Klee looked around to observe the facial expressions of the faculty members to see how they were reacting. She began to circulate around the tables to where teachers were standing and, with a mischievous look, whispered to her fellow teachers, "I think we need something very special added to our coffee today!"

The class celebration was fun for all. Klee was proud of her students, proud of their behavior and thoughtfulness throughout their free time during the party. The goodies were devoured like a vacuum cleaner sucking them in. Klee was showered with gifts.

"Good-byes" were shouted, and "see you next year" was echoed throughout the bus loading area. After the final exodus of buses, Klee felt a sense of merriment as she anticipated her own free days ahead. She would do all that had been put on hold for so long, and yet there was a sense of emptiness as she performed her final waves of adieu.

CHAPTER 34

The planned entertainment at Klee's home for the holiday was a delightful respite. She always looked forward to evenings of adult conversation. Everyone seemed to enjoy themselves.

Sonya filled Klee in on her doctoral work at the University of Rochester and the challenges of writing her dissertation during her visit. Lisa and Rob felt right at home while enjoying the holiday cheer. Rob talked about his recent trip to Rome, Italy, where Kodak had some negotiations in the works.

Klee asked, "Did you like Rome, Rob?"

"I really did, and I regret that my visit was so short. It is a magnificent city. The architecture and engineering layout of the city are superior. There is so much beauty to absorb. The people were very friendly, and the food . . . well, I went nuts for it! I would like to plan for Lisa and me to go to Rome for a two-week vacation."

Lisa smiled broadly and said, "Wouldn't that be just the greatest. How exciting to absorb some of the history of that great city. However, the way Rob goes on about the food, I would probably put on the pounds mighty fast."

"You are so slim now, Lisa, I doubt if a few pounds would matter," said Klee, mulling over Lisa's very orthodox thinking about her personal appearance. She always ate small amounts of food. She never had a hair out of place. The expensive outfits she wore commanded a second look. Without a doubt, she was the fashion plate among the faculty women.

The Hatchers enjoyed the holiday fare, and their love for Muffy Cat was obvious. The gifts they brought for her were more than generous. Harriet and Ernest always took turns playing with the cat. Whenever they came to visit, Muffy Cat was the star. She, in her every move, accommodated the Hatchers. She responded beautifully to their gestures of playfulness. The cat seemed to sense their needs and love of felines. They had always had cats, but they no longer had that pleasure. Health factors changed that lifestyle. Klee was thrilled with Muffy Cat's performance when in the Hatchers' presence.

The holiday recess was skipping by as fast as a stone skimming the water. Klee had to think about what she would wear for her date with Dean on the twenty-eighth. She could hardly put it in terms of a date. She was afraid to let herself go to the date mode. Yet Klee being Klee, she had to face the fact that it was indeed a date! Dating a vice principal was certainly a new and uncommon experience for her and probably for most faculty members.

At six thirty sharp, Dean was at her front door. Why would she ever think that he would not be punctual? Actually, she admired this trait. It demonstrated consideration and respect toward the other person. He wore a dark navy suit, which fit his muscular body to a tee. His maroon necktie with gold flecking complemented the gold clasp that extended from the edges of his shirt collar. A recent haircut accented his jet black, slightly wavy hair. Those cobalt blue eyes were penetrating. The iris of his eyes took on different shadings depending on his mood. She had to admit that he was picture perfect. She knew, too, that she was elated to be escorted by him. Would this actually be a magical evening?

"Hello, Klee," greeted Dean as he stepped inside the foyer. "How very lovely you look. I like your aqua sequin dress, it goes with my suit. That sheath dress certainly displays your loveliness. Are your dancing shoes ready for some exercise this evening?"

Laughingly Klee replied, "Yes, they are, and you look quite sharp yourself, Dean. Aren't you brave with no overcoat!"

The Spring House was a picture with all its beautiful decorations. The fireplace fueled by gas jets gave off a welcoming glow. The extended mantle above the fireplace was adorned with live pine boughs and seasonal antique figurines. The Santa Clauses representing various countries were especially enchanting. Dean and Klee strolled over to the huge Christmas tree. The ornaments, lights, and tinsel made the sight of the tree breathtaking. The magnificence of the restaurant lifted one's spirit. Dinnertime was a pleasant mix of good conversation and good food.

The three-piece combo was perfect, not too loud, and able to perform a variety of styles to satisfy all ages. Dean and Klee danced a great deal. They seemed to fit together with ease and glided nicely on the dance floor.

Dean asked, "Are you enjoying yourself this evening, Klee?"

"Yes, I am," responded Klee. "The evening has been delightful. It has been almost magical, I think."

"I'm so glad you phrased it that way," responded Dean. "I feel the same way. I have enjoyed our entire time together." He drew her closer to him.

Was she in a dream world? Was this really happening with Dean, the vice principal? She realized that she was experiencing feelings toward him. His aftershave was intoxicating and interfered with her equilibrium and thought process. His deep, penetrating, dancing eyes peered into hers, and she felt weak at the knees. She was always so sensible, in control of herself, but she felt that something was being altered deep inside. She repeatedly told herself to go with the flow, but, girl, go slowly.

CHAPTER 35

The holiday recess was delightful, but it sped by too quickly. School beckoned, and the focus turned to business.

Everyone appeared refreshed and ready to begin the New Year. Returning to school in January was always fun. Both teachers and students chatted about their recess and all the interesting things they did. Some teachers had traveled home to visit with their families; others went West or to Vermont to ski, while some remained close to the home fires. The students gushed about the gifts that they had received and the relatives who had come to visit.

Although the first couple of weeks of January began with a kick start, there were months ahead that usually brought about a sense of struggling. The main culprit was the weather. January through March were expected to be cold, snowy, and icy, but the weeks of dark skies throughout this period often deflated one's mood. Leaving for school in the darkness of the morning and returning home from school in darkness got tiresome. Because of this, Klee always planned special projects for her class. This kept them on task and interested.

They missed being out-of-doors regularly each week during the winter months. The fact that they could not go outside for kickball was a sacrifice, but they all knew that once April dawned, Ms. Cato would have them out there playing their hearts out if the weather cooperated. They had a grand time playing during the previous fall term, so they looked forward with great anticipation to April. They loved kickball! Ms. Cato worked with students who were not athletically inclined. Once they got the hang of it, it was a joy to watch their excitement.

During the fall term, Klee had zeroed in on one youngster who was of slight build. He was actually skinny. He was constantly pulling up his trousers. His waist was so small that his belt did little good. He had black straight-as-a-poker hair, wore glasses, and had twinkling black eyes. In addition to his small stature, Randy could not kick the ball. No matter how hard he tried, his foot missed by inches. His timing was off. He was so disappointed each time it was his turn to the plate. He never gave up though. Klee admired his determination.

On a particular kickball day, Klee motioned with her hand and called out to Randy, "Randy, come over to me. I want to show you a couple of methods to use when it is your turn to kick."

"Gee, Ms. Cato, I can't do it. I try and try," Randy replied dejectedly.

"I know you try, but I believe you can have success, Randy!" said Ms. Cato.

While Klee's friend and team teacher, Sandy Osborne, was supervising the game, Klee explained to Randy that a vital ingredient in a sport—in anything in life—is the vision and belief that anything worth the challenge can be accomplished with the right mind-set. She continued, "See a picture of success in your mind, and also it means as your leg and foot poise to kick, you never, ever take your eye off the ball, but follow through with the picture in your mind of a good kick. You must believe that you can do it. You must believe in the goal."

"Okay, Ms. Cato," said Randy displaying a big smile. "I'll try to do it."

Klee knew how important his success would be. He was tiny in stature, but the gray matter was abundant. His intellectual prowess separated him from his classmates, big time, and Randy was sensitive to this fact. Yet because he was intellectually gifted, he had a promising future. He desired to be like the rest of the kids, if that were only possible. Therefore, a triumph at kickball would be his ticket to all-around success. Klee made the commitment to herself and to him that he would have this victory, maybe not this day but one day while he was under her tutelage.

When Randy was called up to the plate, Klee gave him a thumbs-up. She observed his concentration and the determination in his eyes. He drew back his pencil-thin leg, kept his eye on the ball and connected with it. Although it didn't go very far because of his lack of strength, he did engage the ball, and it bounced toward third base. This caught the defending team off guard. The third baseman was startled. No one ever expected Randy to connect with the ball on the first kick and neither did Klee. She assumed he would need more than one attempt. He ran as fast as his wiry legs could carry him. The cheers were thunderous from both teams. Randy made it to first base and his excitement was exhibited as his slight body gyrated in irregular motions. The grin on his face and the fire in his eyes were priceless.

Ms. Cato yelled out toward first base, "Hole-ly macaroni, Randy, that was great!"

Klee knew what this meant to him. She realized that he'd get better each time they played now that he had some confidence. She hoped that he had retained some of the newly acquired skill, and with a little practice, it would return to him during the spring term.

Spring and decent weather for kickball were a long way off however. Something different needed to be worked on during the doldrums months of January, February, and March. Considering this, Klee had done some outlining for a special project while she was at home during holiday recess.

"Class," said Ms. Cato, "today, I want to discuss with you a special project. Since we've been involved with Allie's rescue, I would like the class to divide into teams and get involved in research. The research will center on the study of the dog classification—the Labrador retriever. It will be necessary to investigate the history, the characteristics of the Labrador, the size and measurement, and the special uses of this particular breed."

Greg raised his hand and asked, "What do you mean by special uses of the Labrador?"

"This particular breed is not only loved as a family pet, but also it is a breed that can be trained to assist people with disabilities. I want you to find out more about this extraordinary class of dog. This means we'll work with the encyclopedia, books from the school library, and I'll bring in some materials from the public library also."

Debbie asked, "When do we begin, Ms. Cato?

"Let us agree that we'll begin tomorrow . . . let's say, Tuesday. We'll set up team clusters with five members to a team. Each cluster will decide on what aspect they wish to research. We will need six teams. I will help you with the organization of the team members."

Klee's intention was to embrace every aspect of each specific discipline: Language Arts, Math, Social Studies, Science, and Art. In addition, with the music teacher's plan of a lyric composition for a song about Allie, all learning disciplines would be incorporated. What a terrific interdisciplinary unit, she thought!

The unit will be the jump start for another idea that would naturally follow. It would fit perfectly and the students would ease into it. Yes, a play written and composed by the students would be the final culmination—the final satisfaction! Surely Mrs. Marco would help with the production that would be scheduled to take place in late March or early April.

Tuesday proved to be a busy day indeed. The team unit project commenced with enthusiasm. The hum of conversation, the sharing of ideas went along smoothly. Klee observed the students who were emerging as leaders within specific groups. She had brought in materials for them to use to get started with the project. Later in the day, they would go to the library to seek more material for research.

Wednesday turned out to be a special day. Klee had received a phone call from Bethany the prior evening and had very good news to share with the class.

Ms. Cato said, "First thing I wish to mention this morning is that Mrs. Winslow called last evening to inform me that we all should listen to radio station WHEC at one o'clock on Saturday. Mr. Joe Carter does the Monroe County Humane Society Update. It is a public interest and informational spot offered by WHEC. He is going to tell about the rescue of Allie. If you can tune in on Saturday, please do and invite your family members to listen too. I'll attempt to tape record his message. He is dedicated to his work and often finds his job discouraging with all the pets that end up at the humane society. Mr. Carter, however, is grateful that Monroe County does have such a society to provide for the unwanted.

The students' expressions registered their joy about the broadcast of Allie's rescue. Yet there was something that Bethany revealed during their phone conversation that Klee did not share with the class. Not yet anyway! She hoped that the information of the potential problem Allie could face would naturally evolve as the students became more knowledgeable about Labradors through the unit study.

During the unit study, Klee planned to expand on one characteristic of the Labrador that might be compromised because of Allie's long struggle with abandonment, injury, and surgery. She was certain that she could indicate an impending roadblock that Allie and the Winslows might have to deal with as Allie aged with care. This would be another of life's lessons, more collateral learning.

"The second matter I wish to present to you concerns the explosive pet population we are facing in our United States," Ms. Cato stated. "It will tie in with our study of the Labrador in a sense. I am going to use the overhead projector for illustrations and graphs. You will eventually take notes. As we explore this data, it is my sincere hope that you will all take to heart the information presented. It is my further hope that some of you will become the leading citizens of the future to fight for animal rights and pet population control. Before we continue, let me say this: On the whole, the American people are caring and responsible citizens. However, the pet crisis has not been adequately addressed. Millions of animals must face euthanasia each year. It is obvious, then, that as a nation, we are shamefully lacking in the area of pet population control as the statistics will bear out. Before we view the information on the overhead projector, let's have a discussion."

"Yes, Andy, your question."

"You said *millions*. I never heard that number before."

"It is true. We'll see how such numbers are calculated when we examine the projected information."

There was stillness among the students. Ms. Cato realized that most of the students were stunned with the term *"millions."* Surely there would be additional class discussions to follow once the data was imparted and absorbed.

Ms. Cato felt the students' interest was sufficiently piqued, so she went on. "Do you have any idea how many offspring of dogs and cats are produced every hour?"

The silence said a great deal; no one stirred. Ms. Cato said, "A conservative estimate states 2,000 to 3,500 offspring per hour."

Jessica, with concern on her face, asked, "Where do they put all these offspring?"

"That's an excellent question, Jessica. Bottom line, there are not enough families or households to absorb all these innocent creatures. We'll do the math part later, but right now, you have an idea of the staggering amount of unwanted animals."

Eric blurted out, "No wonder millions are killed."

Ms. Cato gently replied, "Let's use the term *euthanized*. Millions of unwanted animals pass through the nation's municipal pounds and animal shelters each year. The majority are healthy pets that are relinquished or abandoned by their owners. Because of the cost of operating shelters and because of lack of space, each year millions are put down. Cats are of particular importance in the scheme of things because they have three mating periods. There are three distinct mating periods within the mating season of cats. The period starts in the early spring, the next mid-summer and the last ends in fall. A frenzy of mating takes place during these periods which results in an unbelievable number of unwanted cats. A single mating period can result in dozens, even hundreds of unwanted cats."

"Gee, Ms. Cato," Randy said, "I don't think any of us understood the enormous amount of disposal pets each year. The statistics you mentioned are telling us that if we let one stray cat roam the neighborhood, it means frequent breeding and a huge number of unwanted kittens."

"Randy, you've got the idea! We cannot afford to allow strays to roam nor feed them because all we are doing is adding to the problem. We are either part of the problem or part of the solution to the problem. What needs to be done is to capture the stray and bring it to a shelter. That is a humane act, the only civil act to perform," explained Ms. Cato.

"So that's why responsible people spay and neuter their pets, right, Ms. Cato?" asked Robin.

Klee paused, nodded, and let that statement take hold. The students were processing beautifully; she felt the joy!

CHAPTER 36

It had been over two weeks since Klee had been in Dean's company. There had not been one opportunity to speak to him. During school hours, she saw him at a distance, a couple of times in the hall dealing with school matters, but not close enough to say hello. She thought the lack of communication was odd. They both had had such a wonderful evening at the Spring House during holiday break. He said that he would call her soon. What did he mean by *soon*? She admitted to herself that she felt uncomfortable, even hurt by Dean's apparent noninterest. They had seemed compatible talking and sharing all kinds of topics. Dean even got a kick out of Klee's humor. She wondered how everything seemed all right at the time, but she had different vibes as the days passed. She repeated to herself, "I have no right to expect anything. After all, just because we had a magical date, it doesn't indicate any kind of expectations." Klee resigned herself to the current situation and tried her best to release feelings of disappointment. It was necessary to go with the flow; she firmly believed that what was to be, would be!

That evening, Lisa called.

"Hey, girlfriend," said Lisa, "I have something on my mind, and I'd like to come right out and ask you about it."

"Go ahead," laughed Klee. "You usually are candid with me on a regular basis, my friend, and you know I ascribe to frankness."

"Well, each time we've chatted since we've returned to school from the holiday recess, you have not mentioned Dean, not even once. I admit that I am curious about you two. I know it is none of my business, so you need not respond if you prefer, but exactly, what is happening with him and you?"

"In a word, nothing," exclaimed Klee. "I am deeply puzzled. I have not heard a word from him since our date. Frankly, I am disappointed. I don't know what to expect at this point in time. On the other hand, I realize that

I have no designs on him. My stomach feels as though a million humming birds are whipping their wings in a total frenzy every time I think about him, our wonderful evening together, and his inexplicable silence."

"I thought that things would progress once we returned to school. I am sorry you are feeling disheartened, but it is possible that there is a simple explanation. Do not throw in the towel too soon," Lisa offered.

"You are right Lisa. I probably should not jump to conclusions—not yet anyway—but you know too that I am a no-nonsense gal."

"Oh yes, I do know that indeed! I should mention that Rob and I are planning on having a house party in a couple of weeks. We want to have it close to Valentine's Day. It was just natural for me to put you and Dean on our invite list. I still want to do it if it is okay with you."

"Of course, I will come. You and Rob are my dear friends and no one will interfere with that fact. If Dean comes, whether alone or with a date, I'll carry on as usual. We have always had a friendly relationship at gatherings. I never entertained the thought throughout our contacts with each other that we were anything but colleagues. To repeat myself, I have no right of ownership. I do admit that I wish I had just a little piece of the real estate. It would be nice to experience. As you say, I shouldn't throw in the towel yet," Klee sighed.

Lisa and Klee chatted a little longer. Lisa ended their conversation with continued words of encouragement.

How matters of concern usually took care of themselves always amazed Klee. If one is patient, stuff unfolds. Stuff happens. Things happen when they are supposed to happen. Klee's major shortcoming was that she lacked the virtue of patience. Sister Ann Mary reminded her of that fact so often. Klee would hear Sister's comments echo in her thoughts frequently:

"Klee, you are impossible!" Sister would say. "You need to be patient. Remember that patience is an important virtue. You are so quick in your decisions, so quick to act and to get things done with rapidity, while others are still in phase 1 sifting out what the next move should be."

Two days after Klee's conversation with Lisa, she was leaving the library, and as she exited, she ran smack into Dean. They were both startled; each apologized then began to laugh.

"What a way to say hello," Dean exclaimed. "Klee, I have meant to call you, but something urgent has taken a great deal of time. It was a family matter. I have had to return to Ithaca these past two weekends. Because of my trips home, I have been backlogged."

"I am sorry to hear this. I hope matters will correct themselves soon."

"I'd like to phone you and fill you in on the event that called me away. Better yet, can we meet at Geraci's Café again around five on Friday if that is convenient for you? I will not be going home this weekend."

Klee's feelings of neglect surfaced, and she was not ready to let him off the hook so fast. Then she considered, "Am I being foolish and lacking in understanding? That damn ego sure can ruin things!" Obviously something drastic occurred. A small voice within her urged her to go with the flow.

"Friday would be okay with me. I'll look forward to seeing you then," she responded.

As Klee headed for her classroom, she was curious about Dean. Had something happened to his mother? He had such a large close family it could involve any one of the members. She could do all kinds of guessing, but that was a waste of energy. Patience must prevail! Everything is revealed when it is suppose to be revealed and not necessarily when one wants it to be evident.

On Friday, Dean was waiting for Klee at the café. His smile was warm, and he pulled out her chair as she approached the table.

"I am so glad that you were able to come," said Dean. "I have so much to tell you. I feel that I have neglected you. I really did have every intention to call after the Spring House, but things happened."

"Dean, since we spoke at school I have come to realize that you have been under a great deal of stress. I am truly sorry. I did take your silence personally. Yet I told myself I had no right to respond to your distant behavior."

"Thanks, I need your understanding. I think you know from our date that I am attracted to you, and you have so much that I want in a partner. I want our relationship to develop. I hope I haven't blown it."

"I'd like our friendship to progress also. I must say that I am surprised at the new direction in which we seem to be going after all the time we have known each other. That being said, please go ahead. I am ready to listen. Feel comfortable to tell me whatever you wish."

He went on to explain that his nephew and godson, Sammy, had been in a terrible toboggan accident. He had slammed into a huge maple tree. He suffered a bad head injury and was unconscious for four days. There was bruising and swelling on the brain. His brother and the rest of the family were beside themselves. He called home daily for the medical report and went home on two consecutive weekends. It was an upsetting time for the entire family. The good news is that Sammy was doing just fine now, and matters have calmed.

"What an unfortunate incident. I have empathy for you, young Sammy, and your entire family."

"Thanks, Klee. I am so glad you understand. Now can we go on?" Dean asked.

"What do you mean?"

"I want to ask you for another date. Maybe we could plan on a week from this Saturday. Dinner and dancing might be nice again," Dean offered.

"I would like that. Please call me this evening. Let me check my calendar. Okay?"

"I'll do that. I want you to have my phone number too."

Dean walked Klee to her car. She situated herself in the driver's seat, started her reliable Chevy, and with a wave drove off. Patience . . . going with the flow does have advantages!

CHAPTER 37

The month of February kept its annual promise. Western New York state was blanketed with plenty of snow. This was a wonderful time for all the winter activities to get into full swing.

Skiing, ice skating, tobogganing, ice fishing, and cabin parties with the warmth and glow of a wood burning fire were the compensations for the long winter season. The cabin fireplaces throughout most of the area had huge hearths that were constructed with brick. Their façades were crafted with river rock from the Genesee River. Cabin parties for adults and youngsters alike instilled fond memories.

All the various winter activities loosened the grip of the daily house dwelling and nagging feelings of claustrophobia. They provided the opportunity to enjoy what nature offered to them during the wintry weather. It was especially important that kids got out-of-doors on the weekends to release some of the built-up energy. Cabin fever knows no age limits however.

At school, the students within their teams had been working for a couple of weeks on the Labrador research project. The time had arrived, and the team leaders were ready to present their findings. The first two weeks in February would be the culmination of the research reports. Shortly after the reports, the music class special would take place prior to the class Valentine's Day celebration. Each leader would present a fact or facts that the team thought were of most interest to their classmates. Following the oral presentation, the research packets would be passed around to each team so that team members could see and discuss what other teams had prepared.

"All right, which team wants to be first to start with their research report?" asked Ms. Cato.

Hands eagerly shot up. It was evident that Allie continued to be important to her fans.

"Rebecca, we'll begin with you," said Ms. Cato.

Rebecca began in her matter-of-fact demeanor. "There are special characteristics that are particular to Labradors. We have found four main characteristics, namely their temperament, head structure, tail, and coat. We felt that the coat was of special interest because Allie was hiding in the woods for so long. Basically, the Labradors have a double coat. There is a downy undercoat that keeps them dry and warm in cold water and a hard outer coat that helps them repel water. Their coats dry easily. After a few good shakes, the Labrador should be mostly dry. Because of these facts, our team believes that the unique coat structure helped Allie to survive."

"Well done, Rebecca and your team."

Klee had allotted time in order to encourage the class to continue and expand the discussion once the leader finished. The reports and discussions would never be accomplished in one session, but the collective exchange was vital to the experience. There was plenty of time for all the discussion and reports before February 14.

"Eddy, let's have team five's report," announced Ms. Cato.

Rising from his chair, Eddy showed that famous grin of his. "Okay, Ms. Cato. The history part was interesting. Robin drew some good pictures too."

"Illustrations make the content of the report come alive. I am glad that you used your artistic skills, Robin," complimented Ms. Cato.

Eddy went on. "There was a lot of crossbreeding over a long period of time. The breeders were trying to get a specific kind of bird dog. The dog had to be strong, versatile, and able to withstand cold water. We can thank the English breeders for the crossbreeding back in the early 1800s with the Labrador Newfoundland dogs. They crossed the Labrador Newfoundland dogs with different known breeds at the time. One such crossbreed was with black pointers. It seems that there was a lot of crossbreeding until they got the perfect dog for their hunting purposes. Once they did, the breed remained pure. Now we know where the name Labrador came from."

"Thank you, Eddy and team five, for helping us understand some of the history of the Labrador. Robin, please come forward to the front of the classroom. Show us some of your drawings," Ms. Cato encouraged.

The students were very interested in Robin's work. Her talent was awesome for her age. In addition to art, Robin was also athletically inclined; she was fantastic on the kickball field. As a flutist, she showed another side of her abilities. She went about her business and worked hard. She was friendly but reserved. Basically Robin was a dream student for any teacher to experience.

"Eric did the geography section of the report. He's going to tell us about it," said Eddy.

"I'm going to briefly outline some of the interesting geographical features of the region," Eric began. "Labrador and Newfoundland are located in the easternmost part of Canada. Newfoundland is an island located in the Atlantic Ocean off the east coast of Canada and Labrador is considered the mainland. Geographically the Strait of Belle Isle separates Newfoundland and Labrador. Labrador has an irregular coastline. Its highest point is Mount Caubvick at 5, 420 feet, and the longest river is Churchill River recorded at 532 miles. Lots of natural resources and minerals come from Labrador. This following information interested all of us. During World War II in October 1943, a German U-boat crew installed an automatic weather station on the northern tip of Labrador. This was the only armed, German military operation on the North American mainland during the war. Joanie did a map drawing illustrating the Labrador-Newfoundland locations."

The students wanted to see the map. She had done an expert job. She used colors to differentiate land masses, bodies of water and borders, the compass rose to indicate direction and the legend to indicate the coordinates. She offered to have her dad make copies for everyone because he worked at Xerox.

"What a good idea, Joanie," Ms. Cato exclaimed. "It certainly will be nice for each student to have his or her own map. Thank you for asking your dad. Also class, it sounds to me that it would be interesting to delve more into the geography and seek more facts about Labrador. After all, this region is part of Allie's lineage. We can plan the extension of such a follow-up exercise for another time."

Following the map display and discussion, Debbie took center stage for her report. She was a natural before a group. It was amazing to see this tall, lanky, short-haired brunette draw in the group. Surely, someday she might find her way to the theater and maybe even the silver screen. At such a young age, she had the looks and poise for such a career.

"I am prepared to tell you about the coat color of the Labradors. Basically, the American Kennel Society recognizes specific colors. The three acceptable coat colors are black, yellow, and chocolate. The yellow has variations from fox red to light cream color. Black is due to the dominate gene, and the other color variations happen when there is a lack of the dominant black gene. In simple terms, both parent dogs have black genes, then the offspring, the puppy, will be black. When there is an absence of the dominant black gene, the recessive gene can be expressed. Because of this fact, a black dog can produce yellow or chocolate offspring if it carries in its genetic makeup both the dominant black gene and a hidden recessive gene. The most common color is black, but the yellows and chocolates are becoming more popular. Steve Martin, the standup comic has a black Lab."

"Thank you, Debbie. Good information for all of us. Steve Martin is such a jovial, affable guy, so it seems in keeping that he'd select the sociable, even-tempered Lab," remarked Ms. Cato.

There was animated discussion about Steve Martin's dog and Allie's color. The students, who briefly saw Allie during the time of constructing the shelter, concluded that Allie would probably be classified as a yellow Labrador, but of the cream color shade.

Next, Ms. Cato called on Gregory. He was a well-liked lad. His wavy blond hair and piercing blue eyes especially caught one's attention. The girls of the class already thought of him as a dreamboat. Ms. Cato got a kick out of their reactions to Greg.

"I think what our team found out about a special problem that Labradors have might be what Ms. Cato mentioned to us some time ago. She said that due to Allie's hip injury, there could be complications later in her life. It seems that Labradors have few plaguing disorders, which is a good fact, but they do have a tendency toward hip dysplasia. It is referred to as HD. Dysplasia occurs when the ball of the thigh bone does not fit properly into the socket of the hip joint. As the dog ages, movement becomes painful and the back legs become lame. It is a crippling disease, and there is no known cure for it. Allie already has suffered with her hip through an accident of some kind. We wonder, because of this early damage to her hip, if she'll develop HD before she begins to age."

The class entered into intense discussion about this possibility. Andy secured some pictures of the skeletal structure of the Labrador. He placed one on the opaque projector. It showed the hip area and an illustration of the HD disease. Jessica's dad, who also worked at Xerox, had color copies made for the six team research packets. This was a visual hands-on account of HD. During Andy's presentation, he referred to the opaque projector to display the entire skeletal structure to the class.

There it was, Klee thought. They learned about HD during their investigation. Now she could explain some of the concerns the Winslows had.

For several days, a period of time was allocated to complete the reports on the research projects. The interdisciplinary unit was unfolding as Klee hoped it would. However, she realized that as February 14 approached, the students would be focused on matters other than on Labrador details and accounts. Knowing when to "pack it up" with the students came with years of experience. The music class program along with the reports would be completed in ample time before the hearts and flowers celebration.

CHAPTER 38

The Saturday date with Dean came along quickly, but they enjoyed several evenings of conversation before then. The educators were sharing a great deal during these talks, and it seemed that they were getting to know each other. They both began to realize that they were operating on the same wave length on so many issues. Each conversation made them more comfortable with each other.

The teacher-administrator role each had to perform at school was long gone in their private world. They compared, disagreed, and agreed to similar pedagogical methods, procedures, and philosophy. The disagreements were respectful, and the dissimilarities didn't threaten either party. Klee thought this was an indication of real friendship. There didn't seem to be room for resentment, which was good.

Extracurricular activities such as dancing, cross-country skiing, boating, and camping were enthusiastically embraced by both of them. As the conversations expanded into various areas of life, it became more evident that whenever they had been in each other's company at previous school functions, neither of them realized the possibility or the potential of a contented relationship between the two of them.

To take one's time to recognize the personality of the other person and to intently listen was infrequently practiced. It seemed that small talk was the fare for most social situations. Few individuals were willing to go beyond the general social encounter and take the time to engage a particular person or persons on a more personal level. Both Dean and Klee originally fell into that category along with the majority. Often treasures are in our midst, but they are not noticed. The step into discovery is too often avoided. Keep things light and impersonal seems to be the accepted behavior. It's safer that way. Oh, but what is so often missed!

Saturday arrived, and Klee was filled with anticipation. The Treadway Inn was a popular scene for dining and dancing. Sounds of laughter and the general din of chatter filled the lounge as they entered. It was an entertaining place! A large circular bar with ample stools filled the lounge area with small tables occupying a small section within the bar area. Flowing from the lounge was the dining room. The dining tablecloths were solid maroon in color with deep purple napkins as a contrast. Each table held a lighted candle with a wreath of flowers encircling the pewter candle holder. The general motif reflected an old English inn. The pewter and copper adornments enhanced the walls along with paintings of hunters, equestrian riders, and fox hunts. The dance floor was small, but the smallness afforded cozier dancing with your partner. Musically, everyone liked the tempo of the trio that played on Friday and Saturday evenings. The resonant sounds from the piano, bass, and drum were phenomenal. The pianist made the ivory bones dance. The drummer's rendition of "Caravan" invigorated the crowd.

Klee's feelings intensified as Dean held her in his arms. Swaying to the music, she was aware of his athletic body against hers and realized that the scent of his aftershave lotion continued to entice her. Actually, it drove her crazy!

As the dancing progressed throughout the evening, Dean embraced her even more tightly and whispered in her ear, "Are you enjoying yourself, Klee?"

"Yes, yes, I am. It's another magical evening."

"Yes, it is very enchanting, my sweet. You know that you are the kind of woman that a guy wants to marry."

"That is a very correct assessment, Dean," Klee affirmed with an air of firmness in her voice.

Klee never expected his term of endearment. That was the first time he referred to her as, "my sweet." The word *marry* hit her like a thunderbolt. She never expected him to refer to walking down the aisle—not at this point in time anyway. Klee felt good that he understood that she was "the type of woman a man would want to marry" and not a woman with whom to have a casual, noncommittal affair. She expected gentlemanly behavior, and she always received it.

Expressions of intimacy were the acme of human love and devotion, which implied many responsibilities. Klee had those tenets instilled in her for twelve years during her schooling. The nuns saw to it!

Gliding across the floor in Dean's arms, Klee remembered her high school dances. The chaplain would circulate the dance floor. Every once in a while, he would come upon a couple dancing too closely and remind them to leave room for the Holy Ghost. It was apparent that as both Dean and Klee had matured, they didn't adhere to many of the teachings of their youth. They seem to have mellowed and eased up on some of the specific

Catholic school promptings that were taught to them when they were youngsters. They were committed to each other and keenly responsible, but they were also human with human needs, yet they exercised discretion, responsibility, civility, and caring.

If the chaplain could see them now! There wasn't any room for the Holy Ghost! Would she adhere to the old saying of not trying on the shoe before marriage? There was such chemistry between her and Dean. There was a powerful force pulling opposites dead center. What would the next chapter in their relationship bring? Go with the flow.

CHAPTER 39

Although Klee was preoccupied with thoughts of Dean and the sensations she drank in at the Treadway Inn, she had to discipline herself to remain on task at school. The day of the music presentation of "Allie's Song" had finally arrived. Mrs. Marco had selected the last day of the school week for the program. Friday often was selected to culminate the project at hand. Completing the task left the students and teachers with feelings of well-being. The finality of the accomplishment offered a sense of pride as they strode off in various directions for their enjoyment of independence over the weekend.

Ms. Cato accompanied her class to the music room for the special Allie presentation. Earlier in the morning, she had left her guitar with Mrs. Marco so it would be there for the program. Klee planned on playing and singing her theme song at the end of the program. It would be the culmination of the sentiment concerning Allie and all that the students had discovered during the unit of study and class discussions.

The students' excitement permeated the room as they anticipated the staging of the song they had written. Their song was to a simple melody the music teacher put together in the key of C. Klee thought how wonderful it must be to be able to put something together without music to follow. It was a talent—a gift all right—and Klee often wished she had an ear for music so she could abandon all the music books and music sheets.

Jessica stood up from her chair and walked to the front of the room. She scanned the room and stood there waiting for everyone's attention. Klee smiled inside when she realized how perfectly Jessica was mimicking her.

She began, "Ms. Cato, we all welcome you to this exceptional event today. We give special thanks to Mrs. Marco for helping us learn how to write lyrics and to tailor it to a melody that Mrs. Marco composed for us. We have come up with a unique song for Allie. We hope you will like it. Maybe someday we can sing it for Mrs. Winslow too."

Mrs. Marco went to the piano, readied the students, and they began to sing:

ALLIE'S SONG

What do I see . . . could it be?
What is this under the lonely pine tree?
The snow serves as a bed
To where the animal lays its weary head.

The gentle brown eyes peer at me
What do I see . . . could it be?
A dog with shivering body is there
Beautiful Labrador, you came from where?

Let me help you, don't go away
I know something isn't right, so please, please stay.

What do I see . . . could it be?
What is this under the lonely pine tree?
An abandoned, lonely creature
If only I could reach her.

Don't retreat and go away,
I'll help if only you will stay.

Ms. Cato could feel her eyes moisten and her insides quiver like a string on a bow. How beautifully done were the lyrics. The students did a superior job. They captured the essence of this life's lesson.

She believed in her heart that if the students learned about caring, even when it wasn't convenient, they would learn the value of giving of themselves. Her students had witnessed how one person, one leader could indeed make a difference. That is what Mrs. Winslow did with dedicated commitment to an abandoned dog. She carried the banner. They came to realize that others would join the leader to make things happen, do what they could to make the situation better, and resolve it if at all possible.

It was a strong conviction of Klee's to produce an analogous paradigm from the learning of the Allie saga. The nurturing and caring of animals, she firmly believed, was the first crucial step toward the human realm of nurturing. Systematic, gentle, responsible pet care was the training arena for their future lives as parents. Learning the proper rearing skills with pets would set the stage for a natural correlation to child upbringing. Klee expressed this philosophy over the years to her students and parents, to any organization that might listen.

On completion of the student's rendition of "Allie's Song," Klee pulled herself together and did all she could to hide her deep emotions. She went before the class.

"Students, I am overwhelmed with the caring and sensitivity of your song. Words cannot truly express my feelings, but let me tell you that the lyrics made me quite emotional. Thank you for sharing your work with me. Mrs. Marco, thank you for working so diligently with my students and for teaching them new skills. I am proud of you all, and I am deeply touched. Thank you, thank you."

Bobby raised his hand. "Ms. Cato, do you think we will be able to sing our song to Mrs. Winslow and maybe even Allie?"

"I'm glad you asked that, Bobby. I am certain that it will happen. I realize that we all have been waiting for some time now to know if we will ever have Allie come to school, but there are other considerations we need to keep in mind. We'll discuss it when we return to our classroom."

Once the students had settled back at room 119, Ms. Cato readied herself to go into further explanation. She explained that Allie had to go through some physical therapy for her hip after the surgery. This was a careful process and of some duration.

Next, the Winslows had enrolled Allie in obedience school. They wanted her to be trained to be an obedient dog and one that people would enjoy being around. Dogs get excited and, unless they are properly trained, can be a nuisance to others, even destructive to things in their environment and sometimes hurtful to others.

The Winslows were not only caring people but were also responsible individuals. Mrs. Winslow was adamant that Allie learn to follow commands whenever cued by her masters or mistresses. Obedience school would provide the adequate training needed. She also believed that Allie required, after her long period of abandonment, time to trust people again. Once Allie accomplished the inner security to trust humans, Mrs. Winslow felt that Allie would embrace both social and party manners.

Klee went on to explain that there was a certain behavior that needed to be corrected. Mrs. Winslow had indicated to her that Allie was very possessive and protective of the family members. Allie became aggressive with visitors and strangers. She was assured that the aggressiveness would dissipate with positive behavior reinforcement and training at the obedience school. After all, Allie had to get back into the swing of a daily routine with a family and the real world. Ms. Cato felt that this information would help her students understand why they hadn't seen Allie yet.

In conclusion, Ms. Cato said, "As you all understand from your research, the Labrador is known as an exceedingly sociable and family-friendly breed. Allie's ordeal of desertion and the traumatic injury have to be ironed out, but with caring encouragement and professional training, she will do just fine."

CHAPTER 40

"Allie's Song" was like a haunting refrain to Klee as she puttered around the kitchen Saturday morning. The song, she mused, was one more positive to share with Sister. It was usually quite easy to reach Sister Ann Mary over the weekend. Klee had learned that mid-Saturday morning was the best time to call. Klee felt the need to talk to her; Sister was her confidant and a loyal supporter. She felt comfortable with her. She could tell Sister about her innermost thoughts and feelings. Sister loved her for who she was and for what she stood. Sister Ann Mary recognized her uniqueness and could deal with her distinctive personality with ease and love. Sister was her champion indeed! Not only was Sister her advisor and best friend, she also served as Klee's surrogate mother.

"Hello, this is Sister Ann Mary speaking."

"Hi, Sister, it's Klee."

"Oh, Klee, I have been thinking of you. I have kept you in my daily prayers. I hope your guardian angel and you have been walking hand in hand."

"I love how you phrased that, Sister. I do believe my angel is close at hand. I feel its spirit within me. Do you remember the quote from Harriet Beecher Stowe you gave to me a long time ago? It was about angels. I can still quote it:

> Sweet souls around us watch us still,
> Press nearer to our side;
> Into our thoughts, into our prayer
> With gentle helpings glide

"How splendid that you remembered it and retained it as part of your life."

"So now for you, my dear Sister, what is happening with you? How's everything these days?"

"Very nicely I can say. I do have a couple of students that are quite a challenge, but I'm handling them okay. I think my angel is there for me too."

"Why, Sister, after having to deal with me in your eighth-grade class so many years ago, these students should be a piece of cake! I remember you telling me on many occasions over the years that you found yourself on your knees in chapel for guidance when you had me as a student."

"Yes, Klee, you were incorrigible!"

Both Sister and Klee laughed heartily, then Klee went on to speak to her about the important aspects that were occupying her life.

"My students have been doing a fantastic job with all the various learning skills related to the Allie story. I am so proud of them. Mrs. Winslow is steadfast in her drive to do her best for the beautiful Labrador retriever."

"Klee, I am proud of you too. You have evolved into an exceptional teacher. When I look back, I never would have thought your life would be in the field of education. I remember we spoke about you considering the field of research or maybe the medical arena. I was happy for you when you told me that you had enrolled in premed at the university, but I do understand how you felt when it came to dissecting animals to say nothing of what would have happened to you when you were required to work with a cadaver. It seems to me, however, that each of us is guided to the place where we are supposed to be in order to fulfill our earthly journey and to best serve others."

"Thanks, Sister. Saying that you are proud me, and that I am an exceptional teacher, especially coming from you, means the world to me. The word *exceptional* has been surfacing here and there during my career thus far, and I have come to believe that it is not a word being used in a superficial manner. I care a great deal. I am super sensitive to kids and their pain and that of animals too. I have that work ethic that makes me expect myself to do 100 percent with everything that comes my way. I admit that many days I feel burned out."

"I must say that worries me. Burnout is a real danger. We have discussed this on many occasions. I understand that your personality demands you to drive full speed ahead, to be totally responsible for all that is present in your space, but working at that pitch will eventually catch up with you. Remember, dear heart, you had three major surgeries in a four-year period. Dealing with physical limitations takes a great deal of energy and concentrated coping skills."

"Yes, Sister, you continue to give me good advice, but I'm not sure I know how to change my drive, and if I do, who will I become?"

"I would never suggest that you change, dear, but modify. Remember we often speak of moderation and patience. Patience is a word that is often void in your vocabulary, but it is important to practice, so is moderation."

"Intellectually I fully understand, Sister, but to internalize the warning is a different egg in the basket."

"Changing the subject, Sister, there is something else I need to tell you. I hope you'll be at the convent during Easter week. I would like to drive south to Elmira during that break and pay you a visit if you're not going on retreat that week."

"Yes, I'll be here, dear. I'm coming to Rochester this summer. I'll do my retreat earlier on at the Mother House. A week day after Easter Sunday would be wonderful. I'll look forward to your visit, Klee, and I realize that I won't have to worry about dangerous driving conditions for you by Easter time. I hope not anyway."

"Great, Sister. We'll make plans closer to the time. By the way, Dean and I are seeing each other a great deal these days. I believe we are exclusively dating each other at this point. I'll be seeing him during this weekend as a matter of fact. He's coming out to my camp at the lake this afternoon. We're going to hike around in the snow . . . just enjoy being out-of-doors and drinking in nature. I really care about him, but I have some concerns, and I'd like to discuss them with you."

"I hope you will always feel free to do that, Klee. I am here for you. You know that."

"Thanks, Sister. I'll see you before you know it. As soon as we finish our conversation, I'm off to making a thermos of coffee and some sandwiches for Dean and me to consume during our hike. He's also quite the photographer. Dean has a neat camera and likes to do scenes and take photos of anything that flies or has four legs. Some of his works move one's soul. Well, Sister, enough said. Take care. Good-bye now."

CHAPTER 41

The weekend always renewed Klee. She loved her time at her camp in the hills ascending Canandaigua Lake. She was totally in love with this particular exquisite Finger Lake and its surrounding region of western New York state. Although all the Finger Lakes were unique, she was biased in her thinking that Canandaigua Lake was the best! She was delighted that Dean liked it too.

In spite of the many visits to the camp, seeing all her friends each time served like taking an energy tonic. Her neighbors were from all walks of life, and she enjoyed the variety in their backgrounds. She added to her already construction expertise a good number of additional building and repair skills, complements of the men throughout the camp. Her father had been the master teacher in that area in her life however. The women shared campout recipes that were delicious, but Klee never had the time nor took the interest in mastering them. Her concentration was on grilling out on the homemade fire pit, and firing it with maple logs that, when ready for searing the steak, emitted a wonderful smoked maple flavor.

Before the calendar officially proclaimed spring, Klee and Dean once again planned to drive out to camp, but first they would meet in the town of Canandaigua at the little coffee shop for a delicious Sunday breakfast. The shop had a typical fifties motif, and it felt cozy and welcoming. Mr. D'Amico, the owner, was of slight build and energetic with a pleasant smile. He wore wire-rimmed glasses, and his salt-and-pepper hair was slicked back with a part on the right. His narrow mustache was always meticulously trimmed. He made his customers feel as though they had known him for years. Of course, Klee had known him for a long time, and she really liked him. Once she and Dean were satiated with a delicious breakfast of sunny-side up eggs, bacon, freshly baked cinnamon rolls, and baked apple with plenty of hot coffee, they would drive out to the Camp in the Forest.

He would have another perspective of the camp now that it wasn't blanketed with a couple feet of snow. Although many had not opened their camps at this point in time, the real campers were there by the first week in April. Once they arrived, Klee was eager to introduce Dean to her friends. She swelled with pride when introducing Dean to her camping neighbors. She could tell that they were impressed with him. Her friends were cordial toward Dean, and the guys teased him about the little firecracker known as Klee. Dean smiled and gave a wink as he peered into Klee's eyes.

"This is exceptional, Klee," Dean commented. "What a great camp setting. Sure looks different now that it isn't covered with a couple feet of the white stuff. No one would have ever known that the Camp in the Forest with so many sites existed in this vast wooded area. It's rustic and yet so neatly done. I didn't have the full impression of what this was all about. It didn't register during our winter visits."

"Thanks, Dean. I'm glad you like it. It has taken a few summers to get the place where I wanted it to be, so it would be comfortable yet attractive. My cousin, Salena, is an out-of-doors person too, and she has been a tremendous help to me."

"You've both done a terrific job. The idea of using crushed stones is great."

"Yes, Sal and I spread tons of pea gravel. No mud allowed around this site! It makes it easy for us to come here in early spring and late fall, even when the ground is soft or somewhat muddy. It's set up for year-around visitations."

"I never thought of Salena in this light, Klee. Every time I've seen her in the record room at school with her sharp business suit and French twist hairdo, I never got the impression that she was a gal who loved nature."

"I guess that is true of both of us. It runs in the family or something like that."

"I could see you with Allie out here. She'd be in dog heaven."

"Once Bethany thinks that Allie is ready to go off to a different environment with someone other than her family, I've been thinking about doing just that. The pond with the skipping frogs and the schools of minnows would entice Allie. She'd probably dive right into the pond if she weren't leashed. I think she'd love the acres of freedom to walk and roam. I haven't figured out how to handle things with Muffy Cat if she sees a dog come into her domain. I'll probably have to farm her out at Sal's apartment if Allie comes out to the camp."

Klee invited Dean into her twenty-foot travel trailer, which was the focal point of the site. The yellow mallard with chocolate-brown trim was attractive to the eye. Passersby who were visiting often stopped and commented on the mallard and inquired about its floor plan. It slept four comfortably. During the day, the two single beds served as a couch and dining area. The kitchen was adequate with double stainless steel sinks and plenty of cupboards above and below the laminated countertops. The full bathroom with tub and shower was a pleasure to have. After giving Dean a tour of the comfy house on wheels, Klee invited him to sit down. Muffy Cat nonchalantly eyed Dean. She knew this guy. He seemed to be hanging around quite often of late. Klee moved the cat from the couch area and placed her in her basket.

"Muffy Cat thinks that no one has the right to enter her domain. She is especially possessive of her recreational vehicle."

Before Dean went to sit down, he took her hand and drew her near him. Klee began to melt even before he began kissing her.

"Klee, I've missed you so. I've been thinking about coming out to your camp all week."

"I know, I know, Dean."

As they continued to kiss and hold each other, an alarm sounded in Klee's brain once again. She felt a gut spasm. She felt so guilty that she hadn't told Dean what he had a right to know. She never thought that their relationship would have progressed as easily and as smoothly as it had. Things were happening so fast, but it seemed so right. She was even more certain that she needed to get to Sister Ann Mary to sort matters that were pulling her insides in all directions. Thankfully, the Easter visit wasn't far off.

CHAPTER 42

Each time Klee visited the camp, she recalled all the hard work she and Salena had put into the camp site. The camps were permanent sites that were individualistic in arrangement and placement. The area was like a little village, but with the luxury of trees and more trees and space! The trees offered shade and coolness on the warm, muggy days of summer. The temperature could read well into the nineties during the height of the summer, so the trees were a blessing to everyone. Maple logs provided the best flavor when grilling steaks or hamburgers on the open pit fireplace.

During a previous summer, Klee, along with her cousin Sal, built the fireplace between two huge maple trees that were located near the entrance to their site. They borrowed the miniature tractor with cart attached from the camp owner, Jim, and went into the woods in search of just the right sized rocks for the fireplace. The search went along with ease until there was a scream from Salena who was foraging off in the distance.

Klee called out, "What's happening . . . what's wrong, Sal?"

"Oh my, I just ran into a big snake. I don't think it was a good snake either!"

"Come back to the cart. I hope it wasn't a copperhead. They are indigenous to the area. However, in all my years tramping through so many wilds of the natural environs of Canandaigua, I have never run into a poisonous snake. That is to say none that I am aware of anyway. We have enough rocks. Let's drive back to the camp. This is going to be a good campfire story!"

"Right, and the way you expand and embellish a story, it will be a pip to say nothing of the dramatization that will ensue. In the meantime, I'm still shaking."

"I understand how you hate snakes, but they have a purpose in nature too," Klee said. "You never would have made it with me when I was a kid. My pals and I would scout for snakes as we traversed the stream of a particular gully in search of snakes. We'd catch them if we were lucky. Once we examined the snake, we'd let it go. We thought we were so brave."

"Maybe brave with a little stupidity in the mix," responded Salena with obvious annoyance.

"Yeah, you're probably right. I'm sorry you had such an experience. I would have been startled too. You are such a good sport."

They hauled the various sized rocks to camp to build the fireplace pit. Both women sorted the rocks by size and made piles for each size, and one for any rock that was totally irregular in shape. Next, they emptied some of the contents from the bag of cement into an old-fashioned metal tub to mix a smooth, workable mud. They had found the old tub in Jimmy's junk shed. That shed served as a hardware store for Klee. Jimmy was a pack rat. It was amazing what this guy salted away. Deposited in the secluded hidden structure were pieces of lumber, chicken wire, electrical cable wire, galvanized tubs, sheets of metal, motor parts, old nails, assorted screws and bolts, to mention a few items. The only thing the gals had contributed to the project was the bag of cement that they had picked up in Can and, of course, their labor.

Luck was with them. They had gathered enough rocks, and each fit like a charm as the women arranged them in a circular shape to make a fireplace base. They were careful to measure the diameter of the circle in order to be sure that the iron grill would fit properly from edge to edge. Once completed, it looked quite good. It would be serviceable and also look inviting to others.

Before long, there was a stream of visitors stopping at the site to comment on the new addition. Everyone got a kick out of the two industrious women and their various projects. Klee's mind never stopped thinking, coming up with new challenges.

The maple trees had to be at least thirty-five feet in height. Between the two trunks, Klee and Sal's next project would be to rig a metal roof over the open fireplace. Previously, they had gone down the lane that led to Jim's shed where there was always a treasure to be found among the assortment of junk. That's where they had found the perfect scrap sheets of metal.

"These sheets will be perfect for our rustic camp. They're of irregular shape, but that's what will give them camp charm. If we can erect a roof over the fireplace out of this scrap, it will be great," Klee announced.

"Yes, it would. Do you ever stop with ideas? Gee, Klee, you are in constant motion. When do we get to enjoy the weekend?"

"You're right, Salena. No more after this project."

"How come I don't believe you?"

The roof did prove to be adequate to retain the heat from the warmth of the burning logs. Everyone enjoyed this arrangement, especially when it was rainy or on the cool fall nights.

The mixed forest of maple, oak, beech, and chestnut became a spectacular sight in autumn. The autumn woods became nature's canvass. The leaf colors of rich gold, brownish gold, red, deep red that displayed a hue of almost purple in color and various tints of yellow were stunning. The conifers that were mixed in here and there among the deciduous trees were the final touch of nature's brilliance. Without a doubt, nature was expressly observed in all its magnificence and glory as an annual display at the Camp in the Forest. Klee's spirit soared as she drank in all the beauty that surrounded her. She often thought that the angels did an exceptional job with their splashes of hue dust that they scattered most autumns.

In Klee's mind, summers were meant for improving the campsite in order to enjoy more comfortable living. Each improvement paid off during the other seasons. This meant that she and Sal would be able to go out to the camp at any time of the year, open roads permitting.

CHAPTER 43

The 1975 spring break was scheduled for the middle of April that year. It was delightful when the break wasn't too early. Students and teachers often groaned when it occurred in March because it was such a long period from March to June without some kind of break. The students became restless and often less productive. It seemed that the school year did run far more smoothly with the later April spring recess date. Actually, it was an unspoken plus to everyone because the closing date of school on the twenty-third of June didn't seem so distant. Simply put, the April break was more workable. Student production remained on a steadier level and their general interest was apparent with this schedule. It also meant that with the April break, the kickball games would not be far off once the break was over.

The physical exercise was imperative to the students' well-being. The kickball season was welcomed with glee. It would be time in late April or early May to head for the field area to play.

Anticipating the spring season with its outdoor activities invigorated Klee. She threw a load of laundry into the washer as she lost herself in the music from the stereo. She often did this on week nights, especially if she had other plans for the weekend at her camp. She was engrossed in the symphonic sounds of Tchaikovsky's "Swan Lake Ballet Suite" when she heard the phone ringing. She pushed the pause button on the stereo to stop the music in progress then reached for the phone.

"Hello."

"Hi, Klee, it's Marie. I hope I'm not calling too late in the evening."

"No, no, this is fine. I'm doing some laundry while listening to music."

"I'm trying to get my calls out to our friends. Don has been urging me to get on the stick and do the inviting before any more time goes by. We are planning a pre-spring break party at our home the Saturday prior to our spring recess. Of course, we want you to join us. Lisa and Rob will be coming, Jane and her husband, and Salena and you, I hope. I haven't called everyone yet."

"It sounds great, Marie. Thanks for including me. What may I bring along?"

"Just yourself as you always say, Klee. By the way, I understand that you and Dean are an item. Don and I were surprised to hear this, but so happy for you."

"I appreciate your good wishes. Yes, we have been seeing a great deal of one another when our schedules jive."

"We are planning on inviting Dean too. You'll probably come together, and for those who don't know that you are a twosome, they'll surely recognize it when you both make your entrance together."

"It will probably knock a few of them for a loop with the realization. I really haven't said much about out relationship because it is in the early stages, and certainly there are no commitments coming from either side. I like to be private, especially in the area of personal involvement." She hadn't even told Lisa how deep her feelings were running for Dean.

"You are probably wise, Klee. Don and I know that there was a great deal said about us combining the two families when we decided to get married. We were lucky to have tied the knot shortly after everyone became aware of our plans. Once the marriage was accomplished, it voided a great deal of speculation."

"I understand what you are saying. Don has mentioned to me that the two families are doing great together. I am so happy that it has worked out that way for you two special people."

"Thanks, Klee. We feel so blessed. It was quite an undertaking, but it has all worked out for the best. I can honestly say that we are one big happy family."

The two teacher friends chatted a little longer. After saying good-bye, Klee went off to resume her laundry task and to let her heart sing as she continued listening to Tchaikovsky. Muffy Cat peacefully slept in her basket while Klee was busying herself around the house. However, the cat jumped up on cue as soon as Klee went to her recliner. Muffy Cat never let the cozy lap experience pass her by!

After a weekend at camp, Klee always felt renewed. She was ready to face the week with all its challenges. Even doing laundry in the evening was okay with her because this meant more free time on the weekend. Basically she had two laundry jobs to accomplish. One job was doing home laundry and the other, camp laundry. Washing double sets of sheets, towels, and personal items didn't concern Klee because the reward of the time spent at the camp was worth every extra effort.

CHAPTER 44

Canandaigua Lake is the fourth largest of the eleven Finger Lakes. The name, which means "chosen spot," is derived from the Seneca Indian language. The Iroquois, native peoples of North America, originally consisted of five nations or tribes which made up the Iroquois League. The original Iroquois League was often known as the Five Nations. It consisted of the Mohawk, Oneida, Onondaga, Cayuga, and Seneca nations. When the sixth nation, the Tuscarora, joined the League, the Iroquois became known as the Six Nations, an impressive and powerful entity. The Seneca mainly dwelled between the Genesee River and Canandaigua Lake.

Klee roamed the hills, fields, gullies, streams, waterfalls, and shoreline of the Canandaigua Lake area as a child and a teen. As she matured, she was sure that her love of exploring indicated that she had some Seneca in her. The affinity was so strong, her love of nature powerful. Maybe she was a true pantheist.

Canandaigua Lake is approximately sixteen miles in length and one and a half miles wide. The average depth of the lake is 127 feet with a maximum depth of 276 feet. Although Klee often thought of the maximum depth while swimming in the middle of the lake or skimming across the water in her powerboat, little intimidated her.

When Klee celebrated her twelfth year, she was entrusted with her own motorboat. She loved opening the motor full throttle once she navigated the vessel into the open waters of the lake. She was exhilarated by the freedom she felt as she sped along and loved looking back at the wake made from the propeller rotation of the twenty-five horsepower motor. She referred to it as a crystal ice path. The picturesque hills that surrounded the lake warmed Klee's heart each time; they encircled her being. Nature filled her with overwhelming joy.

On a clear day, as kids, Klee and Billy Wingate, her buddy in exploration, would pack up their snacks, boat gear, check the gas tank on his dad's large boat, and navigate north. Squaw Island was situated at the north end of the lake. According to the Seneca legend, this eleven-thousand-year-old island was used to hide the Seneca women and children during the Sullivan Expedition against the Six Nations of the Iroquois in 1779.

Billy shouted over the drone of motor, "Klee, let's anchor about fifteen feet from the island as usual. I need to be sure the propeller will be clear. Remember, it gets shallower the closer we go to the island."

"Okay, Billy, I'll have the anchor and line ready. Let me know when."

Once the anchor dragged and settled on the bottom, the boat steadied. It was a day void of wind. The lake looked like shimmering glass. Billy secured the ladder to the clamps on the gunwale of the boat. It was their pattern to dive from the boat into the sparkling clear water and swim to the island. Later they would swim back to the boat and scurry up the ladder to get their lunch and snacks. Billy entered the water from the stern of the boat while Klee liked the higher dive from the bow. Both were expert in shallow dives.

Billy was twelve years old and two years Klee's senior. She thought Billy was cute with his short brush cut. His brown hair shading almost matched Klee's, but his eyes were a fascinating hazel brown. He wasn't much taller than Klee. He was solidly built and had strength too. Klee could see it when he had to hold the boat at a dock when the lake was rough with waves and the wind didn't cooperate. It was his strength against the force of the churning water.

While sunning on the island, Billy and Klee would fantasize about being steamboat captains. There were fourteen boats that provided passenger and commercial services along the lake from 1827 to 1835. The steamboat, *Lady of the Lake*, was launched in 1827 at Canandaigua Lake.

Billy said to Klee, "Just think of steamboats and double-decker paddleboats along the lake more than a century ago. I'd be crazy for being on one now."

"I could just see you, Billy. I'd like it too. Maybe someday you'll be a captain of a ship. I'm enthralled about anything that has to do with water. I'd like to be a captain too."

"Don't be a silly little girl," Billy firmly stated. "Girls don't become captains!"

"Yeah, I can be anything I want to be."

Even as a youngster, Klee wasn't afraid to tackle what others thought would be impossible. That was her mind-set throughout her life: do what needs to be done with no social qualifiers interfering. However, Klee had to learn, and often the hard way, that she couldn't always be what she wanted to be or to do what she wanted to do if it interfered with tradition and the establishment. Role discrimination operated on all levels and sometimes where least expected. She was clearly made aware of this fact by her father as she matured. Her creativeness and inquisitive mind were sucked out of her more frequently than not. What a waste of a creative mind. What a waste of an individual in the name of role expectations. What a disservice to the female gender!

CHAPTER 45

The city of Canandaigua was a quaint, family town located at the northern shore of the lake. Klee's family had to drive through the entire main street to get to their summer place, which was situated directly on the east side of the lake. She loved going to the town with her dad. Often they would go to the old-fashioned hardware store for new fishing gear. Many storekeepers addressed Klee's dad by his first name, Jared, and often they gave Klee treats. Her dad was a successful businessman in Rochester, and he was an excellent customer to various businesses along the Canandaigua main street. The store proprietors liked to see him coming because his visit meant the cash register would have a full ring.

The store façades were faced with red brick. Casement windows were the focal point to display the many wares of the particular store. Some of the buildings were over one hundred years old, but they possessed such charm.

Klee and her dad went to Mr. Vinci's bakery on Sunday mornings to purchase warm loaves of Sicilian bread. Klee enjoyed listening to her dad and Mr. Vinci's conversation, especially when they talked about going fishing toward Naples, which was at the southern end of the lake. She'd get excited every time there was a suggestion of making the sixteen-mile trip because she knew they would take her along.

Ironically, it was Klee at age eight who had hooked her dad on fishing the day she pulled in a thrashing three-pound large-mouth bass. Being a petite child, the bass almost won out by pulling her overboard as she struggled to land it into the boat. Her determination won out. Her dad was delighted with her prize. Immediately that following weekend, he took Klee into town and bought her shiny new fishing gear along with everything in sight for himself. For the remainder of his life, her dad enjoyed the sport of fishing.

Many of the homes that lined the main street of Canandaigua seemed very high through the eyes of a child with their dormers and cupolas. The lawns were manicured and the properties were enhanced with colorful flower beds that caressed the homes. Flowers were carefully planted so that they meandered down the walkways to meet the city sidewalks.

Klee learned to appreciate flowers and all their loveliness from her grandmother and mother. They had that special touch. Grandma explained that the plants were like children and that meant that they needed time to develop. The beds displayed an array of vibrant colors, heights, and varieties. Annuals and perennials were mixed together. Chrysanthemums, daylilies, peonies, blue salvias, tulips, pansies, geraniums, shasta daisies, and roses made a dazzling picture to behold.

Klee wished that she could develop such attractive beds, but she never inherited the nurturing hand when it came to flowers. Her determination never stopped her from planting, even if many withered under her care. Her ancestors had green thumbs, but Klee always referred to herself as having a black one.

As she peered along the street, Klee was comforted to see folks sitting in large rocking chairs or swing gliders on their front porches. Usually, the American flag occupied a prominent location at the front of the structure. It was such a different lifestyle; family life was the norm, people had roots.

As an adult, Klee continued to cherish the Canandaigua area, and especially the time at her camp in the hills above Canandaigua Lake. She never gave up her beloved lake, however. To maintain the joys of the lake, she and her cousin, Salena, had their boat moored at the marina at the northern end of the lake. It was only a ten-minute ride from the camp to the marina.

They entertained family and friends on the twenty-four-foot boat, which had a below deck cabin that slept two. In addition, there was a concealed head. The one and only time Muffy Cat went out on the boat, she became so frightened when Klee opened the throttle and skimmed the water that Sal had to put her below deck. She stayed with Muffy until they turned around and headed back to the marina.

"Okay, Klee, I know you want the cat to be with you, but taking her on the boat is ridiculous," Sal angrily commented.

"You're right. It won't happen again!"

Canandaigua had changed since she had been a child. Some of the commercial buildings had been modernized, more for convenience and safety than for attractiveness. The general appearance of the homes along the main street also appeared different to Klee. Some of the homes lacked the neatness and pride of ownership so prevalent in bygone years. Although saddened, Klee still could cling to the fond memories of her childhood.

CHAPTER 46

Shifting her mind from memory lane, Klee concentrated on the present. It was nice seeing all her camp friends throughout the seasons. Each season had its rewards and delights. Each season invited new adventures. Each season offered renewal and the continuity of life.

During the fall season, roaring fires in open-pit fireplaces with smoke ascending among the trees that burst with color was a welcome sight on weekends at the camp. Sitting around the campfire on chilly days or evenings chatting and catching up on all the news was enjoyable for the adults and the teens. Snacks, popcorn, hot coffee, and libations were the fare on those memorable cool evenings. The jokes and stories were fun to listen to, especially those with an unusual punch line.

Sal and Klee were usually included in daring group adventures, such as the time they tried to capture and string up a pig that got loose from Jim's pen. It was a hilarious sight to behold! The squealing of the pig, the shouts of the intended captors, and the various missed tackles had everyone in stitches—except the pig, of course.

Often, the cousins would use their camp in the winter for cross-country skiing outings. Not many were that brave to ski back into the 250 acres of the Camp in the Forest on cold bitter days, but Klee and Salena were game.

The soundlessness of the forest, the variety and sizes of animal tracks, and the slick gliding movement of the skis over the snow was an exhilarating and invigorating experience for both women. They followed the roads that Jimmy frequently plowed. He liked to have access to his property—the part that was developed anyway.

What was unpleasant for the skiers or those with snowshoes was plowing through areas that were too deep with snow. This type of exercise was great for burning the calories big time if done on a frequent basis, but there never seemed to be ample time for such regular workouts. Life's indulgences were different for those tending to their careers.

It was evident to most folks who knew Klee intimately that the camp, the lake, and Canandaigua with all its surroundings were ingrained in her soul. She wondered if Dean would come to feel the same way. She was realistic in acknowledging that even if Dean had feelings for the area, his career plans might dictate an entirely different locale. This would be difficult for her.

CHAPTER 47

The last days before spring break were busy with wrapping up lesson deadlines and projects. The students were getting antsy for their break to say the least. They had a wonderful surprise in store for them, but Klee had kept it under wraps. She could hardly contain herself, but she knew she had no choice if she wanted the encounter to have a lasting impact.

She had private conversations with Bethany as to Allie's progress over the winter months. The students were not privy to the conversations. Recently, however, Bethany revealed her intentions to Klee.

"I believe Allie is ready to come to school. She will be leashed, of course. Both Tom and Laurie will accompany me. Tom and Allie have bonded. She responds to his commands in due haste. May we plan a time?"

"Bethany, yes, of course! I was so hoping this would take place before the spring break. What a send-off for the youngsters."

"Good! My children and I would like to bring in cupcakes and some treats for the kids. We'll tell them that Allie is giving them a party."

"What fun this will be. Let's set the date and time now. I'll tell the class about a special visitor a little before your arrival time. If I tell them far in advance, they'll be too excited and antsy. They'd be hanging from the ceiling!"

The women planned on the Wednesday before the spring recess, at two thirty. Arriving at that time would give them ample opportunity for a celebration before the buses rolled in to carry the students home.

Klee also informed Jane Marco about Allie's visit. Jane said she'd work in some practice of "Allie's Song" without suggesting any particular reason for making it part of their class again; it would be offered as a review of their work. This way, the students would be prepared when the visitation actually took place.

"I have a keyboard. I'll see to it that it is in your classroom first thing that morning before the students arrive. I'd like to place the keyboard in the closet in the rear of the room. Then, I'll just slip into the classroom at the designated time."

"Thanks so much, Jane. You have been so supportive. I believe the Winslows will be very impressed. I wonder how Allie will react when the class begins to sing, and she hears the keyboard for the first time?"

"I hope we don't frighten her. I'll play softly, I assure you."

CHAPTER 48

At 2:15 p.m., Ms. Cato told her class that it was time to wrap up the lesson. They had done a good job with the math period. She realized that she would need to review some of the concepts once they returned from spring break. At this point, however, she was satisfied with their accomplishments, and a review upon their return would flow easily.

"Okay, everyone, let's put the books away and clear your desks," requested Ms. Cato.

The students hurriedly did as she requested. There was never a hesitation when it came to packing away books and classwork. Some students eyed the clock with a questioning look. Before anyone asked why they were stopping so early, Klee decided to jump right in. She clasped her hands together before she began to speak.

"I have a special announcement to make. You all have waited so very long for this opportunity. Well, shortly, Allie will be coming through the door."

Before Klee could go on, there was clapping, squealing, and cheering. She was filled with happiness as she watched their reactions. After a minute or two, the class settled down.

"Now you all need to exhibit your best behavior because this will be a new experience for Allie. We do not want to do anything to frighten her. That means we stay calm, no sudden movements or unexpected noise. I am counting on each of you to welcome Allie in a nice manner and to show respect toward the Winslows."

"Ms. Cato, will Allie be on a leash?" Rebecca asked.

"Yes, she will. Tom Winslow, Mrs. Winslow's son, will guide her. Allie follows Tom's commands to perfection, I have been told."

"I guess dog obedience school does work," stated Greg.

Ms. Cato went on to explain to the class that Allie would be led to each student and at that time they could gently pet Allie if they wanted to have

yellow Labrador

the experience or they could just say hello to the dog. She also explained that the Winslows were bringing in cupcakes and some other goodies as a special treat from Allie. Allie was giving them a thank-you party.

"Gee, Ms. Cato, we never thought that Allie would be giving us a party," Eric excitedly called out. "This rescue has turned out to be neat in a lot of ways!"

"Indeed, it has, Eric, but I need to mention one more thing. You will be performing for Allie and the Winslows. Mrs. Marco will come to our class. Her keyboard is already here in the back closet. At last you will sing 'Allie's Song' for the real dog that sits before you."

"Wow, no wonder Mrs. Marco had us sing our song yesterday in class. She said she wanted to be sure we hadn't forgotten it," chimed in Greg.

At the next moment, there was a light rap on the door to room 119. All eyes were fixed on the figures who framed the doorway. Tom, with his sandy blond hair and horn-rimmed glasses, entered slowly with Allie in tow. He appeared somewhat nervous as he peered at all the students, but inside, he believed that Allie would come through as a true trooper. The dog obviously had a recent bath, was brushed to perfection, and sported an expensive leather collar. A heart-shaped pendant dangled from the collar with her name inscribed on it. She was beautiful. Her large brown eyes remained mesmerizing. Allie's family followed Tom.

Bethany wore a lavender tailored suit with a gold silk blouse. Her French twist hairstyle made her appear taller. Her warm smile greeted the students. Her daughter Laurie stood a step behind her mom. Her dress attire consisted of gray dress slacks and a lightweight powder-blue sweater. Her choice of hues accentuated her dark hair.

As promised, Allie went to each student's desk. There was absolute quiet in the room as she made her rounds. Some students were in awe while others showed their pleasure with dancing eyes. Most of the students did pet Allie, and dear Allie seemed to enjoy all the attention. Ms. Cato experienced some anxious feelings initially but Tom did an expert handling job, and Allie went along as if it was old hat to her. Allie displayed a congenial and loving personality. What a positive culmination Ms. Cato thought. What a wonderful experience for everyone involved. All the collateral learning was coming to fruition. These visitors were such role models, and they came in all shapes, sizes, and ages.

At the very last greeting, Tom ushered Allie to Ms. Cato who was standing in front of the room.

Tom said, "Allie, this is the woman who gave you the life you are now enjoying."

The dog recognized Klee and wanted to lurch forward, but she obeyed Tom's command to "stay."

Klee was filled with overflowing emotion. She felt her eyes moisten as she approached the dog. Bending on her knee so she could be at eye level, Klee engaged Allie with a knowing look. It was a look of depth and understanding between a human spirit and that of one of the animal kingdom. It was a moment in time that Klee locked within her memory.

"Hello, precious Allie. How well you look. You are a beautiful creature, and your spirit is part of us all!"

Allie's luminous eyes peered deeply into Klee's. With sensitivity, Klee embraced Allie and the gentle canine rewarded her with enthusiastic dog kisses—profuse, deliberate licking.

Tom spoke to the students about life with Allie, and they had numerous questions to ask. Before he began the dialogue with the students, he said, "I know you are being respectful, but I invite you to call me Tom."

"Tom, was it hard to train Allie at obedience school?"

"Not really. The key was to teach her the learning skills in small steps and with a great deal of patience. She is a smart dog. She caught on and wanted to please. She was good with the commands, but it took longer for her to trust people."

"Does that mean it took longer for her to socialize as Ms. Cato told us?" asked Marvin.

"Exactly! We wanted to be sure that her confidence was restored, and for her to realize that people were her friends, not her foes. Being abandoned for so long can cause undesirable behavior. My mother mentioned to us on several occasions that an abandoned child would have special problems too, just as an animal would when neglected," Tom stated seriously.

"We were so surprised to hear that Allie has pet mates as Ms. Cato calls them. Do the cat, the dog, and the mouse really get along, Tom?" asked Jessica.

"It's amazing, but Allie took to Cleo, the cat, and Charlie, the mouse, without much of a problem. She seemed to want to mother them. Cleo wasn't going to have anything to do with Allie at first, but Allie persisted in following her around and carefully licked her head every few steps. The cat had such a disdainful look on her face each time Allie came around. We would all laugh inside as we watched the maneuvering between the cat and the dog. Although we were amused, we never laughed outwardly because we were sure Cleo would sense our hilarity at her expense. Then she'd really become indignant," Tom chuckled.

Laurie piped in, "One evening after dinner, I went into my dad's study for a specific book from his library collection. As I peered into the room, I saw gathered by my dad's big winged chair all three animals. Allie was stretched out full length. She appeared perfectly relaxed. Cleo was nestled alongside of Allie and Charlie's head rested on Cleo's front paws. It was a powerful picture of contentment and friendship. Once this scene occurred, we were sure that they were all pals. Believe it or not, Charlie followed Cleo's lead most of the time. If Cleo was okay with Allie, then Charlie was okay with Allie too. It touched our mom deeply when I called out to everyone to come and see what I had discovered that evening in the study."

"This peaceful scene made us realize that all the trials and tribulations to save Allie were well worth it," chimed in Bethany.

"Often, the animals teach us what people need to do. We need to accept others even if there are differences," said Robin. "It's all a matter of the heart."

Klee was thrilled with Robin's insightful response. She was a gifted student in many ways and although she was considered reserved, she had a keen sensitivity and could cut right through to the heart of the matter. If she had something important to say, she did.

Klee marveled at the superb job Tom was doing. He possessed such composure and was thorough in his explanations. His role as the debating team captain at his school and an honor student were evident as he spoke.

CHAPTER 49

Mrs. Winslow and Laurie went out into the corridor where they had left the boxes of goodies. They reentered with two large flat boxes, which contained chocolate cupcakes decorated with sprinkles. Tied in little sacks with colorful ribbons and bows were a variety of candy treats.

Randy asked, "Tom, what about Allie's treat? Can't she have one?"

"Yes, she can," said Tom. "She is sitting patiently and is waiting for my command. It is important to be consistent in reinforcing acceptable learned behavior. I will not give her people food, but I have a large milk bone in my back pocket. Once I ask her if she wants her treat and tell her she is a good dog, she knows her special reward is coming."

Right on cue, when Tom went ahead with his comments to Allie and looked directly into her eyes, her large tail began to pound the floor enthusiastically. She gently took the treat into her sizable mouth. The students took in every second as the dog and master worked together with understanding and respect.

The door swung open and smiling Mrs. Marco came bouncing in. She was a tall woman with brown hair that she wore in a ponytail. Her trademark was the oversized earrings she wore. Ms. Cato often overheard the students commenting on a particular set of earrings, especially if they displayed an animal outline or motif.

Ms. Cato introduced the Winslows to Mrs. Marco.

"It is so nice to meet you all. I have heard so much about you and the rescue of Allie. The class and I have something special planned for you today."

"Yes, I understand that we are in for a special pleasure today, and we have been looking forward to the presentation," responded Mrs. Winslow.

Before Jane Marco went to retrieve her keyboard, she approached Tom and Allie.

With bravado, she said, "I must greet Allie. Will that be all right, do you think?"

"Absolutely," said Tom.

Jane loved dogs. She and her husband had three. They all lived in the country so it was a paradise for her dogs. Jane loved walking them in the wooded area that surrounded their huge, old farmhouse with the green shingled roof. Klee had been out to Jane's place a couple of times. She and Lisa did some cross-country skiing in and around the Marco's property. It was a peaceful setting. Virgin snow along the trails was a skier's delight.

The song presentation by the students went very well. How proud both Ms. Cato and Mrs. Marco were with their efforts. It was obvious that it touched the Winslow clan. Even Allie kept tilting her head as certain chords were played. She was reacting with dog emotion by her frequent head movement. Upon completion of the song, the family heartedly clapped. Allie sent out two robust barks and wagged her tail. Thus, the saga of Allie came to a culmination that day. As Klee surveyed those before her in room 119 at Fairhaven Central, she knew the experience was valuable and sustaining.

Shortly after Mrs. Marco said her good-byes and left the classroom, the door swung open once again. Dean appeared. He was wearing a plaid sport coat with light blue-and-black threads accenting the jacket. To coordinate his attire, he donned black razor-creased slacks and cordovan loafers. His gray shirt and black tie complemented the jacket. He was Mr. Fashion Plate or Mr. Movie Star all right! Klee was fascinated with his impeccable mode of dress. She had previously mentioned to him that Allie and the Winslows would be coming to school, and she hoped that he would have the time to stop by. She understood, however, that at the end of the school day, one or two emergencies might arise. She hoped it wouldn't be one of those days. He seemed to do his best, if at all possible, to never let her down. She felt that the demonstration of reliability said a great deal about the person. It also seemed to her to demonstrate respectful behavior in a relationship whether romantic or platonic. The attribute of unfailing dependability would certainly be a plus in his chosen career.

"Good afternoon, everyone," Dean said. "I have been looking forward to meeting Allie and the outstanding Winslow family."

All eyes were on Mr. Cappelli. Tom was located in the front of the room with Allie. Dean strode over to Tom; they shook hands. Dean looked down at the dog. Allie was sizing up Dean, but she maintained her relaxed composure. The tall man bent slowly and spoke in an even, reassuring tone.

"Allie, Allie! So you are the famous dog the students have come to care about."

He stroked the dog, and Allie responded to him in a very positive manner; her tail danced. Klee thought she was a smart dog, all right. Why wouldn't anyone take to Dean? Or was she just biased?

Once Dean and Allie finished their greetings, Klee introduced the vice principal to the family members.

Mrs. Winslow summed everything up, "This has been a wonderful experience for us. May I say that you have an exceptional teacher in Ms. Cato."

"Indeed you may, and yes, I do realize that fact. We are fortunate to have her aboard."

Dean had given her a deep knowing look as he spoke. She prayed that she would not reveal her feelings for him before the Winslows and her class. She began to feel warm then sensed she was about ready to break into a cold sweat. For a split second her thoughts drifted. Her entire mind and body telegraphed to her how much she wanted to be with him, and especially before he left for Ithaca for spring break and his Easter celebration with his family. Klee broke her reverie and took a concealed deep breath to gain composure. Her tone was professional when she spoke.

"Thank you, Mr. Cappelli. The real admiration, it seems, goes to Mrs. Winslow because she never gave up on Allie. She embraced the daunting responsibility in order to make a difference in this canine's life."

"Ms. Cato," replied Mrs. Winslow, "I like to think that each of us in her own way made loving contributions in order to be where we are today. Success starts when someone else sees and reaches for the next step. You grasped the next step!"

Laura and Tom started to clap and the students followed suit with Allie's barks accentuating the happiness—the admiration between the two women.

CHAPTER 50

The April pre-spring break party at Marie and Don's home had been a huge success. They were gracious hosts and fun to be with. The variety of foods and libations was impressive.

Indeed, there were some surprised looks when Dean and Klee arrived together. Marie had been right. Those who didn't know about the twosome would get the message. Klee and Dean were prepared if any comments would happen to surface, but no one had the opportunity to ask, thanks to Rob. He was smooth in his approach and a real friend.

"Hey, Dean, what do you think of Klee's camp? Isn't it the neatest place?"

All eyes turned toward Dean as they awaited his response.

"It's fantastic," Dean replied. "It is so relaxing to be there. I've enjoyed myself immensely on each visit."

Klee smiled inside. *That response will do it*, she thought. When they all returned after spring break, surely the total faculty would be apprized of the romance between Klee and the vice principal. She looked forward to speaking to Lisa about the bombshell Rob had dropped at the party.

Although Lisa and Klee engaged in "party" conversation, there wasn't any opportunity to speak on a personal basis, but Klee indicated she would call her as she and Dean were saying "thank you" and "good night" to all the party-goers.

Things seemed to get busy, and Klee hadn't had a great deal of time for chatting, but finally, the opportunity came along.

"Hi, Lisa, it's, Klee. I have some time this evening to chat. I hope you are free."

"Well, girlfriend, it's been awhile! Yes, I do have time. I take it that Dean has been keeping you busy."

"Yes, I guess he has. Even my cat is having a fit. I think she feels neglected."

"I was beginning to feel that way too. So exactly what's been happening with the two of you, may I ask?"

"Of course, I'll tell you where we are at this point in time."

Klee explained that matters were progressing faster than she had ever dreamed. She admitted to Lisa that her feelings for Dean were running deep, and she believed that from his words and actions, he was experiencing the same emotions.

Klee mentioned how difficult it would be for her while Dean was away with his family for the Easter holiday. He would not return until the weekend before school reopened. She believed they'd spend time together that weekend.

"Wow, Klee. He's going to be with his family almost an entire week? This doesn't leave much time for you two, does it?"

"No, it doesn't give us much personal time. I have received the message loud and clear that Dean is very close to his family. He is devoted to his parents and enjoys his siblings, nieces, and nephews. It is obvious that the cohesiveness of the family unit is paramount to him, to all the Cappellis."

"Hmmm," Lisa sighed. "This could be a good thing and maybe not so good. I wonder what position his future wife will be assigned?"

"Exactly . . . I have thought about that. I sense that he has two different approaches to life. On the one hand, he is A-one in his professional career, his decision making, but there is a 'but.' On the other hand, he seems to be very influenced by his family's expectations and traditions. I have the impression that there is a real European element operating within his family. You know what I mean, family first, absolute loyalty. Truthfully, I can go along up to a certain point. I am always respectful of seniors and the older generation, but I probably won't go along with taking a rear seat in the wagon."

"I would feel the same way," Lisa agreed.

"I have had a positive signal come my way in a form of an invitation for Mother's Day weekend. Dean would like to introduce me to his family. Everyone will be at his parents' homestead. His siblings, their spouses, and their children will be present to celebrate Mrs. Cappelli's special day," Klee revealed.

"That setup might be overwhelming for your first introduction to Mama and Papa with so many people in attendance. I hope that you will be prepared for such a review. Are you sure that you are up to this type of introduction, this exposure? Maybe meeting his parents alone at first might be better."

"I'm really not positive that I am ready for group interaction, but nothing ventured leaves questions, doesn't it? So I'll go to Ithaca. In all honesty, I really want to see Dean in a family setting and to understand his role with his parents and his entire family. So I guess the evaluating will be on both sides."

Lisa and Klee talked for some time. Klee didn't want to tell Lisa what really concerned her. Although Lisa was her best friend, Klee decided to talk to Sister Ann Mary first, which meant baring her soul to the nun. Sister was a reliable sounding board. Could she bring herself to open the wounds once again?

CHAPTER 51

O n Friday, the last day before spring break, everyone had a sense of euphoria. The old jingle came to Klee's mind, and she smiled when she remembered that as a youngster she and her pals would chant, "No more teachers, no more books, no more teachers' dirty looks!" Is the chant the same, or is there a new version? Everyone needed a break. Batteries needed to be recharged. Kids needed the freedom to be kids and get out-of-doors for recreational activities. Teachers longed to have adult time for themselves and their families.

Klee admittedly was eager for the dismissal buzzer to sound. She wanted to leave shortly thereafter because this would be her evening to spend with Dean before he left for Ithaca. She was experiencing some contradictory emotional feelings about his departure. Selfishly, she thought that they should be sharing the Easter holiday. Yet she told herself repeatedly that she had no claim on him at this point to have such an expectation. She was torn between emotion and intelligent thinking. Maybe it was Lisa's adamant reaction to the fact that Dean was going home for the entire break that made her start doubting.

The evening before Dean's departure, Dean and Klee went to dinner, and all the while during dinner anticipating their return to his apartment. This would be a special time for them since Dean would be away for several days.

The apartment was neat and well kept. A tan overstuffed sofa with sturdy corduroy material caught one's eye, and two complementing leather chairs occupied the rest of the living room. He had a large cocktail table in front of the sofa. Sports and photography magazines were neatly arranged on the table along with a TV guide and remote control. A large brandy snifter served as a bowl, which was filled with an assortment of hard candies. An end table was situated between the two large leather chairs. The lamp on the table was massive and sported a chrome exterior. Nature and sporting pictures that had been professionally framed occupied the walls. They were arranged in clusters according to the theme of the paintings or prints. The nature photos he had photographed were displayed on a separate wall. They were good!

The kitchen was small but adequate. There wasn't a thing out of place. The cupboard and appliances were well cared for and gave off a clean glow. Dean was great in the kitchen. A marinara sauce was his specialty, and the baked lasagna was to die for.

The bedroom not only held a king-sized bed but also one entire wall was dedicated to his desk-work area along with shelves loaded with books. The study area reinforced the idea that completing his doctorate was an absolute in his plans. Not even a pair of socks was noticed on the floor.

Klee realized in all her observations over the months that what made Dean, Dean was his fine upbringing in so many areas. What woman wouldn't appreciate his neatness and self-pride in his person and his environment? He was brought up to be a caring gentleman. Yet those eyes of his that so mesmerized Klee, which displayed warmth and empathy, could also be stern.

Their evening together was comforting. They talked the evening away as they sipped wine with the soft hum of classical music in the background. "Clair de Lune" by Debussy and "Because" were their favorites. They both realized that their attractiveness to one another was becoming stronger, and it was exceedingly difficult to imagine a long relationship without marriage. At eleven o'clock they both agreed it was time for Dean to drive Klee home since he was leaving for Ithaca at six the next morning.

Holding Klee and kissing her for the last time, he clung to her as though he were clinging to a lifeline. She felt the power of his grip; she felt his love. It had been a beautiful evening for the lovers, and the parting was wrenching.

"Klee, I'm really going to miss you these next six days. As I said before, you are the kind of gal a guy wants to marry. I am so ripped up about this realization. I know that marriage can't happen until I finish my education. I have promised my parents that I would not marry until I received my Ph.D. After all, they are giving me financial support for my doctorate degree when I have to take a leave of absence for a year or maybe two to complete my on-campus internship and write my dissertation. I have to be fair to them and do what is proper. I wouldn't have it any other way."

Klee was overwhelmed. This was the first time he seriously referred to the marriage bit—the first time he used the word *marriage* in direct relationship to the two of them. This time, Dean had given further explanation about marriage, his obligations, and his torn feelings. She was bubbling inside as his words took hold. The moments of ecstasy slowly dimmed as she thought about what she needed to tell him.

"Dean, I do not want to diminish how we feel about each other, but we each have certain issues we need to deal with before we go too much farther," Klee whispered into his ear.

He turned his head to her and looked directly into her eyes.

"Issues! You have something holding you back, Klee?"

"Please let's talk about it when you return, but right now, I want to savor the evening we have shared."

Dean's jaw set, and he had a disturbed look in his eyes. From his reaction to her statement, Klee realized that she probably had some unpleasant conversations with Dean ahead of her. She was realistic in her thinking, so she accepted with a sinking heart the fact that life is a series of hurdles indeed. This might be her biggest hurdle yet!

CHAPTER 52

The drive to Elmira to visit Sister Ann Mary was picturesque through much of its rural passage. Some of the roads were hilly with ample curves. The trees marched by as she drove along the highway. Some of the deciduous trees were exposing their spring buds. It wouldn't be long before the beautiful maple, oak, and sycamore would be dressed for the spring parade. The crocuses were peaking upward toward the spring sun. Once the crocuses appeared, it was a sure sign that spring was emerging with its new beginnings.

Klee was so in tune with Mother Nature. It was a celebration each time she had moments to communicate with the environment. Nature not only provided spectacular beauty, it also offered hidden gifts, and it was all free!

She came upon many hidden treasures as she explored the lake area when she was a youngster. She collected a multitude of rocks because of their unusual shape or color. In the gullies, she liked to look at how the stream of moving water cut the earth and allowed it to meander where it needed to go. Building a stone bridge from one side of the stream to the other was fun for her and her pals. Bugs, butterflies, and tadpoles intrigued her. She would never tolerate anyone killing a living thing unless it was intended for food. Observing with the naked eye or with a camera was sufficient. Nature provided her a playground. It was peaceful, healthy, and life's teacher if it was viewed with introspection and respect.

The winding roads to Elmira never set well with Klee because she was prone to motion sickness. However, for Sister, she would deal with the discomfort, which meant stopping the car and walking around while sipping a ginger concoction she carried in a small flask. The ginger mostly settled the queasy dance in her stomach. Extricating herself from the car for ten minutes or so did relieve her enough so she could travel forward.

Although she had to deal with the queasy sensations, Klee basically enjoyed the drive because it gave her some quiet time to sort out and reflect on concerns she was harboring. Her comfortable Chevy often had become her confessional box where she audibly talked out what was on her mind and what her heart was experiencing. Sometimes while driving, she was so engrossed in her thoughts that she forgot to keep an eye on the speedometer. She had the reputation of having a lead foot, but she sure didn't want to be stopped by a Smokey on her way to Elmira.

After driving many miles in quiet solitude, Klee decided to place a tape in the stereo deck. Easy music and classical music were food for the soul as far as she was concerned. Klee's senses were electrified when the music for "Ebb Tide" began playing. The melody penetrated her core. Also, it was "our song" as Dean put it one evening when they were at his apartment.

The song had such emotion and tenderness that Klee felt a tremendous sadness washed over her. Before she realized that a nerve had been touched, she was sobbing. Grabbing some facial tissue from the console, she counseled herself with the thought that there aren't mistakes, only lessons. She had another lesson to face in the near future. She had to make herself ready.

Upon arrival at the convent, Klee was ushered into the visiting room while Sister Ann Mary was being summoned. Every visiting parlor at the convents Klee had waited in since she was a kid was always done in exquisite taste. The fragrance of highly polished furniture, beautiful oil paintings on the wall, and religious icons on the tables along with religious printed material made her feel right at home. While growing up with the nuns, she had been exposed to many of the finer things of life. In addition, order, self-discipline, appreciation and kindness had been strongly instilled within her. To add to the mix, Klee had always been a generous child. She was willing to give of herself, to go beyond what was ordinarily expected, and to give financially. The latter was a constant endeavor.

Sister Ann Mary wasn't physically tall in stature, maybe about five feet seven inches. It was difficult to actually ascertain her height because of her habit headdress and veil. The creamy skin of her face revealed a touch of blush on her cheeks. Her eyes were an unusual soft gray, which constantly changed with light exposure and mood. While she was attractive physically, her inner qualities were the treasures. Her kindness, her strength of character, her patience, and her deep understanding were a cluster of lasting gems.

Sister Ann Mary entered the room with her beautiful, welcoming smile and arms outstretched. Both women embraced tenderly. Both had looked forward to the visit for many weeks. Sister Ann Mary had to deal with her disappointment when she had been reassigned two years previously to Elmira, but that's where the vow of obedience kicked in. Like it or not, a nun had to obey whatever was asked of her. Prior to the move to St. Bonifice Convent in Elmira, the Rochester area had been her placement throughout her teaching career. This made her visit with Klee even more enjoyable because Klee offered news from back home.

"Dear Klee, how wonderful to see you in person at last. You look well."

"Thanks, Sister, it is great to be with you too."

The women went through the greeting formalities and situated themselves in the mahogany-framed, ornately brocaded chairs.

"So you had a good drive down, Klee. I hope you weren't visited by motion sickness."

"Just a little bit, but not too bad. I had my homemade brew with me," Klee responded with a chuckle. "The ginger does the trick for a spell anyway. I can't wait until you return to the Rochester area. This drive is not my cup of tea. Do you think there is any hope that a reassignment will occur this summer?"

"I'm praying and hoping it will. I have had contact with Reverend Mother at the Mother House in Rochester. She knows my position, my dire need to return because of my mother. Since my dad died, it seems that Mom is more adrift these days. Of course, Reverend Mother will make the final decision," Sister sighed.

"I hope she fully understands that you need to be back in the Rochester area because of your mother's needs," Klee emphasized in an adamant tone.

"Klee, I assure you, she most certainly does. Now, let's talk about you and what is happening in your life."

Klee didn't know where to begin. Maybe it would be best to start with an Allie update, then move into the topic concerning Dean. Both had occupied much of Klee's life of late. Her nurturing and love had been extended to both—the man and the dog. Klee knew that Sister Ann Mary would let her start where she wanted to begin and end when she was ready. Klee shifted in her chair. She began to speak.

"Well, Sister, all is well with Allie. She is healthy, happy, and energized. The students had quite a learning experience via Allie. It was a teacher's dream to incorporate the event into classroom studies and skills. In addition, the collateral learning was fantastic."

"I'm sure it was, and you had the vision to make it into something special. Your trait of operating at a 100 percent level without hesitation and with that strong determination of yours certainly was the formula for success."

Klee went on to tell Sister about the radio recognition of the rescue, the song for Allie with the lyrics written by the students, and Allie's party for the class. It was pleasurable to share the entire saga with her.

"Sister, I am so happy that all worked out with the Allie adventure, but there is something that occurred in my personal life during the months in which I dealt with Allie, the Winslows, and my students. Let me put it this way. I believe it was meant to happen. Allie, this gentle dog, became the conduit to bring a special person into my life."

"That would be Dean, I would guess," Sister replied while gazing deeply into Klee's eyes.

"Yes, it was quite unexpected how it all unfolded, but we have been seeing each other as much as possible, and exclusively."

Klee told Sister all about Dean. She emphasized his background and strong family ties. She explained the temporary roadblock for them because of his goal to attain the doctorate degree. She chatted on about Dean, but she hadn't worked herself up enough to get at the crux of the matter.

"Klee, you are in love with Dean. Is that an accurate statement?"

"Yes, it is, Sister," Klee blurted without hesitation.

"There is something else you wish to say to me?"

Klee couldn't get over why it was so hard for her to come to the point. She had always been a candid individual. Most people shy away from candor, but candor was the byproduct of her integrity. She looked down at her hand; she nervously began flicking her thumbnail against her index finger. A flash came across her mind at that instant when she remembered that it was Sister who helped her stop biting her fingernails to the quick when she was her student. With courage, Klee looked Sister straight in the eye and blurted the tortured feelings of her soul.

"I haven't told him about the operations. I haven't told him that I can't have children. I haven't told him that I'm not a whole woman," Klee stated in anguish.

Even though Klee had cautioned herself not to break down, the tears streamed down her face. Sister quickly moved from her chair, came to Klee's side, and put her arms around her.

"Oh, dear heart, you mustn't think that way. If Dean is all you believe him to be, the barren state will not be an issue. You have so much to offer, so much love to give. Adoption is always an option, isn't it, Klee?"

Klee banged her hand on the armrest of the chair and bolted from it. She slammed her hands together in full fury. Her anger and disappointment finally surfaced with Sister Ann Mary. Klee kept a great deal inside, but when the inner volcano erupted, it could be frightening to anyone who didn't know her. She realized well enough that Sister understood her and would let her vent, to allow her to expose her soul, to literally allow the volcano to erupt, to have its release.

"That's what has me so frightened, Sister. Dean comes from a large, closely knit family. He wants a large family. Also, I have the distinct impression that Mama rules the roost. Intuitively, I sense that a barren daughter-in-law would be totally unacceptable to her and probably to most of the family members. I do believe that if it is revealed that I cannot have children, the complexion of our relationship will change drastically. Sister, you know about my past and how difficult it was for me when Mike and I broke up over this same issue. Sure we could have married, but adoption was absolutely out of the question as far as Mike was concerned. We couldn't resolve our differences of opinions on the subject. A childless marriage I truly believed would have eventually resulted in an empty, unfulfilled life for both of us. Bottom line is that I can't face the rejection again. The rejection hurts so deeply. I've lost courage to be forthright with Dean because I don't want to lose again! I don't want to be rejected again! Each year that passes, I wonder when it will be my turn. Where's God? Why so much? Why years of illness and horrible, horrible pain and suffering before I was finally diagnosed? My college days were ruined because of it, and I was not able to go on with my doctorate because of all the surgeries. Every goal, every dream has been thwarted. There has to be more positives in life, personal accomplishment without the constant trauma, without the coping with the physical."

There was a long period of silence. Sister handed Klee her white linen handkerchief. The lavender scent was familiar and comforting to Klee. The scent caused her to flashback to when she was in Sister's eighth-grade class.

It was recess time, and Klee was running to second base during their quick baseball innings before resuming afternoon classes. During recess, the students used the large parking lot that abutted the church. It wasn't the safest place to play, but play their hearts out they did. She recalled her slide and fall on the cinders that coated the parking area. Her knees were imbedded with miniscule stones, and the blood oozed while cascading down her legs. That was her first encounter with the large scented handkerchief and the loving concern of her teacher.

Returning to the present, Klee was sorry that her emotions got out of control. She hadn't intended it to happen that way, but apparently, it happened for a good reason.

Eventually, Sister gathered Klee in her arms and directed her to a chair. Sister slowly moved to her chair, drew it closer to Klee's, and sat down. She folded her hands in her lap and a gentle smile appeared on her face.

"Klee, I want you to know without a doubt that I am glad you exposed your inner feelings and frustrations. It is important that you do so. It assists in clearing the muddy waters so that clear thinking can emerge. It is a process. The psyche needs to be dealt with, and with honesty. Facing things head-on has always been your strong suit. You are realistic. You've never given into being a Pollyanna or a superficial person or a mediocre one. Your inner self and your integrity have always shone through each uncomfortable situation and each cross to bear. You've had a great deal occurring in your life besides the rigors of teaching. I believe with all my heart that you will reevaluate, settle in, and do what you must," Sister counseled.

Klee listened carefully to Sister's every word. She could feel the tension begin to release.

"I will do what is right, Sister. It isn't fair not to let the other party know that there is a glitch that needs to be exposed. I never have avoided or made excuses in the past. This matter of the heart has thrown me off course. I think the past negative experiences have blown me in the wrong direction. I'll get back to smoother sailing. I'll get back on course, I'm sure I will, Sister."

"I have no doubt that you will, Klee. As you mentioned, Dean wants to take you to his family over Mother's Day weekend. Surely, it will be best to sit down with him and talk out the matters of concern long before the intended visit. Realistically, if there is a concern after your dialogue with Dean, then it would follow that going on with the visit would be risky and uncomfortable. There will be time for other visits. Right now you both need to talk and have time to think, then talk some more," Sister reassured.

"You're so right. Thank you, Sister, for being here for me, for your loving patience and pragmatic advise. I am so fortunate to have you. I was one lucky kid to land in your classroom so many years ago, even though I caused you to spend many hours on your knees in chapel praying for me," Klee laughed.

"I'm fortunate too, Klee. I am so proud of all your accomplishments and what you have become, even though you tell me that many people who have shared your space don't know 'where you are coming from,' to use your words. To that, I say go forward in your uniqueness and be glad of it.

Klee, let's make a visit to the chapel. The sisters in our choir are practicing for Sister Agnes Marie's golden jubilee, but it will be all right if we slip into a rear pew."

As Sister and Klee lowered the kneeler, the sisters' voices resonated throughout the small chapel with the hymn, "Ave Maria." An irresistible wave of determination clutched Klee's spirit. She covered her face with her hands and whispered, "I admit that I often fail to live up to my own philosophy, but I'll keep trying. And yes, I must repeatedly tell myself that love is the perfect antidote for anxiety and fear."

Upon leaving the chapel, Klee invited Sister and her companion, Sister Mary Elaine, out for a ride and a hot fudge sundae. It was always a special occasion for the nuns when Klee took them out for ice cream treats. She enjoyed doing it and always marveled at their genuine appreciation. The vow of poverty certainly made one enjoy and appreciate the simple things in life!

Sister Ann Mary loved to savor a Mexican sundae. Klee always ordered it for her and asked for vanilla ice cream, dripping with ample chocolate syrup and extra Spanish peanuts. As for Klee, her standby was always a hot fudge sundae with extra fudge, of course. How it would set on her tummy on the way back home was another question!

CHAPTER 53

Klee was fortunate that most of the United States' chronometers had jumped forward to daylight saving time. The extra daylight hours would make her trip back home a great deal easier, especially if she had to make stops to rearrange her tummy sensations. Surely, she would arrive before the twilight hours occurred.

She knew that Muffy Cat was well cared for since she was staying with cousin Salena for the day and possibly the night.

Muffy Cat liked going to Salena's apartment. Why wouldn't she? Sal provided her with her favorite foods, such as fresh shrimp, a spook house that had three floors, and plenty of catnip toys. Not only was Muffy Cat lucky to have such a cousin, but so was Klee. She could always rely on Sal. Besides the reliability trait, she was the type of person who always landed on her feet in a jam. Often, when Klee found herself in a predicament, she knew who to go to for help.

While driving along, Klee decided that she'd leave the cat with cuz for the night and pick her up in the morning. Emotionally, she felt that a great deal had been sucked out of her. A good night's rest was the main agenda.

The next morning, Klee had breakfast and her coffee. She spied the clock and decided that nine o'clock was an appropriate time to make the phone call.

"Good morning, cuz, I hope all went well with you and the cat."

"Hi, Klee, it sure did. She is such a little character and smart to boot. I find her to be a fun companion. Did you have a good visit with Sister?"

"Yes, it was most beneficial and comforting. I'll tell you all about it when I pick up the cat. She sends her love to you and looks forward to seeing you this summer, if you're not off traveling, that is."

"How about it if I bring the cat to the house? I'll come by toward the latter part of the morning if that will be okay with you."

"Sal, thanks. I'd like that. Plan on having lunch with me, and I'll bring you up to date."

Meanwhile, Klee busied herself with household chores. One task was preparing a fresh litter box for the cat after she had been away from home. Muffy Cat seemed to like this routine because she would immediately go to check out her box. It seemed that she had to check out her property. After much scratching, she'd always leave Klee a present. The ritual never failed. Klee was well-trained indeed. Somehow, cats knew exactly how to keep their owners in tow.

A plaque that was prominently displayed in the kitchen said it all: "This house really belongs to the cat; only the deed belongs to the owner." The Hatchers had given Klee the plaque as a gift one Christmas. During one of their summer visits to Vermont, they had a local artisan design and hand paint a cat along with the phrase on a natural piece of scrap wood. It was special to Klee. It always made her smile when she peered at it. It was part of her kitchen. Friends or visitors who meandered into the kitchen while Klee was making coffee or fetching some form of refreshment commented on the saying.

Sal arrived with the cat at 11:30 a.m. Both mistress and cat were joyfully reunited. The cat tore full speed through the house, hitting all levels of the four-level ranch. She was exuberant. The cousins laughed and waited as they watched and listened to this ten-pound tornado fly from level to level. Then there was quiet. She was in the basement seeking out her commode.

"I guess she's not too happy to be home."

Sal began to laugh. "That wry sense of humor of yours is too much."

Sal wore jean shorts and a lightweight red turtle neck. It was a smart outfit.

"Gee, cuz, you are in shorts. It isn't that warm yet," Klee remarked.

"You know me, I'm always hot, and it is the middle of April, so it's like summer to me. I am not fond of hot as you well know."

"Okay, but I'd be freezing in that outfit. I think of Lisa and Rob in Canada too, and the cold weather north of here at this time of year. They must be experiencing cold noses and tingling feet. Well, let's get some lunch. I have some egg-and-olive salad prepared."

"You know I love your egg-and-olive. I'm glad I decided to deliver the cat!"

During lunch, the women caught up on Klee's visit with Sister Ann Mary. Klee explained the emotional catharsis that had surfaced and the resolutions promised. Once Klee finished, she realized that Salena was staring at her with a curious look in her eyes.

"What, Sal, what is it? Your eyes are saying something although nothing is coming from your mouth."

"I just assumed that you had told Dean. I can't believe you have let the relationship spiral to the point that he is planning on taking you home to meet his family on Mother's Day, yet he doesn't know about the children factor. I'm not judging you, Klee, but I've never known you to dodge a situation that had to be dealt with. You have always said meet the circumstance head-on, because if you don't, it just gets worse and it will get you in the end."

"Yes, all that you say is true. I have lost my way. I have allowed my judgment to be clouded because my heart is on cloud nine. I felt helpless every time we were together. I didn't want to say or do anything that would upset the balance of our relationship. I assure you that the matter in question will be rectified when Dean returns. Sometimes I'd like to give myself a swift kick for my lack of disclosure."

"He'll probably be all right with it, Klee. If he isn't, then as much as it will hurt, at least you'll know where you both stand before any further escalation. You survived Mike's reaction, and if necessary, you'll do it again. You are a strong woman, even though you bruise easily within. Outwardly, you always meet the challenge. The part I worry about is that you grieve for so long when things go south. You seem to let go intellectually, but your heart weeps for a long time," Sal said.

"Yes, I'm a survivor, but I don't think I'll be placing myself in this position once again if the relationship dissolves. Age thirty-four is around the corner for me. Dean is five years younger. The few years in age difference have never been a topic of discussion, but the children topic I sense will be paramount."

"Klee, your intuitive sense is 99 percent on target. This time I hope it is not. Does Lisa know you haven't told Dean?"

"No, she does not. I plan on calling her and being completely open when she and Rob return from their mini-vacation in Canada," Klee said.

"Before we close this topic, Klee, let me say once again that I want to express my concerns about Dean. I may be entirely wrong in my assessment. The staunch family and religion mind-set Dean possesses are red flags to me, and I think they should be to you. His absolute loyalty will side with what he knows, what has been ingrained in him since childhood. There isn't room for much flexibility. Damn it, Klee! You are such an idealist—such a romantic!" Salena cautioned.

Klee felt the sting of her words and pondered her repeated warning.

After cleaning up the luncheon dishes, the two cousins went for a walk. Klee wanted to go down to the end of the road toward Bushnell's Basin. It would be good exercise. Bushnell's Basin was a hamlet along the Erie Canal. The Canal House and the Bushnell's Basin Inn thrived during the transportation days of the famous Erie Canal. They had been long abandoned. Only the memories of the past haunted these derelict buildings. Presently, across the road, there was a pharmacy and a little grocery market in what was called the Hitching Post Plaza. Adjacent to the Hitching Post was the home of the Bushnell's Basin Volunteer Fire Department, which gave Klee peace of mind. It made her feel safe knowing that help was minutes away in case of fire. The insurance company liked it too!

A prescription had been called in a few days prior, so it needed to be collected. The pickup was a good excuse for a leisurely walk to the Hitching Post. It was a lovely afternoon for a stroll. The freshness of the air was a signal for the arrival of spring. The early budding of the trees announced new life, hope, and a new season. Neither Klee nor Sal spoke very much as they sauntered down the road. It wasn't difficult to guess what occupied most of their thoughts.

CHAPTER 54

After Sal left, Klee entered her study. The house was quiet; there were no distractions. Methodically she withdrew a blank sheet of paper from her top desk drawer. She sat there for a moment and gazed at the paper. It was time to outline all she needed to say to Dean when they were together over the weekend. What was said and how it was said was important enough to spend some quality time to chart the information. She also decided to anticipate questions that might be asked of her and to be prepared for any emotional reactions that would surface for either of them. It was face-up time . . . and big time!

Evening rushed in. It was time to call Lisa and Sonya to tell them about the part she had omitted in the relationship with Dean. She knew that they would be surprised at her behavior, but they were good friends. Actually, as they conversed, each offered her special brand of advice and support. Klee listened to their comments and warnings. However, she knew that it was up to her to carry through and exercise the method and management skills she was so good at in counseling situations. She had to rely on skills rather than emotions, or she knew she'd never get through the unwanted task she needed to tackle with Dean.

"You know, Klee, there isn't any factual knowledge at this point that Dean will have an adverse reaction once you reveal the information you have been withholding. You're both in love, and that is powerful in itself. Remember, all obstacles can be conquered by love," emphasized Lisa. "Really, I don't want you to give into any speculative notions before you two have a heart-to-heart talk."

"Maybe Lisa, it will work that way for us. I desperately hope it will with every ounce within me. If it doesn't, then I'm going to forget the marriage trip. It is possible that a relationship will have to do without any of the troublesome luggage to haul around. My thirty-fourth birthday is in a few months. Dean recently became a twenty-nine-year-old. Although the age difference isn't much, I do believe that the five-year difference in life's experiences and points of view might make a considerable distinction concerning this particular subject. I also have to keep in mind his family ties and their expectations for him."

Sonya had a different reaction once Klee finished telling her what she was facing.

"Why, Klee, I am surprised in a way that you didn't get to the point with Dean right away," Sonya admitted. "It doesn't seem like you. Now it might be harder to bring him into full focus of the situation. I want you to think that all will be okay though. If his family traditions are more powerful than his love for you, then I say let him go. Be strong on that point, even though it will hurt like hell," Sonya stated with resolve.

Klee no sooner hung up the phone from her conversation with Sonya than the phone rang, breaking into her all-consuming thoughts.

"How's my darling, Klee?" Dean asked.

"Dean, I didn't expect you to be calling the evening before your return home, but I am glad you have."

"Are you kidding? I can't wait to return and get back to you. My visit has been great with all the family members, but, honey, I'm one lonely puppy!"

Klee began to melt. She felt her body respond with heat as his words of love and desire sang through the phone lines. She had been very lonely too.

"It won't be long, Dean. I've missed you so much," Klee sighed.

After their conversation, Klee pondered her situation. She revisited questions that had gnawed at her for years. Would she see the sterile, orthodox world in which she lived with all the restraints on women and their roles ever to be altered and modified? Would the stigmas women had to live with ever be erased so that a woman could function as freely as the opposite sex? Would a woman be free to be her own person without the judgment of all the narrow-minded people? Would it be a big deal if a woman could or could not bear children? It was the mid-seventies. Maybe in twenty-five years or so, there would be noticeable changes in society and the position of women within that society.

In twenty-five years, Klee would be fifty-nine years old. There was a distinct possibility that she would be a witness and actually participate in the movement within the culture toward more equality for women. That would mean authentic changes.

CHAPTER 55

It was Friday already. Only a couple more days of spring recess remained. Klee and Dean would see each other that evening. Klee had decided to prepare a special dinner for him at her home. She wanted it to be a private setting so that meant a restaurant would not do no matter how elegant it might be. They needed to be alone. They needed to be free to embrace or kiss passionately. They needed to be secluded. Klee needed a familiar setting to reveal her secret.

It had been fun shopping. Klee decided to plan a menu just the opposite of the Cappelli's traditional feasts. She realized that Dean had been savoring a variety of Italian dishes while he was at his parent's domicile. For Klee's welcome home banquet, she wanted to start out with a shrimp cocktail. These would be extraordinarily large shrimp that were found at only one establishment in Rochester. Without a doubt, the largest shrimp in town were sold there. She wanted to surprise Dean with her special cocktail sauce recipe too. They both savored scotch on the rocks with the appetizer. It was a good beginning to their first meal together since he had left.

She had ordered porterhouse steaks from Star Market. Tony, the butcher, never disappointed Klee. He would say, "Special cut just for you teacher."

While having cocktails on the patio, Dean would prepare the charcoal fire in the large portable grill. He was an expert griller. The charcoal had to display the right glow, Dean cautioned, before he placed the meat on the grill rack. A fresh toss salad and an artichoke casserole would round off the menu. Coffee and an after-dinner cordial would culminate the delights of their palates.

Klee happily went about her preparations in her large homemaker kitchen, and while doing so, she drifted in thought that she would be in Dean's arms in a matter of hours. It was difficult to concentrate when her feelings were raw.

As she sliced the mushrooms, Klee realized that she had been neglectful.

"Muffy Cat, you have been hanging around the kitchen the entire time I've been preparing. I think you know that I did sneak the package of shrimp into the refrigerator as soon as I retuned from shopping. I'm sure you were in the family room sprawled with your long tail hanging over the edge of the organ. You know the organ is off limits, but I bet that's where you were. So I can't figure out how you know that there is a treat hidden somewhere in this kitchen. I also realize that I should never underestimate you!"

The cat walked over to Klee almost on cue when she finished speaking and began to weave in between her legs.

"Don't worry, my Petite Chat, you have two shrimps with your name on them. You won't be served both shrimp at the same meal if I can help it, but then again, you might because that look you give me usually lowers my defenses."

Before Dean's arrival at five thirty, Klee went about showering, washing her hair, and selecting what she wanted to wear. She decided on her lavender slacks with the pronounced flared, hemmed bottoms and a purple short-sleeve turtleneck. The shades complemented her facial complexion and hair hue.

To top off her outfit, she placed her diamond-cut gold chain with its gold sand-dollar medallion around her neck. The sand dollar was a beautiful piece with its delicate carvings. She reversed it and read the inscription, which she did often: Love, Mom and Dad . . . 1962. Her parents gave this gift to Klee when she had visited them in Florida with the hope that she would return to southwest Florida on a permanent basis one day. Klee had thought about it, but she realized that employment opportunities were slim to say nothing about the low pay scale offered. Her social life was important too, and that would mean going to a larger city like Tampa where the sidewalks weren't rolled up at eight o'clock. A large populated city had its advantages, but Klee really wasn't that keen on big.

Slipping on her low-heel pumps, she strode to the full-length mirror in the bedroom. Yes, she confirmed that simplicity with taste denoted class.

Dean arrived just as the foyer grandfather clock was chiming the on-the-half hour. The Westminster chime pealed five-thirty as if on cue. Klee hadn't been able to figure out how Dean could be punctual. Then one evening, he told her; he always sets his watch to her grandfather clock. This delighted Klee because she would be apt to do the same thing if she were in his position. In so many ways, they were like two peas in a pod. Other times, their approaches to matters at hand could be diametrically opposed. Each would stick to his/her opinion. Klee had some different points of view about religion. Dean was a hardliner, traditional practitioner of organized religion. Klee was less traditional and more spiritual than religious. Luckily, conflict wasn't often. At least it hadn't been so far.

Klee had been unrealistic in her thinking that initially they would catch up and have cocktails after he arrived. That never happened. Once the front door closed, Dean took Klee in his arms and hungrily began to kiss her. The kisses became more passionate, and their bodies were wild for each other. They were totally lost in heat and desire. Klee had promised herself that she wouldn't let this happen because she had to be truthful with Dean, and this was going to be the evening to do so. All her good intentions were shocked out of her mind. Nothing mattered at this point, other than making love. Klee took Dean's hand with deliberation and ascended the stairs to her bedroom. The consummation of their love was powerful, all-consuming and untamed. They were both spent; as Dean held Klee in his arms, they drifted off to sleep.

It was ten minutes to eight before Klee began to stir. The cat was pawing her cheek. When she looked at the clock on the nightstand, she couldn't believe that they had slept for so long. The cat was hungry, and so was she after the physical fulfillment she and Dean had experienced.

Eventually, everyone got to eat by nine o'clock. Dean had been out on the patio with the assistance of floodlights to do the grilling. To appease Muffy Cat for the mealtime delay, Klee did give her both shrimps. She ate her dinner with such relish, and the two famished lovers also savored every bite.

Coffee and after-dinner drinks followed. Both launched into catching up on what each had been doing while they had been separated. Once talked out, they reluctantly moved toward cleaning up. Dean headed out to the patio to clean up the grill and grill utensils. Klee cleared the table and went full speed ahead to load the dishwasher and hand washed some of the special china pieces. Once this was accomplished, she tidied up the rest of the kitchen. The clock chimed eleven o'clock. Dean would be leaving soon. Klee could feel the loneliness overtake her, and he hadn't even left yet.

"Klee, it's been terrific being with you. I thought I'd go insane while we were separated. You've made me so happy. I hope I have fulfilled your needs too."

Klee gazed into his deep blue eyes. She had such love for him. She betrayed him again, however. She still hadn't told him what he needed to know about her.

"Another magical time together and more memories made, Dean," Klee whispered in his ear.

"Yes, more memories for us, and before much longer, we'll have a life together to make oodles of memories to treasure and lots of babies."

Babies! That word shattered the moment; it went off like a firecracker, an inner explosion in Klee's heart.

Klee put her arms around Dean's neck and softly placed her goodnight kiss on his lips. She gave a slight shudder and unlocked her embrace and walked away. Changing gears, she started to talk about weekend plans.

"Dean, I'm heading out to camp and the lake in the morning. I'll be there for the weekend. Will you be able to drive out?" Klee asked.

"Tomorrow won't be good, Klee. Being away has put me behind. I have some matters to get in order before we return to school on Monday. How about it if I come out on Sunday around eleven?"

"Eleven it will be. I'll pack a lunch, and we'll take the boat out for a spin. It needs a run. Dress warmly because it will be chilly on the water at this time of year."

"Terrific! I'll grab my cooler and load it with ice and liquid refreshments."

The post lamplight on the front lawn shone brightly. Klee could clearly see Dean's face as he waved and backed out of the driveway. Her face was hidden in the darkness and shadows of the night. Her tears could not be detected.

CHAPTER 56

K lee was an early riser. Beginning with energetic movement by 5:30 or 6:00 a.m. was natural for her. It went along with her A-type personality. She was busy around the house with early morning duties for herself and the cat.

Muffy Cat knew she was headed for a ride when the carrier came out. She didn't mind the ride like most cats did. The ride out to the camp was only thirty minutes from driveway to driveway.

Muffy Cat loved camp life. The scurrying chipmunks entertained her and at the same time drove her nuts as she observed them from the screened dining enclosure that was situated in a clearing among the trees. Although the gray squirrels fascinated her, the chipmunks really excited her. As a chipmunk approached the screened tent, the cat's body would become tense, not a muscle twitched. The dilation of her pupils gave warning that Muffy Cat was ready to spring on the little creature. It never happened, but the ritual persisted every time she was taken out to the enclosure.

While gathering some of the food from the refrigerator to transport to camp, the pealing of the phone brought Klee from her mental list of what she needed to pack.

"Hello, this is Klee."

"It's Bethany, Klee. I was hoping to reach you before you returned to school. Not many more weeks ahead for teaching, and you'll be off for the summer. Have you enjoyed the recess break?"

"Hi to you, Bethany, and I sure have. I'm getting ready to leave for my camp for the weekend. Let's say it's going to be the culmination of the wonderful reprieve I have enjoyed this past week. I feel energized and ready to the face the last weeks of the school year."

"It sounds good to me. I realize that you are one busy lady, so I want to extend an invitation to you well in advance. Shep, the kids, and I would like you to come to dinner. It will be wonderful for us all to be together. You and Allie will have the opportunity for more bonding time."

"I'd be delighted, Bethany. You know that."

"Then let's plan on a date the third week in May. Look at your calendar and offer me a couple dates. You can call me back. The third week would be after Mother's Day."

The mention of Mother's Day gave Klee a wrenching feeling as the thought flashed through her mind about going to Dean's home for Mother's Day weekend.

"Thanks, Bethany, I'll check my calendar and definitely get back to you."

*　　*　　*

Sunday was a beautiful morning. It seemed to be made to order. The clear azure sky and the puffy white cumulus clouds ushered in a new day. Klee brought her mug of coffee to one of the camp chairs, which were nestled around the fireplace pit. It was chilly enough to start a fire and throw on some hearty sized logs, but she didn't feel like wasting the log consumption for such a short duration. She and Dean would be off to the marina in a couple of hours, so really, there was no need to play Girl Scout and build a fire.

The songbirds with their various calls filled her spirit. Sipping her coffee and feeling relaxed in her wooded paradise, Klee began to enumerate once again the points she wished to cover when she talked to Dean while they were on the boat. She called out to her guardian angel for guidance and strength of character to say what needed to be said. The outcome was up to the two lovers and no one else. If it didn't work, then face that fact she would with a heavy, broken heart.

Klee loved the twenty-four foot yellow fiberglass craft with its white trim and white sun canopy. She and cousin Sal were joint owners, and both gals had enjoyed many hours aboard the *Charade*. The cabin space had never been used for anything but changing out of wet suits. The vessel was fully equipped with safety gear and an aluminum ladder for swimming from the boat in deep water.

"Dean, do you want to pilot the *Charade* from the marina to the south end of the lake?" asked Klee. "We'll travel about sixteen miles before we come to the end of the lake. The beautiful view of the Naples area will be our site for anchoring."

"Yeah, that's good. How about if you drive back? I'm sure I'll enjoy a couple of beers while we're out there, then I won't have to think about bringing the *Charade* back to port."

Once out of the channel and into the open waters of the lake, Dean opened the throttle full speed. The wind caressing their skin felt fresh and cold—actually, frigid! The freedom of the open waters felt even better. Klee sat next to Dean on one of the bucket seats. There were two bucket seats. One was for the captain and the other for the co-captain or passenger. Dean frequently leaned over, placed his hand on her knee, and gave it a squeeze. His penetrating eyes said the rest. Dean varied the speed so they could hear each other speak. He told her about the two classes he would be taking during the summer at the University of Rochester. His excitement was mounting as the goal for the doctorate wasn't that far off. He also said with gusto that once the schooling bit was over, they would marry and have lots of kids.

There it was again: kids. He, with explicit candor and no hesitation, made his dreams known about the two of them. The word *children* surfaced once again. It seemed providential that the word was spoken the day Klee had decided to be candid. Her guardian angel opened the door with that one phrase—lots of kids.

As they ate the ham-and-cheese sandwiches that Klee had prepared, the sun warmed them, and the boat experienced a slight rocking in the rippled waters at the south end of the lake. The Naples hillside with its pattern of farmland and the glorious infant foliage made a perfect setting.

"Dean, I have something I need to talk with you about. I should have brought it up some time ago, but our relationship went into high gear before I realized what was happening to me. I lost good judgment as a result."

"Wow, you sound so serious. What's happened? So let's talk, but remember I love you. I do love you," Dean declared.

"Thank you, my dearest. I am glad you do, and you'll have the opportunity to make those words genuine and golden. I have thought through what I need to say to you, and I have even made my points in a list form. However, I think it's best to get right to the issue at hand. It won't be fair to either one of us if I withhold any longer," Klee stated with conviction.

Dean had such a questioning and surprised look on his face. Then he took Klee's hand, and she began to speak from her heart. She explained in specific terms the extent of her three surgeries and the consequences. She was strong and determined to disperse the entire scenario but kindly in her presentation. When she finished, she withdrew her hand from Dean's hand and brought her index finger up to her lips as to signal that she was finished with what she had to say. Her eyes glistened with moisture.

"Klee, I am so sorry. I had no idea. This disclosure has hit me like a bombshell as you can well imagine," Dean blurted out.

Klee knew it would unsteady him, but after the initial shock, she also knew that his first words would be the key to the direction in which their relationship would veer.

"I understand, Dean. Forgive me for not telling you before this, but in the beginning it didn't seem that we would become so involved so fast, but we did. There never seemed to be a right time. Things moved along quickly. I am deeply in love with you, and I was afraid to tell you because I didn't want to take the chance of losing you," Klee sighed.

"That's true. I kept telling myself that I had school to finish and that a serious relationship couldn't take place. No matter how hard I tried to deny what I was feeling and how serious I was about you, I knew I couldn't let you go and at the same time, I knew I had to fulfill my promise to my parents. That's why I mentioned my commitment to my parents to you. Remember? Because of their financial support during my internship, I gave my word not to marry until my doctorate was completed. I wondered if I could hold out," Dean said as he ran his fingers through his hair.

"Yes, I do remember, and that's one of the reasons why I didn't come forth with the information."

"I . . . I don't know what to say to you, Klee. I need time to digest this revelation and what it means to both of us. We'll need to talk about it a great deal more at another time. You know I come from a large family, and I am family-oriented. I always hoped for a number of children, and my family expects me to carry on the Cappelli tradition," Dean stated unwaveringly.

There it was. The last sentence was poignant: carry on the Cappelli tradition. Clearly he hadn't said that they could work things out or that they could adopt. On the other hand, he didn't absolutely say "no way" to Klee, nor emphatically say they couldn't go on. What he left unmentioned in his response to her, however, seared Klee's heart.

CHAPTER 57

It was a restless and disturbing night at Kilber Road. If the walls of Klee's house could have talked, they would have related all the heartbreak of its occupant. Klee tossed and turned with all kinds of thoughts that raced through her mind since she told Dean the facts. Her head pounded. She experienced a continuous rerun of what was said, of what wasn't said, the body language, and the facial expressions. He never said that their love would surmount any obstacles. There weren't any emphatic words of encouragement. Yet maybe it was too much of a surprise for him to absorb at one time. There were so many ifs and shoulds, but in the final analysis, what was to be would be. Klee understood this with her whole heart. Her ego didn't want to accept it, but regardless, she had no control . . . que sera, sera.

In the early hours of the morning, around 2:30 a.m., Klee pulled herself from her bed and headed for the bathroom. Muffy Cat jumped from the bed and patted right after her. Klee needed something for her headache and sinuses. The crying had taken its toll on her body. Taking a couple sinus tablets would do the trick. Within thirty minutes, she was fast asleep.

The alarm shrilled at six o'clock. Klee reached over to Muffin and snuggled her in her arms.

"It's time to get up, Petite Chat, my faithful furry friend, and ready ourselves for the day. I finally got some sleep and so did you. It's going to be a good day. At least I'll make it appear that way."

The warm water pulsating from the large showerhead massaged and relaxed Klee. While showering, she made herself think good thoughts. The students would be her salvation. They had interesting tasks ahead. She would concentrate on them as much as possible.

She always hid her true feelings behind jokes and humorous antics. This was her shield; it protected her from others seeing what was going on in her life. It has been written and reported so often that comedians are often among the loneliest and saddest people. They hide behind all the laughter while their hearts are breaking. On the other hand, some comics use laughter to pump up their spirits and those around them. Klee often fell into both categories. It depended on the situation at hand.

*   *   *

Faculty members filled the parking lot early on Monday morning. Most looked rested and enthused. Some members were already having coffee in the faculty lounge, and a few seemed sleepy and not quite ready to face the day. Observing the various reactions of the teachers was interesting to Klee. She projected a smile that brightened her face, and she was ready for inquires about Dean. She had made up her mind that she would not reveal that there was trouble brewing between them. It was none of their business. Klee liked to keep her personal life private as much as possible.

The first few days of the week with her students were busy, and she made the lessons stimulating. She hadn't heard from Dean since their conversation on Sunday. She made herself believe that he needed time. Surely she would hear from him in the evening. After all, it was Wednesday already.

After dinner, the phone rang, intruding on her thoughts. Klee was sure it was Dean. She was so happy with this thought that she couldn't get to the phone fast enough.

"Hello, this is Klee."

"Hi there, girlfriend! I haven't seen you at school nor have I heard from you. You aren't avoiding me, are you?"

"Oh no, Lisa! I've been busy and preoccupied."

"Would the preoccupation have anything to do with Deano?"

Klee didn't want to get into what had transpired between Dean and her, but she decided to get it over with. Besides, Lisa had been there for her, and it was only fair to tell her the truth. She relayed the entire scene as it occurred on the boat the Sunday past.

"You mean you haven't heard from him since Sunday?" Lisa shouted over the phone. "Why that heel! What the hell is he thinking?"

"I wish I knew, Lisa. I know he is disappointed and extremely upset. He needs time to process this new information."

"Process, yes, but being caring can still take place while processing! He's one of the most caring guys I know, so the revelation must have thrown him big time, or he's just a jerk who has kept himself well disguised."

Klee knew Lisa didn't actually mean that last comment about Dean. She was upset and, when upset, all kinds of strange remarks spew from the mouth. She was her friend, and she was reacting as a friend would at that moment. Lisa would not allow Klee to put this mess all on herself. Lisa always told it like it was. Klee realized as the two women continued in conversation that Lisa was correct and that she had to reach the point where she would refuse to put the blame entirely on herself. After all, she couldn't help what fate had dealt her.

*　　*　　*

On Friday, Klee ran into Dean in the hall just before he was entering a classroom. He waved to her and called out.

"Hi, Klee, I'd like to call you this evening. Will you be around?"

Klee felt a slow burn at the question and at him in general. She wanted to go right up to him and tell him off. Of course, she would be around. She had devoted herself exclusively to him for months. Where the hell else would she be if she weren't with him?

"Yes, I'll be at home," she replied, giving him a perfunctory wave as she turned and headed toward the library to see Mrs. Martin.

Mrs. Martin had set aside some books for her. Klee had asked Mrs. Martin's assistance when she had returned from spring recess. The subject she wanted to pursue dealt with kickball and sportsmanship in general. It wouldn't be long before the students would be kicking and chasing the ball at recess time. Mrs. Martin was the perfect librarian. She was calm in demeanor and helpful. She was a heavy-set woman who wore large framed glasses and always had a big smile on her rosy-cheeked face. Before long, Klee was chatting with her and making her laugh with her one-liners. They both ended up in good spirits. This was the best medicine for Klee. At last, the boiling tea kettle within her had lost a great deal of its steam since she had met Dean in the corridor.

Dean called at eight o'clock. He was pleasant, but his voice was strained.

"Klee, it's Dean. The week has passed by so quickly. I have been loaded down with one thing or another."

"Okay, Dean. Do me a favor and let's drop the excuses. Spill what's really on your mind." Klee was furious to say the least.

"Sure . . . sure, Klee. I have been thinking about the conversation that we had on the boat on Sunday. Frankly, I have been preoccupied in my thoughts about your revelation. The information knocked me off-balanced big time. I've been in a spin! Please understand me when I say that I don't know how I truly feel at this point. I do know that I want a family. I want my own children. I couldn't handle adopting, Klee. I'm sorry, but adoption just isn't in my nature, my way of thinking. I am torn and miserable because I want us to have a life together, but the kid scenario is a big problem. This is a hell for both of us, I realize, but I also know that you wouldn't accept anything but honesty from me. We both need time. We need to talk more. Can you understand my side just a little?"

"Yes, I can. I am sorry for the shock and all the upset. I truly am, Dean. I guess I believed or I had hoped anyway that our love was strong enough to carry us through this roadblock. I don't know what more there is to say, Dean. I think you have made your position quite clear."

"Is it so wrong to want to have your own kids?"

"No, of course it isn't. Just as it isn't my fault that I am barren. I have to deal with what fate has dished out to me. Dean, you are saying two things to me. One voice says you want us to have a life together, but the other voice says you want your own family and adoption will never be a reality for you. We are both too well-educated to kid ourselves, and we both clearly know you can't have both."

"Are you going to be at your camp this weekend? If you are, I'd like to drive out on Sunday. We need to talk. We need to be together. I feel as if someone has beaten me up. I am miserable. I am disturbed, and I will admit to you that the tears have surfaced. I am sure that they have for you too, my darling Klee."

"You are so right, Dean. The tears come when least expected, and yes, I am going out to the camp. Since I hadn't heard from you all week, I went ahead with plans with Sal. She'll be with me the entire weekend."

Klee's heart was breaking. She was emotionally fractured, but she knew in her mind that she must stand firm.

"So you are saying I can't see you?"

"That's about right. Several days have gone by without any word from you, so let's give ourselves a furlough from one another. Let's take a few weeks of separation. Time is not of the essence, but getting in touch with one's true self is of supreme importance to both of us. We can talk down the road once our emotions have settled, once we have ample time to sort things out. Yet we may simply see each other to say good-bye."

"Damn it, Klee. Don't say that! I can't believe this. What the hell is happening?"

"I understand your reaction, Dean. Only a meeting of the minds will settle this horrible dilemma. It seems that a lapse in companionship is necessary at this point in time. For now, I'm going to say good night. I must. I can't bear to speak any longer. Good night, Dean."

She put the receiver down very gently, even as crushing emotions stirred within the depth of her being. The severe sadness was released by a cry from deep within her soul. The full realization that it was over with Dean hit her hard. The loss of hope, the loss of love brought about a piercing stab to her already wounded heart. She let it all out. As the emotions settled after some time, her mind drifted to what she also knew only too well. Philosophically, Klee fully understood that real happiness was brought about through harmony between one's soul and the path one follows. Obviously, there wasn't harmony between them. Realistically, they would make different choices and write entirely different chapters in their books of life. Klee internalized this truth, but her inner voice repeatedly echoed, *Who gives a damn about the philosophical? I just want to be loved for me. I love him so deeply.*

CHAPTER 58

Early Saturday morning, Salena arrived at Klee's home. She helped Klee pack up the car for the weekend. All of Muffy Cat's gear was readied. The ice chest with the food items was loaded into the Chevy.

"Okay, I believe we are ready to shove off," Sal shouted from the driveway as she hoisted the cat carrier into the backseat.

"I'm glad we are getting an early start. After we unpack at camp, visit with our buddies, and have lunch, what do you say about going onto Can to shop for a new anchor line and maybe a bow cleat?"

"You know I love shopping in Canandaigua," said Sal.

"Oh, I only mentioned boat stuff. How did shopping get into the picture?"

"Well, if we go, I'll enjoy browsing in a few shops at least. I need a new pair of deck shoes for the boat."

"Okay, shopping it will be."

"In turn for the shopping adventure, I'll offer you this, Klee. It will be my treat too. Let's take the boat on Sunday down to Woods Hole and have one of their famous burgers. Would you enjoy that?"

"Why, Sal, you little weasel, you know I'd love it."

Sal was a loving cousin. She was doing everything she could to keep Klee's mind off Dean. The shopping would evolve into more than purchasing an anchor line, cleat, and deck shoes. This would be good for Klee to keep her occupied.

The Woods Hole expedition always delighted the women. They found the personalities of the locals at the lakefront grill hangout fascinating and downright hysterical at times. With luck, they'd run into some interesting characters tomorrow. They were all very friendly, good-hearted folks indeed but different in every sense of the word. The lunch visit would give Klee a chance to observe. It would give her material to do her impersonations of these colorful guys from Woods Hole when they all sat around the campfire some evening.

At Sunday morning breakfast, Klee looked across the table at Sal. She had decided to bring up the subject of Dean. To this point, Sal hadn't asked any questions. She respected Klee's privacy too much. She would wait for Klee's opener.

"Sal, Dean and I spoke on Friday evening. It wasn't a long conversation. We are both upset, I know. I also know that we are at a stalemate. There is no logic to our situation. He wants us to marry, but he also wants a family. His definition of family means his own children. He is strongly opposed to adoption."

Klee paused and bit her lip. She did not want to start crying.

"I really fell deeply in love with him. I know that he will always be part of me. The healing period will be excruciating and may take a great deal of time. You know I put my heart into whatever I do and that includes my relationships. So the disappointment matches all the energy I originally invested," Klee sighed.

"I'm truly sorry, Klee. I wish I could alleviate some of the pain. I had hoped that this wouldn't happen again. You are caught in the middle it seems to me. You can offer Dean a deep love and devotion, which he recognizes, I am sure. But he has other needs too. It is basic. He wants his own family, which is natural for him. You must try not to blame him for this basic instinct. Nor must you blame yourself in any way, Klee. You are not responsible for the surgeries that have altered your life. You must tell yourself this over and over again."

Sal wanted to blurt out what she had mentioned before about the strict religious and family regimentation Dean adhered to, but she held her tongue.

"Intellectually, I can grasp all that you have said, Sal, but when it comes to matters of the heart, the tears continue to escape."

"Will you be seeing him again?"

"I told him to let a few weeks go by before there is contact again. This should give each of us time to get ourselves under better control. I don't think the separation will amount to much, but it is my hope that when we meet again and conclude our relationship, we'll part as friends, if that is possible. After what we have shared, I cannot bear the thought that we would part with angry feelings or indifference."

"Klee, you don't know what will happen over the weeks of separation. Dean may have a different outlook. He may put you first in the end." Sal didn't let herself believe her statement, but out of love for Klee, she let it pass her lips.

"It could be, Sal. That would be the fulfillment of my inner desire. Obviously, I won't be going home with him for the Mother's Day weekend. He'll probably confide in his brother while he is at home. They are very close. I tell myself that if I really love him, I'll let him go on with his own life and dreams. That's what the admirable side is telling me. I must prepare myself to exercise the correct behavior when the time comes, even though it will smash my already fractured heart."

CHAPTER 59

The Woods Hole excursion at the southerly end of the lake had another dimension. Since the women decided to do some fishing before satisfying their palates, they went to the bait shop prior to launching their boat. Klee liked to purchase night crawlers. She had always used them as a kid, and she was a firm believer that the bass were partial to plump worms.

The odors of Mr. Cosgrove's bait shop filled their nostrils. It was a pungent smell, but one that Klee had been around since she was a kid. However, Sal had grown up in a small town void of lakes and fishing, so it was all a new ball game to her in recent years. Both cousins had such diverse backgrounds, but each learned from the other.

Even though it was a shanty bait store, Mr. Cosgrove took pride in neatness and order. Rods and reels were lined up on one wall. Glass display cases showed off all kinds of attractive lures, sinkers of different weights, and pound-tested fishing lines. Another section of the store was occupied with bait pails of all sizes and fishing nets. Not only was the place orderly, it was well-supplied for the avid fisherman.

The gals bypassed the tanks that roiled with minnows and the other tanks with the crawling crabs that plowed over each other as they struggled for space.

"Hi, Mr. Cosgrove," Klee called.

"Hi to you, Klee, and how are you doing, Salena?" asked Mr. Cosgrove. "When are you ladies going to call me Barney like everyone else does around here?"

Both women laughed. It was his age, his white hair, long fluffy white beard, and the denim bib overhauls that made them feel that they should address him in a respectful manner.

"Okay, Barney, we will try to do that from now on. I realize that you have mentioned this fact before, but you seem to us to be a mister."

"Oh shucks, ladies. I'm just a simple guy. Barney is the name. Try to remember that. You make me feel old with that mister stuff. Not that I'm saying that I'm a young guy you understand, but being called Barney makes me feel younger than mister. Now what can I do for you?" Barney chuckled.

"Okay, Barney. Sal and I will make it a point from now on to address you as you have requested. We sure want you to feel young," Klee replied. She winked at Sal as she walked toward the worm tank.

"Sal and I want to do a little fishing. We don't have a long time to enjoy angling today, but we would like some of those fat night crawlers."

Barney grabbed an old coffee can to use as a container. He filled the bottom of it with some of the rich dark soil from the tank. His large hand swooped into the tank and withdrew a mess of wriggling worms. Adroitly, he placed them in the coffee can. Placing the lid on the can, he handed them to Sal.

"Anything else you gals need? If not, you owe me fifty-five cents."

Armed with bait, the cousins boarded the boat. Klee navigated the craft to the high banks on the southwest side of the lake. The water was very deep along this area, even though they weren't that far from the shoreline. Some of the branches from the large maple tree shadowed the water.

Klee's dad had taken her to this area when she was a youngster. They'd leave their dock at five o'clock in the morning and head out for the *deep spot* as they called it. Within two hours, they had a healthy catch. This meant speeding homeward to the cottage with a great number of splashing fish. While father and daughter cleaned and prepared the fish for the open grill, Klee's mom would do her special magic by preparing razor-thin sliced potatoes. She made the best home fries in the world according to her daughter. The freshly baked muffins filled with red raspberry jelly that came out of her mom's oven would disappear with haste. Klee ate them as if she would never have the pleasure again. She consumed a great deal of food generally, and yet she was as skinny as a rail. Her constant motion and activity burned the calories.

Klee threw the throttle into neutral. She was ready to have Sal toss the anchor overboard.

"Okay, this looks to be just about the right spot. Do your anchor thing, Sal."

There was a loud splash. Once the anchor hit bottom and its claws dug in, Sal slipped the line into the bow cleat and made the line secure. The boat turned a few times until it settled in the direction of the prevailing current and slight breeze.

It turned out to be a peaceful two hours of enjoying the solitude, the natural surrounding beauty, the peacefulness, and the opportunity to communicate with nature. Klee had to bait Sal's hook. She would not touch the wriggling worms, let alone thread them onto the sharp hook. The catch wasn't abundant, but Sal brought in a good-sized bass. It was at least two pounds in weight. Klee, for all her patience and diligence, could only show two sunfish as her prizes.

"Sal, you are the winner today. What a beautiful bass. Once these are all gutted and scaled, we'll have a tasty little fish fry for ourselves."

"Yes we will, but remember, you are doing the cleaning, and I'll do the breading and frying."

Klee smiled. Sal hated cleaning fish. She wanted no part of the operation. It wasn't the nicest of jobs, and it was a smelly one to boot. As Klee matured, she began having reservations about killing in the name of sport, but for food, it was okay with her.

The weekend at the lake and camp with cousin Sal's nurturing and company was the best medicine for Klee. Although she had moments when she lost concentration to thoughts of Dean and the tears welled, she was able to talk herself into controlling her feelings for the most part. The constant refrain continued to echo in her mind, telling her that what was meant to be would be. Klee realized that the acceptance of the refrain *que sera, sera* was indeed the mantra she needed.

CHAPTER 60

The weather showed signs that spring had really sprung by the third week of May. The trees were dressed with shiny new leaves for the occasion. The early spring flowers were popping up in flower beds. A sure indicator of spring was the blossoming of the forsythia and lilac bushes. A pleasant medium shade of yellow blossoms on the forsythia attracted everyone to their brightness and gaiety. However, the lavender and deep purple hues of the lilac bushes were Klee's favorite.

As a youngster, she remembered going over to the next street where her maternal grandparents lived. They had a beautiful rock garden with a variety of flowers that enhanced the backyard throughout the springtime and summer. The tiered rock garden Grandpa designed and built for Gram included tulips, crocuses, daffodils, pansies, and Gram's favorite, the calla lily. In addition, there were lilac bushes positioned along the fence. Klee wanted some of those lilacs each year for her classroom and begged for bouquets to bring to school. Her Grandma Catherine would smile at Klee and happily cut a whole bunch of them.

Grandma Catherine had a special love for Klee, and they spent many hours together. On several occasions, she attempted to teach Klee how to sew and mend, but Klee could never sit still that long. They shared their lives in an era in which family and quiet times together were the norm. Klee often reflected on those times as she grew older. Such tranquility and memories warmed her soul. She missed that time of innocence.

When Sister Ann Mary was Klee's teacher, she was delighted to receive the lilac blossoms that were neatly wrapped in wax paper. Klee was so proud to offer them to her. She always wanted to please Sister Ann Mary when she was her student. Klee would present the lavender and purple blossoms with their delicate fragrance to her during the entire growing season. It was Klee's task to arrange them in vases and place them before the shrine of the Blessed Mother that held a prominent place in the classroom.

May, among Catholics, was the month dedicated to the Virgin Mary. It was an important ritual every May at the church and in the classrooms. At this point in her life, Klee would never have suspected that such a ritual would no longer be practiced by her as she grew older.

It was an unplanned convenience that the church celebration of the Blessed Mother in May coincided with the Lilac Festival in Rochester. It was held at Highland Park, which is now on the National Register for Historical Places.

Every spring, the park's abundant display of perennials burst with flowers of every shape and hue imaginable. In addition, the flowering plum and crabapple trees are magnificent in color. However, the park became most famous for its lilacs and rhododendrons. For Klee, the flora of springtime demonstrated that it was a glorious time for newness and for the awaking and lifting of the spirit.

CHAPTER 61

Klee had seen Dean a few times at school during the passing weeks. They either gave a wave, a smile, or a simple hello. Both were keeping their promise to remain distant from one another for the time period agreed upon, and each was doing the best possible to act naturally in order to avoid rumors flying around Fairhaven Central. They didn't need to deal with gossip or lots of questions. Both Dean and Klee were private individuals, and they both ascribed to keeping their business to themselves. Besides, they didn't know which end was up at this point. Neither knew the exact outcome of their relationship, or did they?

Bethany's invitation did come to pass in the third week of May. Klee was looking forward to spending some time with the Winslows and, of course, Allie.

Klee approached their home as she trotted along the lengthy flagstone walkway to the front door. She pressed the doorbell and immediately heard the peal of Westminster Chimes. She had grown up listening to this musical sound from her mom's grandfather clock, and it always made her feel warm and comfortable whenever she was exposed to it. Laurie's smiling face appeared as she opened the door for Klee. Next to her, Allie sat at perfect attention. The only movement from Allie was the swinging rhythm of her tail.

The family and Klee had a lovely dinner and the table conversation was fun and animated. Allie did lie down next to Klee's dining chair. Occasionally, Klee would gently pat Allie on her head. She felt so fortunate to have the spirit that dwelled within this dog part of her life. She often thought . . . if Allie could only talk.

Finishing up with dessert and coffee, the young people excused themselves from the table. It was delightful to spend some time with them, but homework called. Both teenagers took their schooling seriously. They had definite goals for their futures. Their accomplished parents were great role models. That fact was evident.

"Klee, Shep and I have something we'd like to tell you," announced Bethany. "Let's all go into Shep's study."

Each selected a chair; there was a lull for a moment. Klee couldn't imagine what to expect. Her mind raced to all kinds of possibilities, but she decided to be patient and wait without guessing. It would probably be best that way.

"Bethany and I have discussed in length what I am going to tell you," Shepard began. "As you know, we travel as a family, and often we find ourselves in distance places around the world. Now that we have Allie and fully appreciating all that went into finally rescuing her, it seems that we have a responsibility to her in the event something should happen to us."

Klee absorbed every word. She nodded.

"So we'd like to add a codicil to our will, Klee. We'd name you as guardian for Allie. Monies would be provided for the dog's immediate needs and care for her entire life. Of course, full compensation for your services would be provided for and granted as long as Allie was in your care," Shepard concluded with a broad smile as he reached for his pipe.

Klee was startled. She never had expected this. She knew how to care for cats, but she knew little about caring for dogs on a daily basis. She'd have to go to dog training school herself!

"Thank you, Shepard and Bethany, for the honor. I'm so surprised. I don't have an acceptance speech ready, but I do know that if anything ever happened to you, I would be there for Allie. I am sure nothing so tragic will happen, but you are planners and responsible people, so I do understand your concern."

"Thank you, thank you, Klee," chimed in Bethany. "We both appreciate all you have done and what you will do if called upon."

Bethany rose from her chair and went over to Klee to offer a big hug. Shep approached Klee next. He extended his hand to shake hers, and with his other hand, he caressed the top of her hand. His eyes shone with relief, satisfaction, and affection.

Once Klee returned home from her evening with the Winslows, she settled into some easy clothes. It was her intention to get a letter off to Sister. She entered her study and settled in at her desk. No sooner had she withdrawn the typing paper from the top desk drawer, she had a furry visitor. For some reason, Muffy Cat thought it was her job to sit at full attention on the desk and watch the little typewriter hammers click away on the inserted paper. She especially got a charge out of the faint *ping* sound when Klee threw the typewriter carriage in order to begin the next line. Invariably, she would stick out her paw to catch one of the hammers, thus jamming up the works.

"Muffin, you are not making this easy for me," Klee softly admonished. "I'm glad that you are with me, but I can't have the distraction if I'm going to finish this letter in due time."

Klee gently moved her away; Muffy Cat got the message and sprawled out on the desk. Klee knew that the fur ball would doze off before long, but it was so nice to have her company anyway.

Dear Sister,
It's about nine o'clock. All is quiet on the western front as I sit before my typewriter. Muffin is relaxed on my desk as I key my letter. I want to get this letter off to you so I can get it in the mail in the morning before I leave for school.

The Winslows had me for dinner this evening. It was such a pleasant evening. Allie really flattered me because she stayed at my side throughout dinner. Sometimes I wonder what she senses about me. I wonder if she knows that I put my heart and soul into her rescue.

Believe this Sister, the Winslows are making me guardian for Allie in their Will if something should ever happen to them. Of course, I don't believe anything ever will, but I assured them that I'll always be there for the beautiful yellow Lab we all love. Sister, I never expected such an offer and request. I appreciate their trust in me.

Mother's Day has passed without the intended plans to go home with Dean for that special weekend. We decided it was best to let the invitation pass at this point in time. We haven't seen each other for a few weeks now. We have taken a sabbatical from one another. Realistically, we have needed the time away from one another so we could sort things out, to get in touch with our inner feelings for each other. It has been murder for me . . . probably for Dean too.

Many moments I experience a well of loneliness, a loss of concentration, and of course, tears. It's all part of what one often must go through when one is in love. It is true that love brings no guarantees for happiness. Love lost is crushing and offers an emotional setback. Yet many lessons are learned during the separation period and definitely when the loss finally takes hold. One comes to realize that part of one's heart will always be dedicated to the one lost if that particular person was the genuine love mate of his or her life.

Dean and I will be seeing each other soon. Four weeks remain in the school year so we may not only be saying good-bye to the students but to each other. Sure there is hope that the arrivederci will not take place, but I'm a realistic person, so I expect nothing other than what is to be, will be.

Have you received any word from the Mother House about your reassignment to the Rochester diocese? If you have not, please call me when you are informed. Of course, I am hoping for your reassignment.

I know you will keep me in your thoughts and prayers these next few weeks as we approach the close of another school year. Finishing up the school year is so busy with some strain as you personally have experienced for many years and so completely understand.

This year, however, I have some added tension! Believe me when I say that I have been on guard not to allow my personal dilemma to interfere with my professional duties.

I'm closing now with love. Take good care.

Klee

As Klee began addressing the mailing envelope, she lost concentration for a few moments and began to recall the words of Richard L. Evans:

> Among the greatest blessings in life is to be safe with someone . . . someone without evil intent, someone who wouldn't violate a trust, who wouldn't take advantage of innocence or ignorance; someone who isn't planning in his heart to comprise principles, or to deprive another person of virtue, honor, or any price-less or irreplaceable possession. We if have all else in life, but if we can't count on character, on integrity, if we haven't the sense of being safe, we have little that matters very much. Oh the joy, the surpassing joy of having someone we can turn to, someone we can trust . . . someone we feel safe with.

Klee experienced this blessing with Sister Ann Mary.

Klee relaxed with a hot shower and readied herself to snuggle into bed. Once the light on the nightstand was turned off, Muffin jumped on the bed and settled in the crook of Klee's arm. She gently kneaded her paws against Klee's breast. Her purr was soothing and rhythmic, and before long, the human and animal both drifted off into a peaceful repose. And so life goes on.

CHAPTER 62

Klee shared her recent visit with the Winslows and Allie with her class. She told them how well-behaved Allie was and what a pleasure it was to be around her. Klee addressed the demonstration of loyalty as she described how Allie remained stretched out along her chair throughout dinner.

"Ms. Cato, will you see Allie once school closes for the summer?" Eddy asked.

"It is my intention to be with Allie. It would be a nice experience to have some quality time with her. I have mentioned this wish to Mrs. Winslow and said that I'd like to take Allie out to my camp this summer. The country setting, the vast wooded area, and the huge pond would be paradise for Allie. Because of her obedience training, I'd feel comfortable taking her anywhere."

After a few more questions, Ms. Cato moved the students onto another topic that they all seemed to like and absorbed like sponges. She mentioned the plans for kickball, what days they'd go out to compete, and the requirements that they needed to fulfill in order to earn time for the games. She told the students that they would be competing with another class during these last weeks before school closed. They'd have a few games with Mrs. Osborne's class. She had expressed that she'd like her class to challenge us.

Greg blurted out, "They can challenge us all they want, Ms. Cato, we'll beat 'em good!"

"I like your enthusiasm. Let's all have the same spirit," Ms. Cato said with a huge smile.

While speaking about kickball with the students, Randy crossed her mind. She wondered how Randy would do during the spring round. Several months had elapsed since the cold, dreary days of late fall which brought the games to a halt. She wondered if he had retained any of the skills learned during the fall semester.

Little Randy was still little Randy in stature. He hadn't grown but a smidgen in height and remained as wispy as a willow. She was prepared to instruct and encourage him again so he'd have some success during the spring rounds of kickball. He wasn't physically quipped for sports like so many of the other kids, but his brilliant mind made up for what he lacked athletically.

Klee spoke to Lisa while they were on cafeteria duty.

"Hi, Lisa, not many more days remain for this duty."

"Yeah, this is not my cup of tea. I can't believe that all the study and degrees earned by teachers should be applied to playing warden in a cafeteria. No one will ever convince me that it wouldn't be far better for the students and the teachers to have a break from one another during lunchtime!" Lisa averred.

"It will never happen, Lisa. It's a matter of bucks . . . a question of economics. No way will they hire cafeteria monitors. Just think, if we didn't have to be in here to deal with all the din and antics, there would be less gastrointestinal problems for many teachers, it would seem to me," Klee chuckled with a twinkle in her eyes.

"So, Klee, anything new with you and Mr. Movie Star since we last spoke?" Lisa whispered as she gently steered Klee away from the ears of inquisitive students.

"Nothing really. Four weeks remain in the school year. We've both have kept our word and haven't had contact. It has been hell. I have made up my mind to call him and ask that we get together to discuss our situation. The hiatus is over as far as I am concerned. Both of us have had enough time to process the entire situation. The phone call has to be made. I must face reality, and frankly, we've had enough time to sort out matters of the heart and make a decision as to what course to follow," Klee stated with resolve.

"Gee, Klee, I can't believe how this has all melted down. I am sorry that you've had to go through all that you have emotionally and for such a formidable duration. I'm still hoping for the best. I'm sure you have come to some conclusions and maybe you have made a decision yourself."

"Girlfriend, you're right on target. I have!" Klee gave a wave and headed across the cafeteria.

That evening, Klee decided to call Sonya. She hadn't spoken to her in a long time, even though she had promised that she would. Both women were no slackers when it came to work, activities, and involvement, and so chatting often was a luxury. Once supper dishes were cleared and washed, and Muffy Cat's needs were met, Klee headed for the family room to make her phone calls. The cat followed her down the steps into the sunken family room. She knew this was her time to cuddle in Klee's lap once she settled into her recliner while she chatted on the telephone.

At the onset, Sonya and Klee discussed professional matters, teaching concerns, and the general movement in education. With all the informal chitchat exhausted, Klee decided to get into a more personal dialogue.

"Sonya, I want you to know that I have made some decisions about my relationship with Dean. We have taken a break from each other as you know so we could decide on a course of action."

"You mean you have come to a conclusion before meeting with him?" Sonya asked.

"Yes, I have. Of course, I intend to give him every opportunity to express his point of view and to tell me what conclusions he has drawn. I shall listen to what he says to me."

"Klee, you do more than listen. I know you. You'll tune into the body language, the eyes, and what is not said."

"True. I'll let you know the outcome, I promise."

"I can't tell you how sorry I am. The pain has been hard to bear at times I am sure," Sonya sighed.

"Indeed it has. Well, dear friend, I am planning on calling Dean once I hang up with you. I hope he isn't at some community meeting. I'm going to ask to meet with him and set a specific date and time. So I'm going to sign off."

"Good luck, old friend."

Klee got up from the lounge chair, much to the cat's disgust. In the kitchen, she busied herself making a mug of hot tea. Once she finished her preparation in the kitchen, the cat and Klee with mug in hand once again meandered down to the family room. When Klee and the fur person were settled in, she picked up the phone and began to dial. Her heart was pounding. This she hadn't expected, but in fact, she was experiencing a strong physical reaction. She wondered how her blood pressure would read at the moment. She prayed that Dean would be at home. It was time to get the ball rolling. It was time to openly discuss the future game plan. It was time for the story of Dean and Klee to come to a resolution.

"Hello, this is Dean."

There was a faint pause as Klee took a deep breath.

"Dean, it's me."

"Klee, Klee, my darling. It's good to hear your voice again. I have been going nuts. I wasn't going to wait much longer before I called you. This has been a nightmare!" Dean exclaimed.

"Yes, it has been for both of us, I am sure. I have called to tell you that I'd like us to meet to discuss where we are at this point."

"Sure . . . sure, Klee. You say when. My place or yours?"

"Neither place, Dean. I believe we need to meet on neutral grounds. Maybe we can plan on a drive and a walk along the river."

"You want to walk along the Genesee River to discuss our future?"

"Exactly. I know what will happen if we see each other at your place or mine. You know very well too, Dean. Then we'll accomplish nothing once our thoughts and decisions have been clouded by our passion. These agonizing weeks will have been for naught if we allow the physical to reenter."

With great disappointment and resignation in his voice, he conceded, "You are right, Klee. A walk it shall be. I'll pick you up at your place."

"Once again, I must decline. I'd like to meet you at the school parking lot on Saturday morning at ten o'clock, if that would be convenient for you."

"Yes, I am free, and if that's the way you want to do it, consider it done."

Dean realized that Klee was being formal and careful not to let their feelings interfere with what they had ahead of them. He knew she was an intelligent, level-headed woman, a pragmatist. Sometimes her frank facing up to matters, her realism, made him uncomfortable. Sometimes it made him as mad as hell, but that's what he loved about her—her candor and integrity—that certain uniqueness.

Klee put down the receiver. She knew this was going to be a heart-wrenching episode when they met. Her inner sense told her that it was going to be more than she had ever dealt with, even though there had been many no-win experiences in her past. Her heart wasn't foreign to love and romance and all that went with it, but this time, her heart was totally and unequivocally possessed. It would be a new challenge to overcome her obsession and her deep love for Mr. Movie Star.

CHAPTER 63

The next day, Klee kept up a good front, although her heart was wounded. She threw herself into her work, the lessons for the day, and her class.

Mid-afternoon approached and all the students from her class filed out to the playing field. They were milling around, being playful with one another, and some were simply talking a blue streak while Ms. Cato was asking Eddy to set up the bases.

"Okay, everybody, listen up! This is your first game this semester. Today we'll have two new captains for kickball. Eric and Robin have been chosen. Captains, select your team players. Remember to choose the players alternately and that means to select boy, girl alternately too. Captains, let me know when you are ready."

The students had learned in the past to get the selection done fast. The faster the selection, the more time they had to play. They really loved kickball, the out-of-doors, and the freedom.

Klee had worked with Randy a few times after school during the spring term. She didn't make this public knowledge, but she went ahead with the plan because she wanted to give him the opportunity to return to the level he had achieved in the fall or become even better and to build his confidence. Klee appreciated his exceptional mental competence, but she also wanted him to achieve success socially. His mom had agreed to pick him up about four o'clock after his private sessions with Ms. Cato.

It all worked out at game time. Randy went to the box to kick the ball that seemed quite large in proportion to his foot. He hitched up his trousers, which he constantly did no matter what the situation, then rubbed his hands together. All eyes were on him.

"Come on, Randy, make it a good one," some of his teammates shouted.

Klee gave him a knowing smile as she clutched her whistle that dangled from the chain around her neck. The private instruction had to pay off.

He kept his eye on the ball, readied himself, and kicked with every bit of strength his little body could produce. It was a solid connect, and Randy ran as fast as his wiry body would carry him. He actually made it to second base. This was one base more than he accomplished during the fall term.

Because Randy was such a likable guy, everyone began to cheer for him. Team loyalty didn't matter in this instance. Every student shouted with excitement.

Robin strode over to him on second base. He had a grin from ear to ear.

"Randy, that was great," congratulated Robin. "I'm glad you are on my team."

"I am too. I really love this game now."

Klee felt good inside. She was happy for him. She realized that he would never be a last pick anymore. She did her job as a teacher. Indeed, collateral learning was dynamic in the total developmental process.

Driving home from school that afternoon, Klee had mixed emotions. She appreciated the gift of being able to help students grow and reach for their special stars. It was her philosophy that there wasn't a greater profession than teaching in which to be engaged.

Often, it was all the ancillary rubbish that kept teachers from their full potential. She thought it was unfortunate how politics were an integral part of academia, but where there were people, there would always be political maneuverings, jealousies, and plain meanness. To keep focused, she repeated the mantra over and over: "I have great success with kids and animals, and I rejoice that those gifts are in my life." This awareness sustained her and gave her the strength to refuse to be part of the pack. To reinforce her belief, she often recalled Evelyn McClellan's words: "The purpose of life is to matter . . . to have it make a difference that you live at all . . . by using whatever talents you may have to the very fullest." The key word *the fullest* is what Klee dwelled on. She also believed that she would be on the right path if her feet were imbedded in the solid rock of fact and reason.

She had been referred to as a special teacher or an exceptional teacher. She was beginning to wonder if the label also indicated the sum total of her life. Was she so different? Was she too special for those around her? Even matters of the heart weren't working for her—that came under the special category too because of her physical composition. She didn't want to be special and be left behind. What a price when one is different from the norm. The more she dwelled on the concept of norm, average, mundane, the more she felt saddened. What a world, filled with narrow-thinking people who swell their limited brains with bias, prejudice, and set patterns, and heaven forbid if one exhibits just the slightest deviation from that pattern. Life is filled with such heartache if one is even slightly different.

CHAPTER 64

Klee was up early on Saturday morning. The cat didn't expect a five o'clock morning arousal time, but there it was. Usually five thirty or six o'clock was the target time. Felines like routine. They like consistency, so when there is an alteration, it doesn't please them. The expression on the Muffy Cat's face said it all! She wasn't a happy camper.

Klee coaxed the cat along out of bed and downstairs to the kitchen. She went straight to the cupboard in search of a nibble treat to sweeten the cat's disposition. That being successful, she went to the basement area to begin doing the week's laundry. Her intention was to get this chore completed, along with some house cleaning before she met with Dean.

She had made up her mind to go out to camp once she and Dean finished with their rendezvous later that morning. She was sure she'd need the quiet of her camp; probably she'd take a solo ride on the *Charade*. The beautiful lake with its gentle breeze sweeping from the western hills and crossing the lake toward the eastern shoreline would gently caress her body and lighten her soul. The lake would be the place to process what occurred during the meeting with Dean. She clung to the mental image that the breeze would carry away any sad feelings she might have. Even if things worked out for them, which remained a slim possibility, she wanted to go off by herself before she and Dean came back together once again.

Both arrived at the school parking lot at ten o'clock sharp. Klee made herself gain composure as she opened the car door. She flashed a pleasant smile as Dean approached her. His eyes peered at her with tenderness. Neither embraced because there were homes abutting the school property, and surely, someone at just the moment of their intimacy would be peering from a window. They didn't want their actions to be fodder for neighborhood gossip. Observers could observe them driving off together, but that's all they'd see. Any voyeurs would have to make up the rest of the story if they were so inclined.

Dean opened the door of his car for her. She slid into the immaculate, camel-colored interior seat. It was an attractive Oldsmobile with a comfortable ride. At first there was an initial lull, followed by both starting to speak at the same moment. Both began laughing, which helped to open the conversation, and Dean gestured to Klee to go first. She had been talking to her guardian angel all morning. She needed guidance with her words.

"It's good to be with you once again, Dean. How did you do with your second-term final exams? I'm sure you aced them. That is the norm for you, isn't it?"

"Fortunately, I can say yes. I'm pleased with the outcome. Not much more to go. Some course work this summer and fall term. I've already talked to Jay about leaving in January to begin my residency on campus to finish my doctorate. He's such a helpful guy. We are lucky to have him as principal."

"Yes, we are. Jay's great with the kids as well with the teachers. I didn't realize that you'd be leaving Fairhaven Central so soon. Let's see, that would mean that in seven months, you are on your way to complete your ambition. Time does get away."

"Yes, Klee, my dream doesn't seem so distant anymore. What about you, Klee? What have you been up to since we've been on leave?"

Klee chatted about routine things. She wanted to keep the conversation friendly and off anything that had to do with their personal involvement until they were out of the car. Her goal had been met. Only light chitchat filled the car's cavity as they traveled toward the Genesee River Park parking lot. Dean slowly maneuvered into a space and parked the Olds. He came around to open the door for her. The air had a crispness and freshness to it.

As they approached the walking path, they observed the swift current cascading the water toward the direction of the falls. To lighten the situation Klee casually offered information about the Genesee River. The river's name is derived from the Seneca tribe, meaning good valley or pleasant valley. It flows northward through western New York from its source south of the town of Genesee in Pennsylvania. This concept of a river flowing north always surprised students. Surely all rivers must flow south and downward. Klee enjoyed this lesson and the exchange with the students. The main concept they needed to learn was that elevation was the determining factor as to the river's direction of flow. The source was at a higher elevation in Pennsylvania, and therefore, it flowed to reach its lowest point, Lake Ontario.

"Thanks for the geography lesson, Klee," Dean remarked half-heartedly.

The trees along the walking path and the banks of the river showed off their new leaves that had greeted the world in early spring. Dean gently took Klee's hand as they began their walk.

"I'd like to begin Klee. I think it is safe for me to say that we have both been through hell during our separation. I do believe now that it was a good idea to temporarily part. It has given us space and time to reflect and learn from others. I made up my mind to inquire, to seek input from others. When I went home over the Mother's Day weekend, I did talk to my brother, Sam, and to Father Christopher. I made excuses about your absence that weekend, but I think my family was suspicious. My brother certainly was. So I confided in him."

"I'm sure they were all surprised by my absence. I regret that it had to play out as it did. It certainly wasn't a good opener for the woman in your life. What advice did they give you, Dean?"

Dean went on to tell her the important, abbreviated segments of the conversations. His brother had pointed out that it was up to him to do what he wanted with his life, but he also cautioned that his parents wouldn't be happy. They expected Dean to marry a Catholic woman of Italian lineage and to have a healthy-sized family brought up in the faith. He also understood Dean's negative reaction to adoption.

Father Christopher counseled him by saying that if he would not adopt, then he and Klee would be living a selfish life and not fulfilling the true sanctity of marriage. Even with adoption, the true meaning of marriage would not be fulfilled. His seed would be wasted on pleasure only.

His last sentence almost blew Klee away. She was so shocked upon hearing Father Christopher's statement that she could not respond. Her lips would not move. Her voice was constricted in her throat. In what age was this priest living? Her inner rage and indignation roiled her entire body. Wasted seed!

Desperately Dean shouted, "Klee, I don't want to give you up. I don't care what advice I have been given. I love you. Just being separated these few weeks has almost killed me. The suffering has been unbelievable. I've lost seven pounds." His tone was strong and determined. "We can marry and have a good life. We both have careers and so many similar interests that we enjoy. We'll make it together, and the hell with everything else. Please don't give up on me, don't abandon me, please."

There was a brief silence. Klee knew the moment had arrived to make the plunge into reality.

"Your intentions are well meaning, my dearest Dean. I know that's what you believe now that we can make it. I want you to thoroughly understand my deep love for you with the words that follow.

She went on to point out to Dean that his innate desire to have a family would surface down the road. It was only natural that he wanted a family, and since he would not consider adopting, then that need and desire would never be fulfilled. Also, all the religious demands would play havoc with his soul. It would eventually cause resentment, a void in their lives, and ultimately cause them to grow apart. There would be a strain with his family. There were all kinds of pitfalls that would eventually show themselves. As the heartaches surfaced, their relationship would tarnish. The relationship would become fractured, and it would dwindle.

"You see, Dean, I love you too much to let this happen to you and to us. I could not bear it. When one really loves the other person, sometimes it is required, for whatever the circumstance, to let that person go. I believe we have reached that crossroad. It is time for each of us to take separate paths, no matter how painful. We both must be strong and make it happen."

"Klee, please don't throw away the depth of our love, our friendship, our passion, please."

"I'm not discarding you, Dean. I am loving you! You will always be part of me. Your indelible footprints are on my heart. You must realize that. We must always be friendly toward one another. That's the true demonstration of love, and once the hurt is under control, though it may take time, we can remain civil and kind toward one another. That is my hope anyway."

She halted their slow pace and looked into Dean's beautiful cobalt blue eyes. Tear-filled eyes met the other's tears. She took his face in her hands and gently, brushed his lips with a gentle kiss. "I will always love you." She realized that would be their last moment as lovers.

On the way back to the school parking lot, not a word was spoken. Klee repeatedly looked out of the car window so she could hide the tears. She didn't dare speak, for if she did, she knew she would have no control of herself. Dean made frequent deep sighs and repeatedly slammed his fist on the steering wheel. The realization that it was over between them thundered in Klee's brain. Her heart felt as if it was shattering like glass that had been smashed on a hard, unforgiving surface.

Once Dean pulled his car alongside Klee's car in the parking lot, he walked around to open her door. He took her hand to help her out of the car. He leaned into her so his lips would meet hers. She instinctively turned her head.

"No, Dean, we must not, we cannot. Somehow we must move on," Klee whispered.

As she drove home, she contained her emotions. She did not play the car stereo. She didn't dare for she would not have been able to bear the chance of one of their songs adding to the sadness within the emptiness of the car. Instead, she concentrated on the road and getting herself home.

She pulled the car into the garage. She fully realized that she couldn't go out to the camp or take the boat out as she had originally planned. She must have been really kidding herself. She didn't want to see anyone, let alone talk to anyone. She was emotionally upside down. She was drained to the last drop.

Entering the house, she hardly gave recognition to Muffy Cat. She dropped her purse in the kitchen. She slowly ascended the stairs to her bedroom. Looking at her bed, it signaled to her senses that she finally made it to a safe place where she could let it all out. Throwing herself on the bed, Klee's thundering, bottomless sobs filled the room. This was the same bed that was their "altar" of lovemaking.

After this catharsis, Klee got herself under control for the remainder of the day. She busied herself out in her flower garden. Even though she was plagued with a black thumb all her life, she worked on her gardens. While envying her mom and grandmother's green thumbs, she loved her flowers, especially the one's that cooperated with her and did what flowers were supposed to do.

Muffy Cat was on her leash stretched out on the cool grass watching Klee's every move. Even though the backyard was totally fenced, she never put the cat's safety in jeopardy. So like it or not, the cat had to succumb to the leash whenever she was exposed to the out-of-doors. This was true at home and at camp and always with Klee or Sal in close proximity.

The digging and pruning in the backyard felt good. That physical activity eased some of the stress, but every so often, the tears came. They simply came; she had no control over her weeping heart. She knew that it would be this way for some time. It was all part of the thing called the break up—unfulfilled permanence.

CHAPTER 65

S unday morning greeted Klee's world with singing birds, a beautiful blue sky, and nature's loveliness all around her as she peered out the windows. It had been a fitful night with little sleep, but she readied herself for the day. She engaged in an early long walk along the Barge Canal path that was a street block over from her home. It gave her some peace as she walked along in the solitude of the wooded area. She attempted to put her soul to some rest at least.

Later in the day, she played the organ. She keyed her favorite melodies while omitting "their" songs. It would be a long time before she would play "Unchained Melody," "Always in My Heart," "Clair de Lune," "Because," "The Story of Love," "The Way We Were," "Memory" and "Ebb Tide." Those songs belonged to them, and she suspected that it would be a very long time before she would have the courage to play them or listen to them. She knew that each song, each melody would recall precious memories that would flood every inch of her. It would be like rubbing salt into an open wound when particular melodies resounded in her space.

Healing takes time as most agree. What she knew was that the healing period was of a different duration for each individual. She had experienced ramming smack into so many brick walls during the journey of her life so far that she suspected this latest collision would do her in for some time. Of course, she could seek someone out in order to heal her heart, to make her feel good, and to feel loved. Klee was too sensible for such a decision and behavior. A rebound relationship might work, but it would be one that wasn't honest from the onset. She didn't want to take anyone who came along and use that person as her lifeline. Using others for any reason turned her off.

She knew that she had to ready herself for school in the morning. The evening would be devoted to periodically using ice compresses on her eyes. The application with its soothing cold would do the trick to void the sight of swollen eyes from all her crying during the weekend. She wasn't a makeup gal except for evenings out, but she realized that practice would need to be altered in the morning. No way did she want her students or her fellow teachers to recognize that something personal had happened to her. Klee made up her mind to keep in the shadows at school. She'd do all she could to remain as invisible as possible for several days.

Around seven thirty that evening, the phone rang and broke into the quiet atmosphere of her sanctuary.

"Hello, this is Klee."

"Good evening, this is the telephone operator. Are you Klee Cato?"

"Yes, I am Klee Cato.

"I have a long distance call from a Sister Ann Mary. Will you accept the charges?"

"Yes, absolutely I will."

How did Sister always know when she needed her?

"Klee, dearest, I had to call. You have been surfacing in my thoughts all weekend. The pull to contact you, dear, has been powerful."

There was silence for an instant as Klee fought breaking down into profuse sobs.

"Are you there, Klee?"

"Yes, Sister, I'm here. I . . . I never cease to be amazed how you always know when I'm troubled and in need of some nurturing."

Klee slowly related the results of her meeting with Dean on Saturday morning. Although it was difficult for her to get through the content of the Saturday meeting and the crying, she knew she had to get it over with if she was ever going to get back to some normalcy. When she finished, she heard Sister's deep sigh.

"Klee, my heart aches for you, you know that. There isn't much I can say other than it has happened for a purpose. We don't always understand the divine plan. Dear heart, there is something planned for you, and in the end, you'll know great peace and inner fulfillment. It may not happen right away, but before you finish writing the chapters of your life, you'll know."

"Maybe, Sister, but I want a life like everyone else . . . that means now, not some future date."

"You are not like everyone else. Your uniqueness, Klee, demands that your life will be very different because of your makeup, because of your personality, and because of the principles you so fiercely adhere to. You have never been one of the masses, so your life is destined for a different service, it seems to me."

"Thanks, Sister, I'll mull over your words of wisdom. I am so lucky to have you whenever I'm in troubled waters. In return, all I can offer you is my deep respect and love."

"I accept your loving gifts, and I return them to you also. Stay strong, Klee! Good night."

After saying good night, Klee thought for a moment and decided to blast forward. She might as well get it over with. She would make her comments brief and non-accusatory. She would request that no reference would be made about her and Dean until she was ready to talk about it. She needed to dial up Sal and Lisa immediately. She needed to tell them of the breakup. She needed their support; she needed them to secure her secret.

"Lisa, hi, it's Klee. I need to talk with you. Is this an okay time?" Klee implored.

"As a matter of fact, it is. What's happening?"

Klee replayed the conversation that she and Dean had at the park, but in limited detail. There was silence on the other end of the line, so she knew that Lisa was absorbing everything. Klee finally stopped speaking.

"I can't believe what you have told me," Lisa retorted with anger in her voice. "I'm having a problem with the priest, this Father Christopher. What does he know about human needs? He has no experience or real understanding of love. He's been behind that damn collar, so he hasn't the faintest idea what it is all about. What nonsense to dump on Dean. His seed indeed! That comment probably pierced Dean and set him on a real guilt trip. This religion stuff really causes more problems than most people will acknowledge. It sure is evident with the millions of innocents murdered over the centuries in the name of religion . . . in the name of God. It wipes me out. I can't handle it," Lisa shouted. "Please, Klee, promise me that you'll start right now telling yourself that although you acknowledge your deep love for Dean, this has happened for the best. Keep telling yourself that."

When Klee had finished talking to Sal, she realized that she had reacted about the same as Lisa had. No one could really change the situation or make matters better. Bottom line . . . Klee had a mountain to climb, and it had to be solo.

CHAPTER 66

June 23 was the last day of the school year. It was time to say good-bye to students and faculty acquaintances. The end-of-the-year class party was fun. The students were ecstatic, not only with the idea of going off to weeks of freedom, but also because they had contrived with their parents something special for Ms. Cato. They had planned to give her a special gift at the closing party. They wanted it to be a real surprise.

What a surprise it was! It deeply touched Ms. Cato. The students' faces shone as she carefully opened the gift box. Her eyes widened as she peered at the charm in the shape of a heart. The heart was attached to a beautiful gold bracelet. On one side of the heart was inscribed the "Class of 1975." The fourteen-karat gold pieces were lovely, but what they represented gripped Klee's heart. She was surprised and grateful for the love and respect showered upon her that day. The bracelet would become part of her life forever after. Displayed on her right-hand wrist, it was a daily reminder of the permanent mark each student had carved in her memory that particular school year . . . eradicable footprints on her heart.

It had been a good year generally. Of course, there had been frequent ups and downs, which were true for every other year. This school year would always be significant in Klee's mind, however. She had gained the beautiful experience of sharing a love and devotion with an animal, a magnificent yellow Labrador. Through her, Klee was able to enrich the lives of her students with new awareness. The students, in turn, taught her a great deal. Their faith and belief in her made it so much easier.

Man and beast were brought together for a special purpose this particular year. Klee was certain of that fact, and she believed only time would tell the full impact. Also, the interaction with the Winslows was a meaningful occurrence in her life. She learned a great deal from them. She was impressed with the family unity, cooperation, and the love that they willingly gave away.

Dean was a vibrant part of her life that school year of 1974-75. They fit together like a glove, and yet fate was cruel and kept them apart because of the philosophy of one and the biological impairment of the other. No matter, Dean would always be the love of her life. This fact she intrinsically knew. Sometimes, one is fortunate to meet just the right person. Their personalities compliment each other. It seems as though the heavens had made one for the other. But external things get in the way, whether they are society's mores, religion, or some obstacle that can't be altered. No matter what attempts are made to chisel away at the block, the relationship doesn't prosper.

CHAPTER 67

There were many projects Klee wanted to complete at the camp during the summer. She acknowledged that physical activity would serve as a tonic. She could work off some of the hurt, anger, and disappointment. She decided not to take any classes during the summer semester. Her concentration level was impaired, so bodily activity was the ticket for her well-being.

The house on wheels at camp, the mallard travel trailer, needed to be washed. Then it would take several days to wax the mallard followed by days of buffing. This would require a tremendous amount of energy, but it would be the elixir for sound sleeping.

Sal would help out with this project. They both tackled the sprucing of the mallard every summer. It gave the impression of looking new when they completed the task. The yellow body with chocolate trim was attractive to the eye, and the insignia of the mallard on the front was the finishing touch. Klee was pleased that the travel trailer had a duck as part of its logo.

Ducks had a special meaning for Klee. She loved them as a kid. When the mother duck with her brood would visit along the dock at her family's summer home, she couldn't get to the kitchen fast enough to secure slices of bread to feed them. It didn't matter if she were dripping wet when she darted into the kitchen; all that mattered was the goal of feeding the baby ducks. Of course, her mother was anything but pleased with the puddle on the floor. In the end, ducks had a special meaning for mother and daughter. Eventually, as Klee matured, she referred to her mom as Duck and Klee, the Duckling. The duck reference remained until Klee's mom died.

The tire air pressure would be checked by Jim, the camp owner. At the onset of summer, he would bring his air compressor into the site and check the PSI for the women. Jim got a kick out of the two gals and their creative and industrious projects. He told them that he was blessed the day they decided to make Camp in the Forest their special hideaway.

"You gals have everyone around here wanting pea gravel spread on their sites. The expansion of electrical wiring has caught the attention of others. You are transforming this place, that's for sure!" Jim stated.

"Glad to see it, Jim," Klee chuckled. "I would think the improvements would be good for business. The pea gravel gives a nice impression when entering the site area."

He could never get over how well the two cousins cared for Muffy Cat. He'd take off his John Deere cap and scratch his head when he'd stop by to have some coffee and freshly baked corn muffins. Sal was a great baker.

Often he would say, "I'll tell you, gals, one thing that I am sure about, and that's after I die, I want to come back as a cat, providing that I come back as your cat."

Both women would laugh every time Jim made the comment. It pleased them too. Surely, he'd always be offered freshly baked goods at Wathahuk, the name Klee gave to the campsite.

Wathahuk was a name taken from the Seneca Indians. In their language it meant *bright path*. Klee so-named the camp because she liked the sound of the word and its meaning.

She had found the right sized plank in Jim's rat pack shed. She cleaned it, lightly sanded it, and prepared it with some linseed oil. Once she was satisfied, the wood burning gun was put to it to inscribe the letters for the name. Black paint was meticulously lined within the lettering. When it was ready, Sal and Klee hung it over the fire pit between the two maple trees and under the tin roof that gave shelter around the campfire. The Wathahuk sign finished off the rustic fire pit setting. Both women were pleased; both had a penchant for naming things. The neighbors liked the hanging sign too.

Klee would be on her own for part of the summer because Salena was off to a back-home visit in the mountainous area of Maryland then to Europe for a month. She had friends in Switzerland. She had met these folks on a cruise she had taken, and at that time, they had enjoyed each other's company. After the cruise, the correspondence continued, and she was invited on more than one occasion to their chalet with the magnificent Alps as a backdrop.

Klee would miss Sal, but it was for the best. Klee's mood and disposition hadn't been the best these last months. She was so preoccupied, and it was evident that angry feelings found their way to the surface too frequently. She needed be alone until she had better control of herself. She had held so much in while she was at school, but in private life, it had been another story. It is true that one often hurts the ones nearest and dearest. She was glad that Sal was going away.

Journal writing gave some relief. Klee made it a daily exercise. Great sorrow and utter confusion spilled onto the pages. The writing was a means of releasing the volcanic action that erupted within her soul. The written expression became an emotional catharsis for her as she poured out her thoughts and feelings. After many weeks of writing sessions, she had reached the point where she could write these words. She hadn't thoroughly internalized the full connotation of her outpouring, but she would eventually. At the different stages in her life, she would refer to this passage often:

I have absolute belief that when this chapter in my life comes to closure, something wonderful is planned for me. Something beyond what I could imagine. There will be a rearranging of my thought pattern and my dreams. I firmly believe that each negative episode in my life, each swerving detour is necessary in order for me to reach a higher evolution and development of my soul. Eventually, all things will be good. Peace and confidence will reign. It may be a long process; it may take years, but it will happen if I allow my free spirit to find its way and follow its own time line.

CHAPTER 68

A few weeks after Sal left, she wrote Klee a special letter from abroad. Klee reread it frequently. The letter made her realize that Sal had experienced big time secondary damage.

Hi Cuz,

The flight over was fantastic. Every wish was granted and every comfort afforded. At the terminal, Monique and Claude were waiting for me with smiling faces. What a welcomed sight to see them. I admit that I have been on the go since my arrival. Tomorrow we're planning on some hiking. Yes, I am taking photos and making copious notes so you'll have a nice travel log to enjoy when I return. You can't travel, but you will through me.

I want you to know that you are in my thoughts, Klee. I hated to leave you especially this summer, but I also realized that you needed space. Still, I want you to know how I feel. I cannot withhold my feelings, my sense of things any longer.

Life is to be enjoyed or least there should be frequent enjoyment. Observing you over the years, I believe you have had little inner enjoyment, but plenty of hard work and doing for others all the time.

I cannot accept how things go wrong for you so frequently, no matter the area of pursuit. I hate to see the disappointment you too often face. It's like a foreboding presence that surrounds you. Yet you are stoic in thought and behavior and face each challenge bravely. Often, I cannot believe the positions you are put in and how lousy things turn out for you. I hate it . . . I really hate it, and I'm often bitter as an eyewitness. I can't imagine how you stand it! Also, I can't believe the muscular symptoms you are now experiencing. What next? You are a spiritual individual, Klee, this is for certain. I am not. I'm more resentful than anything else. I can't accept the way you do. It's all too much horse pucky as far as I am concerned.

I had to get my feelings out in the open. Believe me, I'd do anything if I could change your path.

Give Muffy Cat a big hug for me, and of course, I send one along to you.

With Love,

Cousin Sal

Klee sensed that Sal was often beside herself with the frequent negative situations and outcomes of Klee's life, but she didn't realize how strong her feelings were. Is it time to make a change and maybe be a loner? It would be less a hassle and fewer people would be upset and hurt because they were in her life. Was it time to make a geographical change? Would a change in location, new acquaintances really make a difference? Can one truly escape one's destiny? Klee had a great deal to consider.

CHAPTER 69

House cleaning the *Charade* that summer kept Klee busy and physically active. She washed and waxed all exposed areas. The portable vac sucked up any unwanted particles on the carpet area. After vacuuming, applying a good carpet cleaner always did the trick. The outdoor carpeting was never that soiled because both women were careful when onboard themselves or when company was on deck to do all they could to prevent soiling.

Appreciating what she had dominated Klee's thinking—that meant taking care of her possessions. She never took her material or emotional gifts in life lightly.

That solo summer, she often took off from the marina with a mess of night crawlers from Barney's bait shop and enjoyed the quiet on the lake as she angled or trolled the waters for that big catch. Although she realized that it was against all safety practices to swim alone, she took pride in being an excellent swimmer and one who could hold her breath for a lengthy duration. She would place the ladder on the gunwale, which provided her with ease once she was ready to get back into the boat. The configuration of the boat was so designed that it was best to dive from the boat using the stern as the dive entry into the cool, delicious liquid. Even in the middle of the summer, however, the lake waters gave her a start upon first entry, but the cold water didn't stop her. The natural springs that fed the lake not only meant pure water but also meant a numbing sensation upon impact. She actually adored the crystal, beautiful water of Canandaigua Lake.

Although she had begun to notice muscular pain after her surgeries, she had pushed it out of her mind as much as possible. However, she had to admit that lately she was experiencing some severe muscular pain after a swim. At first, she didn't realize that it might be the chilly water temperature, but after a water skiing workout, her right leg buckled; there was a sharp pain, and she went airborne while jumping the wake until she hit the water again. This had never occurred before, but the pain engulfed her and she had no control over the skis or the jump of the wake. Being an excellent skier, the experience shocked her.

Klee became suspicious of her muscle reactions to cold, sports, and any physical activity. Afterward, she would be crippled up and needed bed rest with plenty of heat. These occurrences were becoming more frequent, but, because she would never give in, she went forward and dealt with each bout when it visited. Little did she know that these were the first warning signs of what would eventually alter her journey for the rest of her life. Not only the physical side of Klee would be hampered, but it would take its toll on her personal life.

CHAPTER 70

Klee and Muffy Cat would pack up and go back to their permanent residence on Kibar Road for a couple days each week. Laundry had to be done because there weren't any facilities at Camp in the Forest. Wathahuk had many conveniences, but laundry capability wasn't one of them. In addition to laundry chores, mowing and trimming of the lawn was a weekly ritual that she needed to performed. Checking the mail was something she looked forward to each time she returned home. Certainly the bills weren't exciting, but she looked forward to receiving letters from family and friends.

As she sifted through the mail, she recognized Sister's handwriting on one of the envelopes. *What a nice surprise to come home to*, she mused. What a lovely visit she'd have with Sister via her letter.

Could there finally be definitive news about Sister's transfer contained in this particular letter from Elmira? she wondered:

> Dear Heart,
>   I pen this letter feeling great joy and a sense of peacefulness. Yesterday, I received word from the Mother House indicating that I am being reassigned to St. Francis High for the fall semester. I will teach freshman and sophomore English. I am so pleased and truly excited about returning to Rochester, and especially at the high school. I have many of my dear sister friends at St. Francis, so it is a dream come true. I am scheduled to return on August 17. It won't be long before I'm back in Rochester and settled.

We will have a good face-to-face visit before you know it.

Klee dear, you are constantly in my prayers. You are in my thoughts, and I pray that you are doing whatever you can to get through this last disappointment . . . this last blow to your spirit and ego. I have made a list of a few readings that might be helpful to you. I'll send them along shortly, dear, but right now, I wanted to relay the good news to you.

*With deep understanding and deep love,
A. M.*

A huge smile came across Klee's face. The news lifted her spirit several notches. She scooped up the cat and began dancing around the kitchen. Muffy always went along when Klee got into one of her dancing routines.

"Muffy," Klee shouted, "Sister is coming back to Rochester. Both she and Sal will be returning home around the same time. In about three more weeks, we'll be celebrating their returns. Planning a couple welcome home parties for two special people seems to be in order."

The look of "oh please don't continue dancing" reflected on the cat's face as Klee went on with her jig. Muffy Cat, however, was a good sport and especially accommodating when it came to Klee, even when it was far below the cat's dignity to engage in a whirl around the kitchen. Yet their bond was powerful, rewarding, and comforting.

Plans had to be made for the return of the two people who especially shared Klee's life. Her mind went into full spin as she began to formulate ideas for welcoming both Sister and Sal. She considered having a cookout for Sal and including some faculty members. This would be a great opportunity to hear about Sal's visit to her home state and family and the month abroad. It was fun to pore over the photos she took. Pride in her photography made Sal's shots special. She had the ability to capture spectacular compositions of scenery and people.

Klee's thoughts came to an abrupt halt. There was no way she could invite faculty associates. She was not ready to face the Dean breakup. At the gathering, asking about him would be the natural course to expect, especially with his lack of presence. She was not sure as to what her responses and reactions might be. So that plan was deleted as fast as it had come into her thoughts. After Labor Day, school would resume, and then it would take awhile before most realized that she and Dean had gone their separate ways. She expected to be a great deal stronger by that time. She'd probably be better prepared to face any questions or comments. Of course, Lisa and Sal were privy to the breakup, but they would be loyal to Klee and offer little or no comments.

The next plan was to have a shindig in Jim's dining area in his little country store at the camp. He and his wife whipped up a delectable barbeque every Sunday. Klee would ask them to incorporate the Sunday fare as part of a celebration for Salena's return. She would provide appetizers and libations. It would be fun decorating the dining area with vases filled with wild flower arrangements on the tables, and of course, there had to be balloons. Klee would ask Jim's son to get his group together to provide the musical entertainment. The piano, guitar, and banjo would have the place jiving.

Inviting all their camp friends would be a pleasure and a chance to bring everyone together. She'd make a few posters inviting the campers and hang them in strategic locations. Klee loved to decorate for parties and plan menus.

As for Sister, she would ask permission to take her for a ride to the lake. They'd celebrate with a delectable lunch and, of course, an ice cream treat at the old soda fountain in Canandaigua before returning her to the convent. Sister would relish every minute of her special visit.

Nuns had so few pleasures in life. The vow of poverty saw to that. Realistically, if they had to go the poverty route, which meant forever begging in a socially acceptable way among friends, family, and parishioners, then so should the priests. Klee often stated this point of view. She vehemently opposed the double standard. The priests enjoyed the material conveniences and pleasures of life while the sisters had zilch! She also resented the roles assigned to girls and women in the Catholic Church. She thought it was unfair and biased toward the female gender. It seemed totally insane to ascribe to such prejudices and unchristian practices.

CHAPTER 71

Before Sal's and Sister's return, Klee decided to ask Bethany if she could take Allie to her camp for a weekend. The acres of woods and the large pond would be delightful for any dog to explore. This wouldn't be Allie's first visit but a longer one at the camp. New areas were available to snoop around, and Allie loved snooping. Besides, she would be good company for Klee for the entire weekend. She loved Allie and respected her intelligence, her courage, and her loyalty. Feelings of warmth and well-being engulfed her whenever Allie was in her presence.

The weekend before the arrivals of the two dear people in Klee's life, she and Allie took off to the camp. Allie loved riding in the car. She sat in the passenger seat constantly peering over at Klee and also watching the passing cars whiz by.

"You are enjoying the ride aren't you, Allie?" Klee observed. You are my co-driver, my co-pilot. I should get a cap for you to wear when you drive with me. Allie, how about a pair of sunglasses too?" Klee laughed. "That would be some picture for those to see as they passed by."

Klee patted her head, and Allie answered with a joyous but controlled bark. Klee had the windows ajar but not entirely opened because she didn't want Allie to stick out her head. The rushing breeze was not good for an animal's eyes, so that meant enduring less coolness and air movement within the Chevy. That was okay with Klee. Allie's welfare came first. Keeping the rear windows more ajar helped.

It was nice having Allie around. Klee missed Muffy though. She was being looked after by a neighbor. This circumstance was tolerated by Muffy, but she always let Klee know how ticked off she was for being left behind, and with a stranger in her house to boot. It took Klee a day or maybe two to get back in her good graces.

Regardless, she wanted this time with the dog before she went back to school in September. There wouldn't be opportunities once school was in session to take her for the entire weekend or before the mallard was winterized. Often, cold season came early in the fall and that meant the water lines of the Mallard had to be flushed and replaced with special antifreeze.

Anticipating that there would be questions about Allie as she greeted former students at the commencement of the fall term, she would have plenty to tell them after sharing her weekend with the Lab. The kids would be enthralled with Ms. Cato's tales and recaps of her adventures with Allie.

Klee continued to be a great storyteller at camp in spite of having her inner foundation cracked and her heart shattered once again. The laughter during the long tales served as putty to hold her splintered inner foundation together and also served as a cushion to her wounded heart.

Late Sunday afternoon before the weekend came to a close and the dog and Klee had to return home, Klee and Allie loped along to the pond. The pond was located in a peaceful and isolated area of the Camp in the Forest. Campsites were off in the distance and far enough away so that the pond area served as a private natural sanctuary. For Klee, it was a place to reflect, meditate, or simply to observe all the creatures of the pond.

Peering into the water, schools of little minnows darted at high speed whenever anyone approached the water's edge. Frogs rested on lily pads until they saw approaching figures, then there were splashes and circular ripples in the water as the frogs dove to safety. This action put Allie into high gear. She was ready to do her dog thing and jump right in to play with the frogs or whatever she could find. That's where the leash and commands came into play. It didn't take much to keep her under control. Besides, Allie had her swim on Saturday when she and Klee went to the lake. Getting her back into the *Charade* was a real challenge for Klee. Coaxing her and pushing her hind quarters up the ladder was as funny as all get-out! Klee began laughing so hard at the entire scene that she almost drowned herself.

Klee sat down in the soft grass as she surveyed the pond. Allie sat right next to her and nuzzled her head on Klee's shoulder. She would paw Klee's arm so Klee would eventually put her arm around her. The dog seemed to like this position. She sensed that this was going to be a quiet time with Klee, and she was forever obedient to Klee's mood and gestures.

Stroking Allie's head and robust neck was comforting to her. Throughout the weekend, it felt good to hug her and hold this precious creature. The dog offered her special affection without reservation or judgment.

At times, her inner feelings of emptiness took Klee's breath away. She could feel her heart sob within while her outward appearance never portrayed the inner turmoil. She wasn't sure of the direction she should take. She did know that she was fed up with being stoic and always exhibiting valor. Why, why all the unsuccessful experiences in so many phases of her life? She intellectually knew the answer to her question . . . she hadn't, however, thoroughly internalized it yet or, more truthfully, accepted it.

Klee changed position and stretched out on her back. Allie responded and positioned her head on her shoulder as she elongated her beautiful dog frame. Klee peered through the canopy of trees to glaze up at the white, fluffy fair weather clouds passing by. She wanted to be free of grief. She wanted to drift away as a cloud might. She vigorously had to work out the newest roadblock in her life, but her spirit was tired.

Throughout the weekend, Klee found herself having a heart-to-heart conversation with Allie. Of course, the dog couldn't respond but her presence, her dog caresses, her eyes did speak. This satisfied Klee.

"Allie, I need direction. I don't know if I should try to help myself and start anew or remain with the status quo and see what happens. Honestly, I'm afraid that I'm not patient enough to play the wait-and-see game. I'm not getting any younger, that's for sure. I wonder where I might go to start a new life. Yet how can I give up my relatives and friends, my beautiful home, my camp, my beloved lake, and all that has been part of me since I was a kid? Most of these fall into the category of material things, which in reality mean nothing, but they are a vital part of me. Each aspect has, to a large extent, shaped my life and shaped who I am.

Yet the spiritual plane must be tended to, and there is no way getting around that fact. I also am certain that a geographical move does not change the inner upheaval. The turmoil of the spirit persists until resolved and so a new location will solve little, maybe just offer the enjoyment of new adventures and new people."

As all these thoughts flooded her brain and flowed from her lips, she whispered them to Allie. She felt the sharp impact of what she had just uttered. She felt a lump in her throat, a thundering inside, then the sobs poured forth. In alarm, Allie sat up on her haunches and began to whimper as she nuzzled Klee's face and licked the rivulets of tears.

"Oh, Allie," Klee cried out, "I have so much love to give, but nowhere to place the depth of it. It is a truism that love is measured by the amount given, not by what is received. I have given so much during my life, and yet I am lacking in fulfillment. I know that I should encourage myself to never stop offering my love, to follow my heart, to love whomever is sent in my path, but I am afraid. I am intimidated to try again. Sure to offer love means that there is no guarantee that it will be returned, but maybe there are too many wounds that I have experienced for me to attempt any further relationships."

Gently, Klee took Allie in her arms. Her beautiful yellow coat absorbed Klee's tears. For a long time, they lay in the grass with the breeze caressing them and with the clouds in the August sky drifting along.

CHAPTER 72

Klee often recalled that special weekend at camp with Allie. She remembered her confusion and her struggle as to what decisions she should make to get her life on an even keel again. Although it was ten years ago, and she was in the process of returning to the scene, she realized that her life had, indeed, found a new direction and purpose. She had moved forward.

Klee had left her Florida home in her Chevy station wagon two and a half days ago, and she looked forward to the last leg to back home. She still referred to the Rochester area as "back home." Often she would reminisce and see herself speeding down Canandaigua Lake on the *Charade* or sailing from the yacht club. The breezes, sights, and sounds were still real to her. Frequently, she felt twinges of homesickness. That would last all her life. Her soul was forever deep-rooted "back home."

She wondered how much more her old stomping grounds had changed since her departure a decade ago. The year 1976 seemed like ages ago to her. The nation that year celebrated its bicentennial, embracing its freedom and the pursuit of happiness, and so had Klee. She moved away from her Pittsford home to sunny Florida to begin a new chapter in her life.

While residing in Florida, she had heard via long-distance telephone calls and some written greetings from a few camping buddies that the lake was becoming more populated. In addition to all the people cramming every available space for building cottages and opulent homes, the quality of water had succumbed to the pollution from the boat spillage of gasoline and oil. This was sad news. She was so grateful that she knew the lake long before all the commercialism. She was privileged to have experienced the beauty and magnificence of an unspoiled creation of nature. In her vivid imagination as a youngster, she pictured the roaming of the Seneca people along the shoreline and their hunting ventures in the magnificent hills. She felt so akin to these images of the past history of the area.

Klee hadn't kept in touch with too many faculty members except Lisa and Marie. Judy, the school secretary, wrote her a lengthy letter every Christmas. She was anxious to see Lisa and Marie in particular. They had traveled many journeys together. She wouldn't see Sonya because she had taken herself and her doctorate degree to the University of Hartford some years ago. Actually she and Sonya left the Rochester area within months of each other in 1976. Their friendship continued via mail and lengthy phone conversations.

At the university, Sonya met a fellow professor, and before long, they had married. He had been previously married, but they seemed quite compatible. From her letters over the years, she sounded content with married life and enthused with the requirements and responsibilities of her professorship. She and her husband, Harry, decided not to have a family. Klee thought this was ironical. What joy it would have been for her and Dean if they had had such a choice. Sonya and Harry were both career-oriented and any spare time was devoted to study and travel. Klee was happy for Sonya. She had found the right partner from all that Klee could discern.

Lisa and Rob, to Klee's amazement, had been facing some difficulties in their marriage. His travel time increased, and it kept him away too much from the hearth and home. The pressure and stress built over the years until they finally called it quits. That happened in 1984. So Klee was anxious to spend some quality time with Lisa, although it would seem strange seeing her alone.

Lisa was not, nor had she been, the single type. She needed a man. She loved to flirt. Klee wondered if the divorce had changed her. She pondered the thought that maybe it was her time to give some face-to-face advice to Lisa. Lisa certainly had done it for her when she broke up with Dean.

Sal had indicated in her letters that during and after the divorce Lisa had lost weight, which meant that she was really underweight now. She had moved on with her life and purchased a condo. According to Sal, it was beautifully furnished. Lisa not only had exquisite taste in her wardrobe selections but also was a tasteful interior decorator. Sal believed that Lisa was very lonely and felt utter betrayal. Life has so many twist and turns.

Dear Salena would be there for Klee when she arrived. She would stay with her at her apartment. It was the same apartment she resided in when Klee had moved south. It was the same place that Muffy Cat stayed when Klee needed a place for her for a short period of time.

Muffy Cat lived for eighteen years with Klee's loving care and devotion. Klee finally had to succumb to the euthanasia procedure in 1983. It was absolutely devastating to her. It was like losing her child, the child she could never have. They had been inseparable for such a long duration. Her heart ached; it was shattered and her breast felt the emptiness of the little, purring body she could no longer hold.

Sal continued working at Fairhaven Central in the records department. She had advanced to supervisor of the records on the district level. She traveled a great deal, and was okay with not having any permanent relationship. Klee was often in awe of her independence. She was one savvy gal about life. On the other hand, her cousin Klee was the sensitive one, possessing a childlike heart as Sister Ann Mary often echoed.

Sal had maintained Wathahuk for three years after Klee's move. When she realized that Klee wasn't coming back, she petitioned her to dissolve the camp and all its possessions. They both agreed that it was time to let it go. Because it was such a desirable site and the mallard so well kept, it turned over quickly. The new owners were delighted with the charm of Wathahuk.

Bethany was ecstatic when she received word from Klee that she was returning. Bethany and the family had been doing well over the years. She was a grandmother four times and loving it. Precious Allie died in 1984. She had a good life with the Winslows. Her harsh beginning really didn't seem to interfere with her longevity. They figured that Allie lived somewhere around thirteen or fourteen years, which realistically was good for her breed.

Klee realized that when she went to the Winslow home to luncheon with Bethany, she'd see all the ghosts of the past within the space she visited. Allie would be lying along the dining table chair where Klee sat. She'd see in her mind's eye beautiful Cleo, the cat, and Charlie, the mouse cuddled by the fireplace in "their" special basket. The cognitive part of the brain is indeed useful in remembering loving experiences, not only the sad ones, Klee would often remind herself.

She would miss seeing the Hatchers. While Klee had been out of the area, dear Ernest had died with a sudden heart attack, and Harriet, five years later, succumbed to hip surgery complications. Klee had maintained the possession of Ernest's published poetry verses and the textbook on creativity he had written while he was a professor at the University of Rochester. The Hatchers had been important influences in her life and wonderful role models.

Chapter 73

The visitation back home would be exciting for Klee, no question about it. There were so many friends, family, and acquaintances to see. She also looked forward to going out to the Camp in the Forest to see old Jimmy, and maybe some of the old timers who were still camping.

Of course, she could hardly wait to spend some time with Sister Ann Mary. Ten years was a long time. She wondered if she physically changed very much. Now that the nuns no longer wore full habits with the wimple, she was curious to know how gray her hair would be. Discarding the wimple would make sister look quite different, Klee mused.

When Klee did see her, she realized that she hadn't a gray strand of hair anywhere in her soft brown, permanent curled head. She thought that part of her was quite attractive. What was less attractive and alarming to her observation was an extreme weight loss from what she remembered about Sister. She had always been healthy looking with a beautiful complexion and certainly appropriate weight for her height. Now she was so thin that one could see her sideways. Klee was unsettled with what appeared before her as she hugged Sister with warmth and caring but with a soft gentleness as she caressed her frail frame.

At their initial visit, Klee learned that Sister had been diagnosed with breast cancer two months prior to her arrival. She had waited for Klee's visit before she released the news. She did not want to reveal her challenge via a long-distance call. She knew if she used the means of a telephone to tell all, it would be harder on both of them. It seems that most people dread the bad news phone calls in the first place, so why add to the upset. Klee could hardly deal with what Sister was telling her and asking her.

"Klee, what do you think I should do about treatment?" Sister asked.

Overwhelmed with Sister's plight and her question, she felt her throat constrict. Her inner voice shouted out that this was not happening. This should not be happening to such a good, dedicated woman of the cloth. Klee did finally respond.

"Sister, I firmly believe that it's totally a personal choice. As for me, I would live the best I could for my remaining days. I would live each day to the fullest, be with those I love, and then go naturally without all the scientific intervention other than to accept pain management."

Again, Klee placed strong emphasis on the fact that it was her personal philosophy that she was stating. With sadness in her eyes, Sister nodded when Klee had finished.

Klee would always remember the precious visit and shared love of that day and the days that followed during her visit north. Klee spent as much time with her beloved nun as allowed. Her heart was heavy, and she wondered again exactly where was this personal God she had been taught to believe in. Klee asked herself repeatedly that same question many times as she traveled her life's journey. Is there really a personal God?

Since she had been Sister's student many dreams ago, she had been such a support, such a friend, so loving and kind to her that Klee could already feel the void if Sister didn't make it.

There had been some advancement at that point in time in the battle with breast cancer, but the odds for success in 1986 really weren't that good. Sister did go the chemo and radiation route, much to Klee's sorrow. After all the agony of treatment, two years later, in the summer of 1988, Klee received word that her beloved Sister Ann Mary's spirit passed on to the next phase of her journey. According to the letter from Sister Dorothy, she had suffered an agonizing death, which broke Klee's heart once again. It would take a number of years before Klee had full closure and let her dearly loved Sister Ann Mary go.

CHAPTER 74

It was nice in one way to know that a number of the former faculty members were planning on attending a luncheon in honor of Klee's return. Once Lisa learned of Klee's visit, she got on the horn and planned a special time for a long overdo visit. In another way, the visit would be difficult. The luncheon was scheduled for the Spring House Restaurant. Klee realized that it would bring back many memories of her and Dean's magical evenings spent there. She thought of their time during the Christmas season with all the beautiful adornments throughout the restaurant while drifting on the dance floor within the secure arms of Dean.

She had learned that Dean had been appointed assistant superintendent in a school district in the Albany area. In 1979, he had married a gal from an affluent suburb of Albany. Klee was happy for him. It took him four years from their breakup before he married. It said something about the depth of their relationship it seemed. Klee found that thought comforting. Although she never really wanted to let him go, she knew in her heart that real love required such a sacrifice. She still wondered why their two hearts crossed paths.

Yes, she had learned to love again. It was a satisfactory and a decent relationship, but not what she had once known. She would not engage in a traditional marriage. Neither a church nor an official document made a marriage as far as she was concerned. It was commitment and faithfulness that made a true union. It was the meeting of the minds, and a loving friendship that made the union and kept it functioning.

Dean, without a doubt, would always be the love of her life. She had given in some time ago and accepted that fact. Acceptance, she learned along the way, was the restorative remedy that healed the spirit. Embracing and accepting the heartache was the first step in the healing process. The time period for internal acceptance is different for each individual, but if one works at it, it will eventually fall into place. She had come to accept that sometimes in one's life one has the opportunity to experience someone very special and the two souls will forever linger regardless of what life threw at them.

Over the years, Dean and his wife Joan had been blessed with a girl and twin boys. The little girl had been named Kleah. When Marie had written this information to Klee, it struck hard and was blatantly shocking, but neither Marie nor Lisa made any comments on the name other than just mentioning it. Surely they had drawn their own conclusions regarding the name selection, but being the friends that they were, they never entered into any dialogue about Kleah. Although knowing that she didn't have any right to, Klee still felt that her spirit and Dean's remained connected, and the naming of the daughter confirmed her feelings.

Initially, Klee had mixed emotions upon learning the name. The hurt, the heartrending disappointment and outcome of their love resurfaced with all the impact and vengeance, as though it were yesterday. It was a natural, immediate response for Klee. However, she also came to realize in a short duration of time that the information about the child was comforting if she would allow it to be, and she did. Actually, there was a little girl so named to be a reminder of a love that did not become fulfilled as both had wished. She often dreamed about having the opportunity to see the child, to see Dean once more, but it was only a dream. She would always wonder about Kleah. What would she be like? Would she have Dean's good looks, his winning personality, and intelligence? Who would she become?

CHAPTER 75

Klee continued to be confronted with an extraordinary number of hills to climb as her journey progressed. Little did she know that there was lurking in the near future a huge mountain that she would be required to ascend. However, she'd make it no matter what was thrown at her. She would challenge any hurdle. That's the kind of drive she had. No matter how much hurt existed within her soul, no matter what negative physical revelations were presented to her, and no matter how often disappointments found their way to her door, she would never stop trying. She would not give up. She continued to give 100 percent of herself. Mediocrity was not an option. Excuses she found tiresome. She'd continue to remain the comedy relief act, all the while concealing what only her heart and mind knew.

In her journal writing, she wrote this passage. She often returned to it and silently meditated on the written words:

> Life frequently doles out what I would rather not accept . . . nor deal with. It's just a natural response for me, actually for most human beings. Some of the stuff in life is just plain rotten! Yet I know it is up to me as to how I respond to the situation, and what I have learned from the event once the emotions have settled down. Everyone needs to take time to let the feelings mend.
>
> Besides the emotions, I have learned that the ego has to be put into check also. The ego sure can add fuel to an untenable situation. The ego can play tricks on the mind. The ego can be dangerous and can cause all kinds of trouble. So being aware of the pitfalls of the ego is a task in itself! Guarding against it takes super vigilance. The discarding of the thought pattern of the "me" . . . and the "I" isn't an easy task. It takes practice and a keen alertness as to when it is ready to rear its ugly head again and to

get in the way of finding self or mutual solutions. Once the "me" is generally under control, the victory is stunning, a new outlook emerges, solutions have a chance of coming to fruition, and the soul enjoys more peace.

At another time, while walking along the beach one weekend, Klee went into herself and this image surfaced. Upon her return home she wrote her reflections in her journal:

> I am observing multiple sets of footprints in the sand. I am seeing all the different sizes and shapes of the foot impressions. I begin imagining the traveler . . . matching the footprint size and shape to a conjured type of individual in my mind's camera. Regardless who the traveler is, regardless the size and shape of the impressions in the sand, I realize that there exists a commonality among them.

> No matter on which beach footprints are observed, no matter which hemisphere, which continent traveled, the mysteries of life encompass all imprinters. There is no getting away from that fact.

> It is true that each footprint is a symbol of the passing person who possesses his/her own signature, his/her own personality, own uniqueness, but not one can escape life's design and claim an idyllic existence. For life is meant to be filled with moments of love and joy on the one hand and, on the other, times of sadness and disappointment. Life cannot be all rainbows. The positives and negatives eventually lead one to the whole self if allowed to without bitterness, and that is the treasure—to find the real self and be proud of what is realized, to live in peace and contentment within one's self.

POSTSCRIPT

The year 1990 was waning and a new year fast approaching. All the Christmas ornaments had been placed on a six-foot folding table. The box lids had been removed. Each box was placed in an orderly fashion so it was easy to choose and select what was needed for each tree limb.

Klee was placing the last Christmas ornament on the tree. During the trimming she had thoughtfully returned to many Christmases of the past. They were vivid in her mind. They had remained in her heart, never to be diminished by the seesaw ride of life: Lisa, Rob, Sonya, Marie, Don, Sal, Sister Ann Mary, the Hatchers, Muffy Cat, the Winslows, Allie, and always Dean. Dean would be forever engraved in her soul. Some had passed on, but they remained in her special memory box. They all left forever footprints on Klee's heart.

The recent death of Salena was an unexpected blow for Klee. She was shocked that cousin Sal would be taken at what one would consider an early age, but that's what automobile accidents do. At least her end happened while she was doing what she loved best. Traveling was her passion.

Klee embraced her past with love and acceptance by remembering all the good situations, all the love she had given and received, and all who had been part of her journey. The personal human treasures she experienced during her travels of her life and also the hard knocks in her life made her what she was. She was pleased that she had evolved into a woman of substance as her friends put it.

Yes, at least she had evolved; she understood and she definitely had changed dramatically over the years. She embraced a spiritual level that could not be diluted by any exterior impact nor could it be sustained by organized religion.

She came to the full realization that the golden dreams one might possess often were diminished to dreams of copper. However, she discovered that the real golden treasures were patience and inner strength. She embraced that life was indeed a mystery. Going along with the flow of life as it presented itself was the best approach, while at the same time maintaining one's integrity.

As she matured, she experienced more often than not that her heart burst with delicious glee, ecstatic excitement, and the joy of inner peace. Finally, she had reached the place where she always wanted to be. She was getting closer to home in a peaceful heart.

She revisited a frequent statement that Sister had repeatedly said to her over the years. It became part of her inner thought pattern. It helped her look at herself and other people in a different light. It made life easier.

"You know, Klee, that you are a high achiever, a woman of drive, and perfectionism," Sister A. M. would say. "As you journey through life, you will find dear heart that average is okay . . . it really is good enough for most people. Try to accept this fact of life and lessen your burden to drive, to achieve. Good is good enough, but if you must, strive for excellence, not perfection."

Although Klee didn't entirely ascribe to Sister's words for herself, she learned to make modifications. It had helped her alter her thinking as far as her thoughts and actions were concerned and most definitely assisted her in understanding the common approach of others. She had learned to be more accepting of others and with what satisfied them.

During the trimming, Tangie had remained close by guarding all the ornaments until they were completely and artistically placed on the Christmas tree. She had a knowing expression on her face as she watched Klee's every move. Did the cat with her uncanny ESP understand all the levels of cherished memories that had just transpired through Klee's mind while once again she prepared for another Christmas in her Florida home?

Upon finishing, Klee looked down at the cat and deep into her eyes.

"Well, my precious, it's time to retreat a little distance from the tree and look at it from a different perspective, wouldn't you say? Bertie will put away all the boxes and remove the portable table when she comes to give us lunch. She had everything so conveniently laid out for me, which I deeply appreciate," Klee said in a soft tone. "We are so lucky to have her. I am truly thankful for all the nonmaterial gifts that have been showered upon me throughout my life and continue to feel that way every day of my existence, my little feline friend."

As Klee prepared to withdraw a distance in order to observe the tree, there was a familiar clicking sound. The two clicks became a signal that the cat had readily learned some months ago. Klee had released the two brakes on her wheelchair so she could retreat from the tree. The snap was Tangie's indicator that it was time to scale the lower protruding leg rests of the chair on wheels. It was time to nestle on Klee's lap to soak up all her warmth and love.

Que sera, sera...

ABOUT THE AUTHOR

Kathleen (Kathi) Cellura graduated from the University of Buffalo, Buffalo, New York, in 1959 and began her teaching career in the Rochester, New York, school district. She completed her graduate studies at the University of Rochester in 1964.

She demanded much of herself and sought assignments to different grade levels and within predominately different ethnic/religious communities in the district in order to glean a full understanding of the city's public school educational system. In addition, she wanted to observe firsthand the maturation and learning developmental levels of the students as they progressed through the grades. Her experience spans kindergarten through eighth grade. She was considered a visionary and was creative in her approach, introducing new exercises that would stimulate the students. Parents and students expressed their appreciation. She was independent in her thinking and methods, and those that disagreed did not deter her

She was a teacher in the inner city during the civil rights riots of 1964. This experience was life altering. A sensitive person, she absorbed to the core of her being the lessons learned as an inner city educator. That experience can be another entire novel.

In 1976, she moved to Florida and continued a dual career. Along with her interest in the academic realm, she also enjoyed the business community. She was a real estate broker in Venice, Florida, taught real estate ethics, and organized various workshops for realtors.

Animal welfare was an important part of her curriculum. She has always believed in spaying and neutering programs. Regarding pet ownership, she taught her students and emphasized with parents that proper care, with a heavy emphasis on responsibility and love, was the stepping-stone to grooming young people into becoming responsible loving parents with their own children. There is a correlation, she would state, between pet rearing and child rearing.

The author is qualified to present this story of Klee Cato's journey because of her teaching diversity and often unusual experiences as a teacher.

She taught students across the learning spectrum, in assigned settings, from those with poor academic abilities to those who were gifted.

She has spent many years involved in philanthropic endeavors. Since her retirement from teaching in 1994 and the business world in 2005, however, she has devoted more time to community good works. She is referred to as the hat lady because of the multitude and variety of chapeaus she wears, as observed around town and in the local newspapers.

All proceeds for the novel are slated for the benefit of nonprofits through the Kathleen F. Cellura Foundation at the Community Foundation of Sarasota County, Sarasota, Florida.

Kathleen (Kathi) Cellura

INDEX